Dreaming of S

Dreaming of St-Tropez

T.A. Williams

CANELO

First published in the United Kingdom in 2018 by Canelo

This edition published in the United Kingdom in 2018 by

Canelo Digital Publishing Limited
57 Shepherds Lane
Beaconsfield, Bucks HP9 2DU
United Kingdom

A CIP catalogue record for this book is available from the British Library.

Print ISBN 978 1 78863 167 9
Ebook ISBN 978 1 911591 93 1

Look for more great books at www.canelo.co

Printed and bound in Great Britain by Clays Ltd, Elcograf S.p.A.

To Mariangela and Christina, with love as always.

Chapter 1

'Mr Drugoi says you are very beautiful, Miss Milton.'

Jess snorted silently, but kept the smile plastered on her face.

'Please thank Mr Drugoi, but could you ask him if he has a preference as to where we situate the windows in the master bedroom suite? Would he like to look out towards the river or towards the houses of parliament?'

Dmitri relayed her question to his boss and a short conversation in Russian ensued. Finally, Dmitri reported the result of their deliberations.

'Mr Drugoi would like to be able to lie in bed and look out over the river.'

Mr Drugoi made a further comment in Russian that elicited a snigger from Dmitri.

'He says you're welcome to come and try it for yourself when it's finished. He says he can imagine you lying on his bed.'

The smile on Jess's face was wearing thin by now, but she managed to maintain it as she ignored the comment and moved to the next item on her clip board.

'View towards river. Fine. Now, does he still want the *two* ensuite bathrooms leading off this room?'

The interpreter didn't need to refer this to his boss.

'Yes. He always likes one bathroom for himself and a separate one for his companions.'

Jess couldn't stop her eyes from flicking across the face of the expressionless blonde girl standing at Mr Drugoi's elbow. She looked as if she was less than half the Russian's age and she was stunningly beautiful. She had not been introduced so, presumably, she fell into the category of anonymous 'companion'.

Jess gave an involuntary shudder before returning to business.

'Two bathrooms.' She added a brief note to her list and moved on to the details. 'And he still wants to go with the idea of a glass bath with blue LED lighting?' She did her best to keep the distaste out of her voice. Dmitri nodded, so she continued. 'And gold bathroom furniture?'

'Bathroom furniture?'

'Taps and so on.'

'Definitely. Mr Drugoi always chooses gold. He likes gold.' Dmitri grinned at her. 'He has a lot of gold.'

'Gold, it is.' She ticked it off. 'Now, shall we take a look outside on the terrace?'

The survey continued for the best part of an hour and the innuendo from Mr Drugoi didn't decrease. By the time they reached the basement, Jess could feel his eyes all over her as he muttered comments sotto voce to Dmitri in Russian. Somehow she felt certain these were not remarks about the conversion of this magnificent Georgian townhouse from traditional Old English to twenty-first-century kitsch. She glanced at her watch and saw it was getting on for lunchtime. By the look of Mr Drugoi's waistband, he was unlikely to want to miss out on a meal, and she wouldn't be sorry to see him go. She tried to accelerate things, adopting her no-nonsense architect-in-charge voice.

'You'll see from the plans that we intend to transform this whole basement area into a swimming pool, sauna and gymnasium complex.' Not, she felt sure, that Mr Drugoi would be making much use of the gym. 'If we knock down these walls, we'll have a few fairly complicated structural problems to overcome, but it's feasible – although I'm afraid it won't be cheap.'

Dmitri relayed the message and she saw Mr Drugoi shrug his shoulders dismissively. He said nothing, but Dmitri translated all the same.

'Mr Drugoi has no money problems.'

Jess had already worked that out earlier that morning – the moment she had spotted the white Rolls Royce as it purred up to the front of the house to deliver Mr Drugoi and his retinue. No, clearly, money was not a problem for Mr Drugoi. Whether his money was a problem for other people was a different matter.

The oligarch said something to Dmitri and both men laughed. It was the sort of laugh you hear at the end of a dirty joke, and Jess had a feeling she might be the subject of the joke.

'Mr Drugoi says he wants lights under the water so he can watch the people swimming.' Dmitri was still smiling. 'He says he can imagine you swimming. He says you would look very good swimming.'

Mr Drugoi added another adjective and this time even Dmitri looked a bit embarrassed.

'He says you would look very good swimming... naked.'

Jess bit her lip so hard she almost drew blood. Finally, after a few deep breaths, she replied.

'Please tell Mr Drugoi that I'm an architect and I'm here to discuss the restructuring of this property – nothing else.' As she spoke, she subjected Drugoi to a withering stare, but his dead fish eyes just remained fixed on her body, not her face – totally unapologetic. She heard the interpreter speak to his boss, but very briefly, and she had little doubt that Dmitri had opted not to translate her remarks word for word.

The tour of the property continued, as did Jess's discomfort in the presence of the billionaire. Finally, at just after twelve o'clock, she reached the end of her queries and brought the meeting to a close. By this time she was feeling soiled and slightly sickened, and her only desire was to get away from Drugoi as soon as possible. She shook hands with the expressionless girl, then Dmitri and, finally, Drugoi, and was just turning away when she heard a brief exchange between the oligarch and his interpreter.

'Please, Miss Milton.' She looked back over her shoulder and noted that this time Dmitri actually had the decency to blush as he passed on the invitation from his boss. 'Mr Drugoi asks if you would like to come back to Claridge's with him for a party.'

'A party?'

'Yes, just you, him and Natasha.'

Jess was dumbfounded. Never in her professional or personal life had she had to face anything like this before. She was just beginning to formulate a suitably frosty, if restrained, response – Drugoi was one of the firm's most important clients, after all – when he added a few more words in Russian that Dmitri hastily translated.

'And Mr Drugoi says to tell you he is a very generous man.'

Jess's breath whistled out of her lungs as her hard-won self-control finally deserted her. She walked back until she was standing right in front of the billionaire. Although not as tall as the blonde girl, she was still a couple of inches taller than him. She looked him square in the eye.

'Mr Drugoi, you may think you're able to buy anything or anybody you like, but it doesn't work like that with me. I wouldn't go to your hotel with you if I had a gun to my head.' She took a deep breath. 'You are a disgusting human being.' For a moment she had the distinct impression that he had understood – interpreter or no interpreter – but, to be sure, she glanced across at Dmitri. 'Translate that to him – word for word.'

Dmitri looked appalled, but then evidently followed her instructions. She listened to a rush of Russian from him to his employer and this time she saw Drugoi's expression darken. But instead of shame or contrition, the puffy face registered surprise and then, quite clearly, anger. He hissed something to Dmitri and turned on his heel even before the translation had been rendered.

'Mr Drugoi is very angry with you. He says he will speak to your boss.' As Drugoi and the blonde girl headed out through the door to the stairs, Dmitri added under his breath. 'I'm afraid you're going to be in a lot of trouble.'

–

Jess hit the gym hard that evening. She was still furious at the way Drugoi had behaved – clearly, he was convinced that his money allowed him to say or do whatever he chose. In fact, she was so engrossed in her thoughts that it took a while before she realised that Hope was sitting on the next exercise bike to hers, but not pushing the pedals anything like as furiously. Jess sat up, released her grip on the handlebars, and ran a hand across her forehead, feeling it come away soaking wet.

'Hi, Hope, how long've you been there?'

'I wondered how long it would take you to notice. I've been here eleven minutes.' She grinned and pointed at the screen in front of her. 'If you don't believe me, look!'

Jess gave her a weak smile in return.

'Sorry about that. It's been a rough day.'

'Want to talk about it?'

Jess realised that she did. Over the next ten minutes they pedalled sedately side by side while she told Hope all about the Russian. She didn't leave anything out – she didn't need to. She and Hope went way back and they had few secrets from one another. When she finally finished, Hope was, predictably, supportive.

'Little rat.' She looked across and caught Jess's eye. 'I can think of a few less savoury things to call him, but I don't want to get us thrown out of here. So do you think he's going to cause trouble for you?'

'I wouldn't be surprised. That sort always want to get their own way.'

'What if he goes to your boss?'

'Graham? I'd like to think he'd have the guts to stand up to him, even though Drugoi's contract's likely to reach well into seven figures.'

'Wow. That's serious money. And if he doesn't stand up for you?'

'Then I suppose I might find myself looking for another job.'

Jess did her best to keep her voice level. Her mortgage payments were high and she knew she wouldn't be able to afford to keep them going for long if Graham really did cave in to pressure from the Russian.

'That would make two of us…'

Hope had lost her previous job a couple of months earlier and was doing temporary work while still trying to make up her mind what to do next.

After a pause, she looked across at Jess and winced. 'Do you mind if I get off this damn thing now? My bum's gone to sleep.'

Together, they climbed off the bikes and finished their routine. After a shower, Jess was feeling a bit more relaxed and she offered to buy Hope a drink at the bar. They normally tried to avoid this as it was all too easy to put back on the calories they had just spent ages losing. However, under the circumstances, she felt she deserved something. She bought two glasses of Prosecco and they settled down in the comfortable armchairs, looking down through the glass panels at the other gym users still slaving away below them.

'You know your trouble, Jess? You need a big hunky boyfriend to defend your honour – you know, like they did back in medieval times. He could go along to see your Russian, slap his face with a glove, and then beat the crap out of him in a duel.'

Jess had to smile at the image.

'I'm all done with big, hunky boyfriends, thanks. Been there, done that, don't want another one.'

'Not never?'

'Not for a good long while. Not till I get Rafael out of my head.'

Her long-standing relationship with handsome, wealthy property developer Rafael had finally hit the rocks six months earlier – around the same time Hope and her long-term partner had also split up. In Hope's case, it had been mutual. In Jess's case, she had been the one to dump him, but it had been tough all the same. And it hadn't really been him so much as the increasingly glitzy, phoney lifestyle he insisted upon living, along with his equally ostentatious friends. After two years, she had finally had enough and told him so. His reply had been predictable – he was what he was, take him or leave him.

She had left him.

'They're not all like Rafael, you know.'

'I know they aren't. But, for now at least, as far as men are concerned – and rich men in particular – I don't want to know. They're more trouble than they're worth.'

'They have their uses.' Hope gave her a wink, but Jess shook her head.

'If it's just sex I'm looking for, there are two or three men here at the gym who've made it quite clear that they'd be only too willing. All I'd have to do would be to snap my fingers.'

'You? Casual sex? Don't give me that, Jess. We both know that's never going to happen.'

Jess smiled. Hope really did know her so very well.

'What you need is the love of a good man – not just a quick one-night stand.'

Jess made no comment. They had had this conversation over and over again recently. After a while, Hope returned to Jess's unpleasant experience that morning.

'So what's his name, this Russian? Anybody famous?'

'Drugoi.'

Jess was unprepared for Hope's reaction.

'Drugoi, did you say?' Hope looked up sharply.

'Yes, do you know him?'

'Not at all, but I wouldn't mind betting it's a fake name.'

'What makes you say that?'

'I did two years of Russian at school and I'm sure I remember that *drugoi* means *another*. I reckon he's using a pseudonym so as to keep his real identity secret.'

Jess nodded slowly. 'Wouldn't surprise me in the slightest.' She managed a smile. 'You never know – maybe he's got a whole load of angry women after him.'

'Or their big, hunky boyfriends...'

—

Jess had appointments all the next day and she didn't get back to the office until mid-afternoon. She exchanged pleasantries with Deanne on the front desk and then took the lift up to the third floor, wondering if Drugoi had carried out his threat to talk to her boss. Either way, she knew she needed to speak to Graham herself about the previous morning's events. She had had it with this particular oligarch.

To her surprise, as she came out of the lift, she found Caroline from HR waiting for her. Warning bells started sounding in her head.

'Jess, hello. Listen, we need to talk.'

'Of course, Caroline. What about?'

'Could we talk in your office?'

Jess led her along the corridor to her office and offered her a seat. Caroline closed the door carefully behind her before sitting down. She waited until Jess was also seated before delivering the body blow.

'I've been talking to Graham, and I'm afraid we're going to have to let you go, Jess.'

Although Jess had half been expecting it, this demonstration of her boss's total lack of backbone came as a shock.

'You're what? This is about that slimy toad Drugoi, isn't it?'

'No, of course this isn't because of Mr Drugoi, or any other client. It's just restructuring.' Jess noticed that Caroline didn't meet her gaze, keeping her eyes down as she opened the folder she was holding. 'You've been with us now for almost five years?'

'Yes.' Jess felt the anger rising in her veins. She leant forward, resting her elbows on the desk. 'And you're firing me? Why? I think you'd better tell me what I'm supposed to have done.'

Caroline looked up, but only briefly, and Jess noted that she surreptitiously pushed her chair back a few inches. 'Not *firing* you, Jess. Please don't think that. Like I said, we have to restructure the business. I'm afraid it's just that you're surplus to our requirements. Business is down in the wake of the Brexit vote and we have to be prudent.'

This didn't accord with Jess's assessment of the situation. She had been busier over the past six months than at any time since joining the company. She struggled to get her head round what she was being told.

'You don't need me? Who's going to do all the work I've been doing? I've got six projects ongoing as it stands, and if we get the Drugoi contract, there's well over a million pounds' worth of work in that one job alone.' Caroline finally raised her eyes and Jess held them. 'Have we got the Drugoi contract?'

She caught a flicker of something on Caroline's face, but it disappeared immediately as she replied in a bland tone. 'I have no idea. Contractual matters are not part of my remit.'

Jess stared at her for a few seconds until the other woman's eyes dropped once more. Suppressing a desire to reach across the desk and strangle her, Jess did her best to keep her tone level.

'So, when do I have to leave? And what about pay and all that?'

Caroline looked up again, clearly relieved to be able to talk about practical matters. 'We've put together a generous severance pay package for you. You've been a valued member of staff and we want to reward you for your efforts on behalf of the firm. Graham told me to make that clear to you. Here… see for yourself.'

She removed a sheet of paper from the folder and slid it across the desk. Jess took it and cast her eye down the figures. It soon became clear that Caroline hadn't been joking. The settlement was, indeed, generous.

Suspiciously generous.

Dropping the page onto the desktop, Jess raised her eyes towards Caroline.

'And when am I expected to leave?'

'With immediate effect.'

'Now? What, this afternoon?'

'Yes. I'll get somebody to bring you a box for your things. You are to clear your desk and leave.' She caught Jess's eye. 'Graham told me to tell you that he will provide you with a glowing reference, without any stain on your character.'

'Why should there be a stain on my character?'

The cold sensation in the pit of her stomach was turning to anger.

'No reason.'

Jess got the feeling Caroline was regretting her choice of vocabulary.

'It'll be a glowing reference, Jess, but he did ask me to make it clear to you that, in return, he expects you to leave quietly and without fuss. And without contacting any of your colleagues, or any of our clients, now or subsequently. Do I make myself clear?'

'Crystal clear, thank you, Caroline. I think the expression you're looking for is *gagging order*.'

The urge to throttle somebody rose up again and if Graham had been in the room, Jess felt pretty sure she would have been tempted to launch herself at his scrawny neck. She was dimly aware of Caroline standing up and offering her hand across the desk. She took it automatically and shook it, resisting the temptation to squeeze it until the bones cracked.

'Goodbye, Jess, and thank you on behalf of the firm for all you've done.'

'This is Drugoi's doing, isn't it?'

'Mr Drugoi? How could you possibly think that?'

Chapter 2

'So they're kicking you out and buying your silence?'

'It couldn't have been made much clearer.'

'And you think it's all down to this Russian letch?'

'I'd stake my life on it. Horrible, horrible man.' Jess reached for her wine and took a big mouthful. 'You should have seen him. The repulsive Mr Drugoi – or whatever his real name is – was like something you find floating in a septic tank.'

'And so now this man has screwed you good and proper. Although not in the way he was planning.'

Jess looked across at her best friend.

'He has, and he hasn't.'

She saw interest in Hope's eyes and decided to try to explain how she was feeling, now that the news had started to sink in. That afternoon she had followed Caroline's instructions and cleared her desk, leaving without uttering a word to anybody, not even to Deanne at the front desk. She had taken the cardboard box containing her personal effects and the accumulated memories of five years and hailed a taxi to take her home. Only then, in the seclusion of the back seat of the taxi, had she finally succumbed to the tears she had been repressing ever since her conversation with Caroline. Nevertheless, by the time she got home, she had managed to dry her eyes and think rationally again.

No sooner had she got back and dumped her things than she picked up the phone and called Hope, who had immediately invited her over. Now, here in her friend's cosy kitchen, sipping red wine, she did her best to put into words just what she was thinking.

'I'm not supposed to talk to anybody from work, but I know I'll get to hear about it sooner or later. I'd lay money on it being Drugoi, behaving like the bully he is. He probably told Graham he'd give him the contract as long as he fired me. The whole "surplus to requirements" story was probably concocted by Caroline, just so I couldn't take them to an employment tribunal and allege unfair dismissal.'

'But surely you still could, if you want to?'

'Maybe... I don't know, but I don't want to go through all that. Besides, the thing is, Hope, I'll be quite honest, I've been feeling more and more uncomfortable working there of late. I've enjoyed the work and some of the projects have been a real architectural challenge, but there's something about the filthy rich that sticks in my craw.'

She caught Hope's eye.

'Yes, I know, they're not all like Drugoi, or Rafael for that matter, and some of my clients have been genuine people – one or two really nice – but increasingly I've been given the big budget jobs and, almost without exception, the people I've been dealing recently with have been creeps.'

'Surely money doesn't automatically mean creeps?'

'No, of course not, but I seem to have been getting more and more of the Drugois of this world.'

'Drugoi sounds grim, but I wouldn't mind a billionaire of my own, you know.' Hope nodded towards the old poster on her wall. Jess had seen it hanging there for years. 'I bet there are any number of them in a place like St-Tropez.'

The photo on the poster was of the atmospheric little town on the Côte d'Azur, its quayside lined with luxury yachts. Happy people in summer clothes were strolling around, while others were sitting at harbour-side cafés, sipping cool refreshing drinks. The sun shone down from a clear blue, cloudless sky and the sea itself was a perfect, transparent aquamarine. It looked idyllic, but Jess knew that real life wasn't like that. She returned her eyes towards her friend.

'Still dreaming of St-Tropez?' As Jess knew only too well, the one fixed point in Hope's firmament over the past few years had been her dreams of this iconic holiday resort. 'I can't think of anything worse. Imagine a place full of millionaires and their yachts, the over-privileged few living in villas that cost the earth, and all of them doing nothing but lounging around all day long. Are you really sure you'd like to go there?'

Hope nodded. 'Definitely. And you're just biased. You've had a few bad experiences and you've convinced yourself they're all like Rafael or your Russian. There are some lovely people in this world, with or without money, and I'm sure St-Tropez has got just as many good folk as anywhere else.'

'Keep telling yourself that, Hope. We all need our dreams.'

Hope shook her head. 'Well, I'm sticking to my dreams, and I'm going to go and see for myself sometime soon, I guarantee it. Anyway, leaving St-Tropez out of it, are you saying you're glad they fired you?'

Jess grimaced. 'I wouldn't say I'm glad. It's been one hell of a shock. But, when all's said and done, I now find myself with a whole heap of redundancy pay, and the knowledge that I'll still get a glowing reference to wave in the faces of future employers.'

'You sure your boss'll keep his side of the bargain?'

'Graham's a cowardly little wretch, but he'll keep his word. I'm sure of that. And if he doesn't, I'll be going in there with a meat cleaver – and he knows it!'

'So you think he's maybe done you a favour?'

'I'm not sure I'd go that far, but at least it means I can take my time and look round for a new job that appeals to me more, while still being able to pay the mortgage.'

'So, are you planning to go off on a long holiday, or might you be interested in a little stopgap job for now?'

'Working with you? Why not?'

Hope had been working for a dog-walking agency for some weeks now, since losing her job at a big insurance company. The dog-walking was just to tide her over while she considered her options, and she claimed to be enjoying it. She loved animals and had always taken a lot of exercise, so it suited her fine. She nodded at Jess.

'It's only minimum wage, but it'll get you out and about – and it'll pay for a few bottles of wine. Maureen's hurt her ankle and she'll be off for a few weeks, and I'm up to my eyes with so many dogs I'm in danger of being dragged under a bus one of these days.' She grinned. 'If two bull mastiffs decide they want to cross the road at the same time, you cross the road – bus or no bus.'

'When do you need a hand?'

'What're you doing at eight o'clock tomorrow morning?'

–

April that year was the coldest and wettest in England since records began. The rainfall in the first week alone was in excess of the normal figure for the whole month, and it just didn't stop. The rivers were overflowing, towns were being flooded, the ground everywhere was sodden and muddy. Every morning, Jess and Hope drove round southwest London in the van, collecting a motley assortment of dogs from owners too busy, too lazy, or too infirm to walk them themselves. They drove up to Richmond Park and exercised them, rain, shine or thunder – and there was precious little shine.

Then, in the afternoons, Jess took another half dozen dogs on leads for a walk in the local park, doing her best to prevent them from either fighting or humping each other as they walked through the rainy streets to the park.

Ironically, one day she spotted something familiar.

Just before the turnoff for the park, there was an empty shop on a corner. It had obviously been a travel agency once, but now it was a pathetic shell, the windows boarded up – all but one corner. Through this, Jess was surprised to spot a poster that rang a bell. On closer inspection, with her nose pressed to the glass, she saw that it was none other than St-Tropez, and not dissimilar to the poster on Hope's wall. Its corners were curling up and the ink was fading, but the brilliant sunshine, the blue sea and the luxury yachts were unmistakable. Fat cats or no fat cats, Jess had to admit that it looked appealing.

Every day, as the English skies continued to pour rain down on her and her collection of dogs, she glanced ever more enviously at this little slice of paradise. Maybe Hope wasn't so wrong after all.

She started trawling though the Situations Vacant on specialist architecture websites, without finding anything that immediately leapt out at her, but she wasn't worried yet. With the financial cushion provided by the payoff from Graham, she was able to take her time, confident that, sooner or later, the right thing would come up. She even started to consider taking a holiday somewhere warm and sunny. That had a distinct appeal. Anything to get away from the impenetrable gloom of England.

Then one day, as she was standing in the limited shelter provided by the branches of a massive oak tree, her phone started ringing. She was in the middle of wiping herself down after separating a German shepherd called Klaus from a golden retriever called Betty – she hadn't been able to ascertain whether Klaus's intentions had been amorous or aggressive, but Betty hadn't appreciated them one bit. Jess, still smarting from the Drugoi incident, felt a considerable bond of sympathy with her. However, in the process of wrestling with them, she had slipped on the grass and now had a soggy bottom and muddy hands to show for it. Still muttering to herself, she wiped one hand on her jeans, pulled the phone out, and answered it.

'Yes, hello.'

'Hello, Jess?'

She immediately recognised his voice and wondered what he wanted.

'Graham, I didn't think I'd ever hear from you again.'

'Well, yes, Jess… I know.' He sounded apologetic, and for a moment Jess wondered if he was calling to offer her her old job back.

'So, is there a reason for this call? I'm working at the moment.' She kept her voice cold.

'Working?' He sounded surprised, but not half as surprised as he would have been if he could see her now, covered in mud. 'It's sort of about work that I'm calling.'

He hesitated, but Jess wasn't doing him any favours. She remained silent until he started up again.

'You remember old Mrs Dupont? The single floor extension in Highgate.'

'Yes, of course.' Mrs Dupont had been one of Jess's favourite clients. Although no doubt worth quite a few million, she was pleasant, friendly, and totally unpretentious. 'What about her? The job was finished three, four months ago and it's all been signed off.'

'I know, I know. It's just that she wants you to contact her.'

'I thought I was expressly forbidden from contacting any former clients.'

'Yes… yes indeed, but she tells me this is something personal. Nothing to do with work.'

'Something personal?'

'Yes, personal. That's what she said. Anyway, have you still got her number?'

'No, I deleted it, along with all the other work-related numbers. I assumed that's what you would have wanted.'

'Yes, of course, good. But, if I give it to you again, please could you call her?' Graham sounded almost pleading.

'Yes, of course, but what's this all about, Graham?'

'I really don't know, but she's an important client and the customer's always right.'

Jess couldn't resist a jab. 'Even when the customer insists you fire one of your employees?'

An awkward silence ensued. Jess waited until he broke it, and was unsurprised to hear him ignore her question.

'Erm, thank you, Jess. I'll text you the number.'

'So, did Drugoi give you the contract?'

'Erm, yes. Thank you again, Jess. Goodbye.' She could hear the haste in his voice.

As she returned the phone to her pocket, she heard it whistle to signify the arrival of Graham's text, but the call to Mrs Dupont could wait. She would make it later on, once she was somewhere dry and warm.

'Right, come on, Betty, let's carry on with our walk. And as for you, Klaus, just leave her alone. All right?'

As the golden retriever stood up, the German shepherd's nose headed unerringly for her backside once more, but Jess was ready this time. She gave his lead a hefty tug and addressed him in her sternest pack-leader voice.

'I said leave her alone, Klaus. Who do you think you are? A bloody oligarch?'

–

The upshot of the call to Mrs Dupont was an invitation to tea on Saturday afternoon. In the course of the brief telephone conversation, Jess hadn't been able to glean any further information about just what the personal matter to be discussed might be, and she was feeling quite curious as she walked up the fine, tree-lined road to see her.

The house itself, while not in the Drugoi league, was a very desirable old property in Highgate and was, no doubt, worth a lot of money. Jess had been responsible for the addition of a single-storey extension to the rear – part conservatory, part lounge. It had gone in very well and both she and Mrs Dupont were very pleased with the result. During the build, she had often visited the house to check on progress, and every time the old lady had invited her to stay for tea and a chat. Jess felt she knew her really quite well as a result, coming round to thinking of her as a nice old grandma, and she looked forward to seeing her again.

She pushed the iron gate open and went up the over-grown path to the front door. Here, in the midst of the trees and bushes, it almost felt like she was in the countryside, and she always enjoyed coming here. The thick foliage cut the noise of the traffic on the road behind and it felt really tranquil. As usual, this sense of tranquillity only lasted until she rang the doorbell. This resulted in a tumult of barking from within. It would be a brave burglar who would risk breaking in here.

She had a good long wait until she heard footsteps and a hand at the lock. Then the door opened a few inches, held by the chain. Mrs Dupont's old face appeared, level with Jess's shoulder, while a black nose and a handsome set of gleaming white teeth appeared at knee level. As Mrs Dupont recognised her visitor, her face cracked into a broad smile, and as the dog realised who it was, the barking suddenly stopped, to be replaced by a plaintive whine.

'Jess, my dear. How kind of you to come and see me. Just a moment now. Get out of the way, Brutus.'

The dog's head was yanked out of the way and the door closed. The chain rattled and then the door opened once more and Jess stepped into the hall.

'Good afternoon, Mrs Dupont. And hello, Brutus.'

The black Labrador came waddling towards her and Jess saw that he hadn't lost any weight since the last time she had seen him. She reflected that he would definitely benefit from joining Hope and herself with their pack of privileged pooches, getting some much-needed exercise. He wagged his tail amiably and nuzzled her hand before she straightened up and greeted his mistress. Mrs Dupont grasped Jess's hand with both of hers and gave her another smile.

'Good afternoon, my dear. How lovely to see you again. Do come in. Shall we go and sit in the new garden room? I call it Jess's room, you know.'

'No Mrs Forsythe today?' Normally the door was opened by the housekeeper – a kindly lady in her sixties, or even early seventies.

'Glenda's in the kitchen. She's been baking, and she told me she couldn't leave the cake in case it burned.'

As they walked through to the back of the house, Jess studied her former client covertly. Mrs Dupont was probably in her late seventies, maybe even older. In spite of her advanced years, however, she still looked pretty sprightly. As usual, she was immaculately turned out – even wearing earrings today that glittered the way only real diamonds glitter.

'Come and sit down beside me, my dear. That way we can both look out over the garden.'

Jess and Mrs Dupont sat down side by side on the fine old ottoman. As they did so, the dog pottered over and slumped down heavily at her feet. Jess scratched his ears as she listened to what Mrs Dupont had to say.

'I'm so glad you've come, Jess. I was very sorry to hear that you lost your job.'

'Who told you that?' Jess sat up. She had been under the impression that her departure from the firm remained a closely-guarded secret, but it would appear that the news had already got out.

'Glenda met Mr Jenkins the builder in the supermarket a few days ago and he told her. Apparently you took a swing at a Russian oligarch who pinched your bottom.'

Jess couldn't help laughing at how well embroidered the story had already become. She wondered how Robbie Jenkins had heard about her dismissal, but she knew him of old. They had worked together on a number of projects over the years. He always seemed to know everything about everybody and there was nothing he loved more than a bit of gossip. Under the circumstances, she decided she had nothing to lose by giving Mrs Dupont the true story.

'I didn't really hit anybody, although I'd be lying if I didn't say I wanted to. The man in question propositioned me as if I was a hooker. I refused his offer in no uncertain terms, and he bullied my boss into firing me.'

'How disgusting.' Mrs Dupont shook her head sadly. 'I don't know what the world's coming to, I really don't. And you're such a good architect, too. What did your husband, or boyfriend, think about that?'

'No serious boyfriend, Mrs Dupont. I had one of those and it didn't work out. And I've been really busy over the past few months, so I haven't really had the time, energy or the desire to go out and find myself another one.' She grinned. 'To be honest, there aren't many good ones around.'

Mrs Dupont didn't look concerned to hear that she was unattached, but was kind enough to express surprise.

'That surprises me – you're so pretty. How old are, Jess, if you don't mind my asking?'

'Twenty-nine.'

'Oh, well, you've got all the time in the world to find yourself a good man.'

'I might need it. Like I say – there aren't many good ones out there. Besides, I'm in no rush.'

'You'll find one, I'm sure. So, now that you're out of a job, what are you doing these days? What are your plans? Have you got another job?'

'I'm going to start looking, but I'm in no hurry to do that either. I'm doing a few bits and pieces, helping a friend at the moment, but I've been wondering about maybe taking a good long holiday while I have the chance. The weather here's been so foul this month.'

'It's been awful. And yes, a holiday sounds like a splendid idea.' She caught Jess's eye for a second. 'Yes, indeed, a splendid idea.'

At that moment the door opened and Mrs Forsythe came in, pushing a trolley. Jess gave her a big smile.

'Hello, Mrs Forsythe. How nice to see you again.'

The dog pulled himself to his feet, nose pointed at the cake on the trolley, his tail wagging hopefully.

'Good afternoon, Jess. I've made a Victoria sponge. I remember you telling me how much you liked sponge cakes.'

'What a memory! Thank you so much.'

The housekeeper unloaded the teapot, cups and plates onto a low table in front of the sofa and set the magnificent-looking cake on its fine china stand in the middle. As she did so, she glanced down at the dog.

'Make sure you keep an eye on Brutus. Last week he stole a whole joint of roast beef, complete with Yorkshire puddings, and ate the lot.'

Once she had left, Mrs Dupont returned to the matter in hand.

'You've probably worked it out for yourself from my name, but many years ago I married a Frenchman.'

Jess nodded and smiled. 'Dupont doesn't sound terribly English.'

'He was a lovely man. I married him when I was twenty-two and, after a few years in London, we moved over to France. He came from a very wealthy family and we were fortunate in being able to choose where we wanted to live.' She waved her hands vaguely around the room. 'That's why I've got all this now.'

Jess remembered what Hope had been saying about not all rich people being bad and nodded to herself. Mrs Dupont was a sweet old lady – money or no money.

'Anyway, that was sixty years ago. My son still lives in France now.' Mrs Dupont looked and sounded nostalgic. 'Alas, Marcel, my husband, died ten years ago, and I've been on my own since then. Anyway...' Jess saw her straighten up again. 'Anyway, I'm digressing...'

'Shall I pour the tea while you tell me all about it?'

'Thank you dear, that would be kind. The thing is, the news here isn't very good. I don't know if you heard, but Glenda's husband died rather suddenly two months ago, I'm afraid. It was a heart attack.'

'Oh, I'm so sorry. I didn't know.' Jess looked up from the cups. 'So she's left on her own?'

'She's got a daughter who lives in Canada but, yes, other-wise she's very much on her own. Just like me really.' She caught Jess's eye. 'Or, at least, we've got each other. She's been with me for so long, she's really become my best friend.'

Jess poured the tea and set a cup down in front of the old lady.

'Would you like me to cut a couple of slices of cake?'

'If you would, dear, but you'd better make that three slices.'

'A slice for Mrs Forsythe?'

'No, she can help herself later on. The third slice is for Brutus. He likes cake.'

Jess began to understand just why the Labrador was so podgy. Clearly, if he was feasting on slices of iced sponge cake, it was no wonder his figure was suffering. Mrs Dupont pointed at the dog, but not to remark upon his obesity.

'Anyway, I wanted to talk to you about Brutus. You see, I'm thinking about going off and doing something I've always wanted to do, and I thought I'd take Glenda with me for company, and as a treat to her.'

Jess took her own cup and sipped the tea.

'And that is?'

'A round the world cruise. My husband and I used to do a lot of cruising, but, since his death, I haven't been away much. I thought to myself that this was the moment to go for it.'

'And how long's a round the world trip going to take?'

'I haven't booked anything yet, but the travel agent tells me these things last about three months.'

'That sounds amazing. I'm sure you'll love it.' Inside her head, Jess was wondering how many thousands of pounds a trip like this would cost. Mrs Dupont was certainly providing her friend with quite a 'treat'.

'I'm really looking forward to it, but there's a problem.' Mrs Dupont looked down indulgently at the Labrador whose eyes were still trained on the cake, a small pool of drool forming on the floor in front of him.

'The problem is that I can't take Brutus on the boat with me. I've had him since he was a puppy – that's almost five years ago now – and he's as much my best friend as Glenda. I know I'll miss him terribly and I really can't countenance the idea of him being locked in kennels for three months. It would be like sending him to prison.'

Jess nodded sympathetically, but, inside, she was digesting the fact that Brutus was not yet five. With his excessive weight and his geriatric waddle, she had assumed he was twice that age.

'I was wondering if you might be interested in a little proposal I have for you?' There was a twinkle in Mrs Dupont's eye. 'Have you ever been to France?'

'France? Just on a school exchange trip for a couple of weeks, years ago.'

'Well, you see, my husband inherited the family home in France when his father died. He and I lived there for a good few years and it's a lovely place. My son lives there now. As you were talking about maybe taking a holiday, I was wondering if you might like to do me a big favour by taking Brutus over to France while I'm having my cruise. My son says he can look after the dog, but, to be honest, he's a bit absent-minded these days and I'm worried he might forget to feed him. I was wondering, in view of your present circumstances, whether you might like to look after him yourself and stay on for a nice long, restful holiday while you're at it. After all, Brutus knows you and likes you.'

The dog, his eyes still trained on the cake, had now slumped down until he was lying on the floor, one heavy paw resting on Jess's foot.

Jess nodded. 'And I like him.' She reached down to stroke his head. 'That sounds like a wonderful offer.' Her mind was racing. The idea of a three month holiday was really, really tempting, but the pragmatic part of her was telling her maybe she should concentrate on finding a new job. 'So how would you suggest Brutus and I get there?'

'Do you drive?'

Jess nodded again. 'Yes… though I don't do a lot of driving. Living in London, a car's more trouble than it's worth, but I'm sure with a bit of practice, I'd be all right.'

'That's excellent. The car's almost new. I only bought it last year for Brutus's sake. My old car was getting too small for him. Of course, I no longer drive, but Glenda's husband used to drive it as and when it was necessary – since his death, it hasn't been used. But the thing is, Brutus knows the car, and he knows you, so he would feel comfortable. So do you think you might be prepared to do that?'

'I'll certainly drive him over there and maybe stay a few weeks, if you're sure I wouldn't be any bother to your son.'

Mrs Dupont beamed. 'Of course not. That's wonderful, Jess. Thank you so much. You can stay in the guest house. It's quite independent, tucked away in a corner of the grounds. We used to use it for guests, but he rarely has anybody visiting nowadays, and it's been empty for ages. You and Brutus could stay there for as long as you like – hopefully all the time Glenda and I are away, if you like it and you have time – obviously free of charge. It's a lovely place for a holiday. How would that sound?'

That sounded amazing to Jess. And, just in case she might have any doubts, the universe chose that exact moment to deliver a downpour of biblical proportions, reducing the view across the garden to a grey mist.

'I should really be looking for a new job, but I suppose as that's all online nowadays, I could do it from pretty much anywhere.' Jess turned to Mrs Dupont with a smile. 'And the idea of getting away from this weather is really appealing – specially on a day like today.' She made a decision. 'That sounds absolutely marvellous. I'll be delighted to do it. Can

I say I'll definitely stay a month and, if all goes well, I'll try to stay for the full duration? If not, I'll happily pop back to bring Brutus home to you when you return from your cruise.'

'That's absolutely excellent. And, of course, do feel free to bring a friend, or friends, with you. Is there somebody you'd like to take with you to France?'

Jess had been thinking about this. 'Yes, thank you, there is. My friend Hope deserves a holiday. She's also between jobs so she could probably take a good long break as well. She and I are working for a dog-walking company at the moment, so she's got lots of experience with dogs, which could be useful.'

'That's wonderful. Now, the cruise that interests me sails from Southampton right at the end of May. That's in, what, just about four weeks' time? Is that maybe a bit short notice for you? Could you manage to get away so soon?'

Jess nodded. 'Yes, I'm sure that would be all right. So, tell me, Mrs Dupont, whereabouts is your son living?'

'You may have heard of it. It's a nice little place on the Côte d'Azur between Toulon and Cannes. It's called St-Tropez.'

Chapter 3

The next few weeks turned out to be very busy, and full of surprises. The first surprise, of course, was for Hope, who was blown away by the chance of visiting her dream destination, rent-free. She immediately set about trying to sublet her flat so she would have money to keep her going at least for a good few weeks. Her excitement was clear to see and Jess felt very happy for her.

As for Jess, in spite of her reservations about St-Tropez almost certainly being full of filthy rich, objectionable people, she began to feel a growing sense of excitement as well. The weather in London had improved slightly, but it still felt like winter in the mornings, and the idea of some Mediterranean sunshine was very appealing. As long as the sun shone, she felt sure she would be able to tolerate the people. As for money, the golden goodbye from her old firm would be more than enough to keep her all summer if she chose to stay in France for the full three months.

The next surprise was Mrs Dupont's car. The following Saturday, Jess went over to the old lady's house to pick up the car for the weekend, so as to get a bit of practice driving again. The surprise came when she opened the garage door and discovered that the vehicle in question was an absolutely enormous dark blue Range Rover. It was twice the length of anything she had driven before, and so high off the ground that she had to physically haul herself up into the thing. Apart from its size, the added complication was that it was automatic, and she had never driven an automatic car before.

Inside the vehicle – she couldn't bring herself to refer to it as a car – everything was sheer luxury. It was a symphony of cream leather, burr walnut and thick-pile carpet, and this opulence felt as daunting as the size of the thing. After an embarrassing delay while she had to consult the handbook to discover how to start the engine – apparently you had to keep your foot on the brake at all times – she manoeuvred her way very gingerly out of the garage and into the traffic.

She immediately made two discoveries.

When she put her foot on the accelerator, the big heavy vehicle instantly turned into a Formula One racing car, and she found herself speeding along and in imminent danger of ramming the cars in front. It went like a bat out of hell. Fortunately, the brakes worked equally efficiently.

The second discovery was more welcome. Other road users appeared to be awed by the sheer mass of the Range Rover and she found that, from the commanding height of the driver's seat, she was able to cut through the traffic pretty effortlessly. By the time she had negotiated her way through the crowded roads of northwest London and onto the M25, she was beginning to relax. And after her initial concern, driving an automatic turned out to be wonderfully simple, and she soon got the hang of it.

The next surprise came a few days later. Jess and Hope were on Google Earth, checking the address of the house in St-Tropez that Mrs Dupont had given them. They discovered that this was a villa, set in huge grounds. But the surprise was where it was situated. It occupied an absolutely fabulous position, only a few short metres from the sea. It was just outside the town, directly overlooking the Mediterranean. The views from the house had to be unbelievable.

From what they could see from the satellite image, there was a swimming pool, and what looked like a private pathway to secluded beaches. It was hard to make out any more than just the roof of the little house in one corner of the grounds where they would be staying, but they could see that it was separated from the villa by a wonderful, verdant garden, containing a number of statuesque trees, including tall palms. Hope raised her eyes from the screen and glanced across at Jess.

'Wow, what a place!'

'You aren't joking. It's amazing.' Inevitably, as she looked at it, Jess put on her architect's hat. 'I can't see much of the villa from above, but from the roof tiles, I reckon it's probably old traditional Provençal style. It's called *Les Romarins*, which apparently means rosemary bushes, and that sounds pretty traditional, doesn't it?'

'It's hard to judge from the air. Is it very big?'

'It's biggish, but not too massive. I'd say the footprint's about one-fifty to two hundred square metres. To give you an idea, this flat of yours is maybe forty square metres. And I'm talking footprint – you know, the area of just one floor. Although it's difficult to judge from an aerial photo, it looks like this villa's got a second storey, at least for part of the length of the building, so it's a good size house. But it's the position that's amazing. It's right beside the sea, on the Côte d'Azur of all places.'

'So it would appear that your Mrs Dupont's son isn't short of a bob or two.'

Jess was beginning to get a bad feeling about this. 'To own a place like that, he must be worth an absolute bomb.

What have I been telling you about my not wanting to get involved with the filthy rich again? Maybe this trip to France isn't such a good idea, after all, Hope.'

'This trip to France is a bloody marvellous idea, Jess, and you just remember that.' Hope took hold of her arm and looked her firmly in the eye. 'Now, don't you go getting all bitter and twisted about things, all right? The man's the son of your Mrs Dupont, and you keep telling me she's a sweetie. He's probably just as nice. So, he's loaded – that doesn't mean he's automatically bound to be another Drugoi.'

Jess repressed a shudder.

Jess visited Mrs Dupont regularly and they promised to stay in touch over the next few months. She liked the old lady a lot and dearly hoped that her son would be equally pleasant.

Finally, the end of May arrived and Jess and Hope went round to collect the dog and wish Mrs Dupont and Mrs Forsythe well. As they climbed into the huge car, Mrs Dupont handed Jess a little package, containing the registration and insurance documents for the car, Brutus's pet passport, and dietary and care instructions for him. The dog himself stood in the boot, surrounded by doggie toys and his luxurious bed, wagging his tail as his mistress disappeared from sight. Jess had no doubt the old lady would be in tears, even though she knew he would be in good hands. She glanced across at Hope.

'We'd better take damn good care of our four-legged friend. She obviously loves him to bits.'

'He'll be fine. I see what you mean about her being a sweetie. He's a lucky dog to have a mistress like that – although she hasn't been doing him any favours as far as his diet's concerned. Do you want me to open this package and see what she says about what we're supposed to feed the dog?'

'Good idea.'

As Jess manoeuvred the car through the London traffic, Hope opened the package from Mrs Dupont and perused its contents. The first thing she found came as a huge and very welcome surprise to Jess. It was a thick envelope marked *Expenses*, and it contained five thousand euros in cash and a scrawled note saying, *Please keep what's left over and have a wonderful holiday*.

Jess was totally awed by Mrs Dupont's generosity. Hope, on the other hand, was equally awed by the sheet indicating the dog's dietary requirements. She read it out loud, disbelief in her voice.

'Our hairy friend back there has a bowl of muesli and a big helping of dog biscuits for breakfast every day. He prefers full cream milk with his muesli, but skimmed is also acceptable. If he's still hungry, he also has two or three slices of unsmoked back bacon.'

'I've never heard of muesli as part of a canine diet before. He's a Labrador, for crying out loud! Of course he's hungry. They always are. So, we can safely assume he gets bacon every morning as well. Little wonder he's a bit paunchy.' Jess shook her head as she squeezed the big vehicle past a red bus and followed the signs for the motorway.

Hope was still reading.

'It's called killing with kindness, but listen to this. He has two main meals a day – taken at one o'clock and seven o'clock. At least one of these must include half a pound of best steak, medium to well done, allowed to cool, but not too cold. As a treat, every day at four o'clock, he's allowed a slice of cake or, his personal favourite, a doughnut (jam, not jelly). Blimey, Jess, this dog eats better than I do.'

'Poor Brutus. Carry on like this and he's on course for a heart attack.'

'Or some sort of awful stomach disorder.'

To reinforce Hope's point, a horrible smell came floating forward from the boot. Clearly, Brutus's diet was going to impact on his fellow occupants of the car as they drove down through France. Jess hastily pressed the buttons to open the windows.

'Are you really going to give him bacon and doughnuts, Jess? It's killing him.'

Jess shook her head with decision. 'It'll kill us as well if he goes on farting like that. Nope. We'll stop before we get onto the motorway and buy some sensible dog food. He isn't going to be happy, but, whether he likes it or not, Brutus is going on a diet.'

They made good time down to the Channel Tunnel, stopping on the cliffs just before the tunnel to give the dog a run. Or rather, as it transpired, to give the dog the chance to have a slow, asthmatic trot. Both girls were appalled at his unfitness and another problem only became clear when they returned to the vehicle. Back at Mrs Dupont's house, the Labrador had climbed into the tall car up a specially-constructed ramp at the back of the garage. Now, it instantly became clear that there was no way Brutus was going to be able to jump several feet into the air so as to get into the back of the Range Rover. Hope took hold of his front end and Jess the rear and they hoisted him manually into the car. It was unfortunate for Jess that she picked the back end of the dog, as he almost asphyxiated her in the process.

'Brutus, we are so going to change your diet.'

Jess had to take a few deep breaths of untainted air before climbing back into the driving seat.

They got through the tunnel remarkably quickly, barely having to wait more than twenty minutes or so. As they reached the other end and moved their watches on an hour, the time was half past one. By six o'clock, they had already covered over five hundred kilometres on motorways that were almost empty, compared to the crowded roads back in England. They had to stop for fuel part-way and Jess was relieved she wasn't having to use her own money to fill this monster up. The big vehicle's appetite for fuel was not dissimilar to the dog's appetite for food. After refuelling, they stopped to let Brutus have a brief walk and Hope demonstrated what a good friend she was by opting to take his rear end when they lifted him back in this time.

It was a remarkably easy journey, apart from their being almost deafened by the loud snores from the boot. This didn't bode well for a good night's sleep later on if they had to share a room with Brutus. They discussed sleeping arrangements and decided to see if the dog could be persuaded to sleep in his bed in the car. Neither of them was very hopeful, but in view of the assault on their ears and noses he was likely to produce, it seemed worth trying.

They finally turned off and looked for a hotel for the night, deciding to go for one right beside the motorway, for simplicity. The place they found was a low, modern building and they were able to park the car directly outside their bedroom window. Pets were allowed in the rooms so Brutus accompanied them, at least for now. Jess found it somewhat disconcerting a few minutes later when the bathroom door swung open, just as she was going into the shower, and she heard the dog's nails clip-clopping across the floor towards her. From the expression on his face, it was pretty clear that he would have been happy to join her in there, but she managed to wedge the glass door closed with her bottom. Luckily, Hope realised her predicament and managed to lure him out with a biscuit from the hospitality tray.

Once they were both dressed again, they took the dog for a walk round the edge of a nearby hayfield. At least, that was the intention, but the Labrador only walked for a hundred yards or so before sitting down and refusing to budge. They cajoled and even bullied him, but to no effect. In the end, Jess had to go back to the car and pick up a packet of dog treats in order to persuade him to pull himself to his feet and walk slowly back to the hotel.

'The sooner his diet starts, the better.'

To reinforce the point, Jess pulled Brutus's shining stain-less steel bowl out of the car and filled it with dry dog food from the sack they had bought earlier. To her relief, he didn't hesitate, and set about emptying the bowl in record time. She filled another bowl with water and he drained that in its turn. Once both were completely licked clean, he sat down, scratched his ear with his hind leg, and looked up at her as much as to say, 'So, where's the steak then?'

'That's your lot, dog. All right?'

The look he gave her was a picture of canine pique.

Their meal that evening in the restaurant alongside the hotel produced an interesting moment.

The dog spent the evening slumped under the table, snoring, but at least it looked as though he was going to let them eat without interruption. That was, until they were just starting their desserts. As Jess dipped her spoon into her ice cream, the table suddenly shot off sideways, upending their wineglasses and sending her ice cream flying to the floor. Hope's reactions were obviously a bit faster and she managed to catch her sundae glass before it joined Jess's on the floor, but a wave of red wine poured into her lap as she did so.

The reason for the seismic shift was the appearance at the door of another dog. This dog – a large standard poodle – must have issued some sort of olfactory taunt to which Brutus had reacted violently. Displaying an unexpected burst of vitality, Brutus had leapt to his feet and set off in the direction of the dog at the door. The fact that he was tethered to the leg of the table didn't discourage him in the slightest, and if Jess hadn't made a grab for the lead attached to the table leg, he might well have made it all the way across the room, the table wreaking havoc in his wake. As it was, she was almost yanked out of her seat as seventy pounds of overweight Labrador threatened to pull her arms out of their sockets.

Both of them had done French at school, but this hadn't really provided them with the necessary vocabulary to cope with apologising for spilt food and drink and a Labrador involved in a tug-of-war with a table. In consequence, they were only too glad to pay up and leave as soon as they could after that incident. Ironically, by this time, Brutus had gone to sleep again and they almost had to drag him out under the disapproving eyes of the other diners.

Finally outside in the fresh air, they both agreed that the best place for Brutus that night would be in the car. After persuading him to come with them for a short walk, in the course of which he hopefully voided himself, they lifted him into the back of the car and saw him settle down in his bed. It wasn't a warm night, but Jess opened all the windows a few inches, including the window in the tailgate, so he would get enough air. Apart from anything else, on his showing so far today, he was likely to asphyxiate himself if he was kept in an enclosed environment.

Jess pressed the button to lock the car, but they hadn't even got as far as the door of the hotel when the car alarm started going off and, along with it, the lights started flashing. She scrabbled for the keys and hastily unlocked the doors, silencing the alarm, but not before several faces had appeared at windows overlooking the car park. Jess shook her head ruefully.

'There must be some kind of motion sensor in there. I'm afraid it rather looks like we've got company tonight, Hope.'

'Well, one thing's for sure – we're sleeping with the window open.'

'Earplugs might have been a good idea, too.'

Chapter 4

They had an unexpectedly good night. Brutus seemed quite happy to curl up in his fancy dog bed, strategically positioned as close as possible to the open window, and even his snoring didn't bother them too much. They were both tired after the drive and had little trouble getting off to sleep. Jess only woke once or twice and on both occasions was reassured to see the dog fast asleep.

Next morning, Brutus was visibly disgruntled that his breakfast only consisted of a small serving of dog biscuits and a bowl of water, but he did, at least, manage to accompany them on a full circuit of the hayfield before they lifted him back into the car and set off again. They stopped twice en route to the south of France to refill the fuel tank and to give the dog a chance to stretch his legs. By now, Jess had got the hang of reversing up to a bank or bump in the ground so that the lethargic dog could climb into the back of the Range Rover without exhausting himself – and that way, they didn't have to lift him up.

By the time they got to the Mediterranean coast, it was late afternoon, but the sky had cleared and the temperature outside was twenty-eight degrees. Considering it was just the end of May, Jess had no doubt the full heat of the summer in July and August would be intense. Inside the luxury car, with the air-conditioning turned on, even with the back window partly open for the dog's benefit, the temperature was very comfortable. Although Jess had been driving all day, she felt pretty relaxed. Their only stressful moment had been on the motorway around Lyon, where the traffic had suddenly swollen to London proportions, but, since then, it hadn't been too bad.

At just before five-thirty, they turned off the motorway, paid the exorbitant toll, and followed the signs towards St-Tropez. At first they found themselves on a good, fast, road that climbed through tree-covered hills, before beginning a winding plunge towards the sea. As they dropped down the other side, the view opened up — and it was spectacular. Jess found a lay-by among the pine trees and pulled in so they could appreciate the scene laid out before them in all its magnificence. The sky was a completely cloudless clear blue, unlike the grey, overcast skies of northern France and England, while the sea in the distance was a wonderful aquamarine. The wooded hills extended down towards the shoreline where glimpses of pale golden sand had them dreaming of sunbathing on the beach. Jess shot a glance across at Hope, who was looking entranced.

'Remind you of anything?'

'They say the camera never lies. Jess... it's gorgeous. It's just like I've always dreamt it would be. And, look, over there in the distance, at the mouth of the bay, that has to be St-Tropez itself.'

Jess followed her gaze and immediately recognised the famous pink and yellow tower of the church, poking up amidst a multitude of weathered pink-tiled roofs. There wasn't a high-rise block to be seen and the houses themselves were a mixture of every possible shade of yellow, orange, ochre and pink — all bleached by the sun. The harbour looked as though it was packed with boats of all sizes and the white of the yachts contrasted pleasantly with the deep blue of the water. She breathed deeply and found herself smiling.

Beside her, Hope was equally ecstatic.

'What a view! And up here, amid all these trees, it's so quiet, so uninhabited. I was expecting a whole mass of houses and people, weren't you?'

They sat in silent appreciation for a few minutes until they were roused by a cavernous half howl, half whine from the boot. Clearly, Brutus was keen to get to the end of their journey. Jess pulled the gear lever into Drive and edged out onto the road again.

'It's all right, Brutus. We're almost there.'

As they dropped down to sea level, the whole mass of houses and people was waiting for them. Down here, it was far from quiet and peaceful. Along with people and houses, they also suddenly found themselves in the midst of a whole lot of slow-moving traffic. The closer they got to their destination, the slower it all became. As they joined the stop-start queue of traffic driving round the bay towards their destination, Jess opened all the windows and allowed some fresh air to come into the car. This even roused Brutus, who stood up, stretched and uttered his long drawn-out half-whine, half-howl again. Clearly, he too had had enough of being cooped up.

'Just a few minutes more, Brutus.' Jess glanced in her rear-view mirror and could have sworn he nodded his head in comprehension.

Jess – and no doubt the dog as well – was then surprised to see Hope unclip her seatbelt and scramble back over the seats until she could lean into the boot and hug the dog.

'Thank you, Brutus. You may be a smelly old hound, but you're the reason I'm finally here in the place I've been dreaming about for so long. I love you, Brutus.'

The Labrador stood up on his hind legs and did his best to lick Hope's face as Jess smiled at the two of them in the mirror.

In fact it took them all of half an hour to do the last ten kilometres, and Jess found herself wondering how much worse the traffic was likely to get in mid-summer. If it was this slow in May, then August was likely to be total gridlock.

As they drove into St-Tropez itself, they started to catch glimpses of the sea between the houses, gardens and reed beds to the left of them. The town was positioned on the southern end of a delightful horseshoe-shaped bay, with green, tree-covered hills rising up behind. The deep blue waters of the bay were dotted with all manner of boats, ranging from local fishing boats festooned with bright orange floats and piles of nets to luxury motor yachts, sleek speed boats, sailing yachts, and a massive white cruise ship, whose layers of decks made it look like a distant wedding cake.

With the windows open, the smell of the sea came rushing in – a not particularly pleasant aroma of long-dead fish. Jess wrinkled up her nose and smiled at Hope.

'It's just as well posters don't give you smells. Your kitchen would be a bit fishy by now.'

'I must admit I was rather expecting the scent of suntan cream, expensive perfumes, and cordon bleu cuisine, rather than this pong.' Hope grinned. 'Although I think it's rather nice that it smells like a real fishing port, don't you?'

Jess nodded. The sight of the big flashy yachts had been confirming her fears that she was about to enter the domain of the super rich and spoilt. Somehow, the fact that it was still evidently a working fishing port made St-Tropez a bit less exclusive and a bit more down-to-earth. Maybe it wouldn't be too ostentatious after all.

'I know what you mean. So this means there must be at least some ordinary people living here.'

Just as she spoke, a high-pitched howl, not dissimilar to Brutus on a bad day, filled their ears, and a bright yellow sports car came screaming towards them from the opposite direction. As it swept past, Jess checked out the handsome driver, his sunglasses perched on his stylish mane of jet-black hair, a gold watch glittering on his bronzed wrist. Alongside him was a woman wearing a skimpy orange top that left very little unexposed. She had tied a scarf over her hair, Thelma and Louise style, and Jess could have sworn she saw the sunshine reflected from her exquisitely painted nails. As the car roared past, Jess turned to Hope with another grin.

'I may have spoken too soon.'

'Mmm, not a lot of fishermen drive Ferraris.'

'Is that what it was?'

'I'm pretty sure. Do you realise, that car probably cost more than my flat?'

Jess nodded morosely. Rafael had had a Ferrari at one point and she didn't want to be reminded of him. Luckily, she didn't have time to reflect, as the satellite navigation sent them shooting off to the right, away from the centre of the town. She squeezed the big vehicle through narrow streets, gradually climbing, roughly in the direction of the massive old citadel, until they crested the hilltop and began to drop down the other side.

'Wow! Take a look at some of these houses.' Hope's voice was awestruck.

They were now running down a gentle slope, slowing as they went over speed bumps designed, no doubt, to prevent Ferrari drivers from turning the road into a racetrack. The road was lined on both sides with high, meticulously-pruned hedges, bushes and trees, securely situated inside metal fencing. Just visible behind this protective barrier, they caught glimpses of a fine selection of luxury villas, ranging from old Provençal-style houses to far more ostentatious mansions, at least one of which appeared to have been modelled on the White House. Every single one of them was protected by hefty gates, some with video cameras and notices attached to the high fencing, warning that the premises were patrolled by dedicated security companies.

'Bloody hell, Jess. Talk about Millionaires' Row...'

Jess nodded morosely. This was pretty much what she had been expecting in a place like St-Tropez. However, this was no time for introspection. The satnav had given up trying to get them any closer to their destination, so she scanned the left side of the road until she saw their turning coming up. She indicated and swung the car off the road onto a dusty track running between iron fences and impenetrable hedges. The track wound sinuously up the hill for a hundred metres or so before reaching the top and beginning to descend. Suddenly, the hedges and villas receded behind them and the hillside opened out – and, with it, the view.

'Wow!' Both of them spoke in unison and Jess slowed the car to a halt. The tiredness she had been feeling slipped away in an instant and she felt a surge of excitement. It was an amazing view.

The hillside was covered with a mass of vegetation that, on closer inspection, appeared to consist mainly of low, wind-blasted trees, wild rosemary, and thorn bushes – all interspersed with a stunning display of bright red poppies, purple thistles and a mass of other wildflowers. The coast immediately below them was rocky and the water so clean and transparent, the rocks, sand and seaweed on the seabed were clearly visible for some considerable distance from the shore, before the browns, greens and blues all merged into a rich cobalt as the water deepened towards the horizon.

Beside her, she heard Hope's voice, full of emotion.

'It's so beautiful, I think I'm going to cry. Thank you so much for bringing me with you, Jess.'

Jess turned towards her and saw her looking almost as emotional as she had been after her break-up. She stretched out her hand, caught hold of her friend's arm and gave it a squeeze.

'What was that you were saying about the camera never lying? That poster of yours hasn't been photoshopped after all. The sea really is this colour. I honestly didn't believe it, but it's quite amazing. But don't cry, Hope. We're here, and we're staying for a whole month, maybe all summer.' She pointed down the hill. 'And, unless I'm very much mistaken, that's us down there.'

The track curled gently down the hillside towards a pair of wrought iron gates, set between hefty brick pillars. Wire fencing stretched out on either side, behind it a mass of greenery, topped with the unmistakable shape of massive old umbrella pines. Just visible among these were glimpses of pink roof tiles. And the whole estate was positioned virtually at the waterside.

'Blimey, what a place...'

Jess coasted down to the gates and stopped. Sure enough – there was a wooden sign on the gatepost marked *Les*

Romarins. She was just about to get out and ring the bell, when a yellow light on the gatepost began to flash and the gates started to open inwards. The two girls exchanged glances.

'That's a bit creepy. There must be video surveillance or something.'

Jess peered around, but couldn't see a camera. The sensation of being watched was a bit spooky, but a few seconds later, she discovered that the explanation was far less sinister. As the gates opened fully and she was about to pull the gear lever into Drive, the nose of another vehicle appeared, coming out towards them. Presumably this was why the gates had opened – not some clandestine surveillance operation, after all.

The car that emerged from the gates was amazing. It was an old open-topped sports car and it looked like something out of a James Bond film – slick, silver and very sexy.

'That's an E-Type Jaguar.'

Jess was mildly surprised to hear Hope demonstrating a hitherto unsuspected expertise in identifying classic sports cars, but what was even more surprising was the fact that she found herself much more interested in the driver. He was probably around her age, maybe a little older, maybe in his mid-thirties. He wasn't classically handsome like the Ferrari driver back on the main road, but there was something about him that stirred sensations in Jess she hadn't felt for a good long time. His face wasn't particularly tanned, he didn't look particularly cheerful, his short-cropped brown hair wasn't particularly stylish, and his nose looked as if it had been broken at some point, but she just couldn't keep her eyes off him.

As his car drew level, she leaned towards the open window with a smile, ready to introduce herself, but, to her surprise, he didn't stop. For a second he glanced in her direction and they made eye contact, but then, just as quickly, he looked away. The next moment, there was a throaty rumble, the noise of wheels spinning in the gravel, and the silver car shot off up the hill, raising a thick cloud of dust in its wake. As the cloud rolled towards them, Jess hastily closed the windows again, but not before a good bit of dust had made its way into the car. She reached for a tissue to blow her nose and heard the dog in the back start sneezing.

'That was a bit rude.' Hope coughed to clear her throat.

'That was *bloody* rude.'

Jess blew her nose and glanced in the door mirror just in time to see the silver car disappear over the crest behind them, the dust plume in its wake making it look as though the car was on fire. But even through her annoyance, she couldn't stop thinking about the man in the car and, in particular, his amazing cornflower-blue eyes. She had only glimpsed them for a second, but she felt sure she would be able to pick them out again from among a thousand others.

She ran her hand across her face and wiped the dust from her brow, shaking her head to return her thoughts to the here and now.

'So who do we think that was?' Hope asked the same question that was running through Jess's mind. 'He's surely too young to be old Mrs Dupont's son, isn't he? Might he be a grandson? Did she talk about a grandson?'

'Nope, but you're right. Her son's got to be in his fifties or sixties. Maybe that guy was just visiting.'

'Well, he can come and visit me any time he wants. What a hunk!'

Looking out of the windscreen, through the dissipating dust cloud, Jess noticed that the gates were once more closed. She opened the windows again and glanced over at Hope.

'Feel like jumping out and pressing the button?'

Hope climbed out, went across to the bell on the gatepost and pressed it. She had a pretty long wait. After a while, she pressed it again, glancing round at Jess and shrugging her shoulders helplessly. Then, finally, there was a crackle and, even from the driver's seat, Jess quite clearly heard a disembodied voice answer.

'*Bonjour, oui?*' It was a woman's voice.

'Um… *Bonjour, nous avons porté le chien.*'

'*Le chien?*'

'Yes. *Le chien de Mrs Dupont*. The dog from London?'

Hope's schoolgirl French was beginning to fray at the edges.

'Mrs Dupont in London? Did you say London? You've brought a dog – *un chien?*'

Jess was relieved to hear that the woman's English sounded fluent – certainly more fluent than their French – but she was dismayed that the voice on the other end of the line didn't appear to be expecting them. She slipped out of the driving seat and went over to provide moral support to Hope.

'*Bonjour.* My name is Jessica Milton. We've been asked by Mrs Dupont in London to bring her dog over to her son for three months, while she goes away on holiday.'

There was silence for a few moments, before they heard the voice again, unmistakable exasperation in her tone.

'Ah, I see. Well, you'd better come in. I will open the gate.'

'*Merci*.' They both climbed back into the car as the yellow light started flashing once more. They looked at each other. Jess was the first to speak.

'I'm glad she speaks English, but it doesn't sound good, does it? I rather think nobody's told them we're coming.'

'But your Mrs Dupont said she'd spoken to her son, didn't she?'

'Yes, but she also said he was a bit absent-minded. Maybe he forgot to pass on the message.'

'Oh, bugger.'

Chapter 5

Once the gates had swung open, Jess manoeuvred the big vehicle in through them and onto a gravelled drive, bordered by colourful oleander bushes – some of them bigger and taller than their car. The pink, red and white flowers made a delightful display as they passed through them, and provided welcome shade. After a short distance, the drive widened into a large circular area of gravel in front of the villa, with a massive umbrella pine in the middle, providing more shade.

The villa was recognisably the same one they had seen on the computer but, close up, it looked even lovelier. As Jess had deduced, it was built in the old Provençal style – ochre walls, pink roof tiles, and dusty green shutters. It looked as if it had some rooms in the roof and, presumably, wonderful views of the sea from the far side. It was difficult to tell whether this was a genuinely ancient property or a modern recreation of something traditional. Jess's gut feeling was that it wasn't very old, but, either way, it was amazing.

They drew up in front of a short flight of steps leading to the main door, tucked beneath a pillared porch, with rose beds on either side. Jess turned off the engine and climbed out, stretching as she did so. She felt a bit dishevelled after so long in the car, but she had to admit that the eight hundred kilometres they had driven that day had been remarkably smooth in the big vehicle.

She walked round to the back and opened the tailgate. Brutus greeted her with a wag of the tail and an attempt to lick her face as she helped him down to the ground. Clearly, the journey hadn't done him any harm. Jess made a mental note to call Mrs Dupont to let her know all had gone well. As the dog sauntered over to the base of the pine tree to relieve himself, the front door opened and a dark-haired woman, probably in her forties, appeared. She looked stressed.

'*Bonjour.*' She glanced across at Brutus dubiously. 'You said you have brought a dog?'

Jess went over to her. 'Yes, I'm Jessica, but everybody calls me Jess. And this is my friend Hope. We were asked by Mrs Dupont to bring her dog over here. She said we could stay here for a few weeks to look after him.'

'Stay here?' The woman looked positively shell-shocked.

A feeling of foreboding descended upon Jess.

'She said something about a separate guest house in a corner of the garden?'

Comprehension dawned in the woman's eyes. There was a pause while she took stock and then she ran a tired hand through her black hair, before holding it out to them in greeting.

'Welcome to *Les Romarins*, Jessica... Jess – and you, Hope. My name is Antoinette and I'm Monsieur Dupont's housekeeper. I'm afraid Monsieur Dupont must have forgotten to mention that you were coming. I'm so sorry. I haven't prepared anything. If I'd known you were coming...'

From her tone, it was pretty clear that this wasn't the first time Monsieur Dupont had forgotten to keep her informed. The exasperation they had heard earlier was now under-standable. Jess was quick to reassure her.

'Don't worry about it, Antoinette. Just point us in the right direction and we'll be fine. Anyway, you can tell Monsieur Dupont that Brutus the dog has arrived safe and sound.'

They both glanced across to the pine tree, where Brutus, mission accomplished, was still sniffing around happily. Sensing himself being watched, he turned and trotted across towards them, tail wagging lazily.

'Brutus, this is Antoinette. Say hello nicely.'

'What a handsome-looking dog, although…' Antoinette still sounded a bit uncertain. She glanced up at Jess as she scratched his ears. 'Although it looks as though he likes his food quite a lot.'

'Oh yes. Brutus certainly likes his food. In fact, Hope and I feel he would benefit from going on a diet. I'm sure he doesn't share our opinion, but it'll be in his interests.' Jess glanced around. 'Is Monsieur Dupont at home? I bring greetings to him from his mother in London.'

'Monsieur Dupont is home, but he's in his room. He told me he didn't want to be disturbed.'

So not only did he forget to mention we were coming, he can't be bothered to come down and say hello. Jess was saddened, but unsurprised. By the sound of it, he was out of the same mould as the driver of the silver sports car – money but no manners. She did her best to banish memories of Rafael and suppressed a sigh as Antoinette carried on.

'Now, just let me pop back into the house to get the keys and I can accompany you to your house. I'm afraid it'll be a bit dusty, but we'll soon have it looking clean and tidy again.' For the first time, she managed to muster a smile. 'Actually, I'm very pleased you're going to be staying for a while, although it would have been nice to have been told.…

We so rarely get visitors these days.' There was regret in Antoinette's voice. Glancing over her shoulder to be sure she wasn't overheard, she lowered her voice. 'Monsieur Dupont lives a very solitary life nowadays, I'm afraid.'

'We saw another man, just as we arrived. In a silver sports car?' Jess couldn't restrain her curiosity.

'That was Monsieur Dupont's son – David.'

Jess waited for Antoinette to say more, but she didn't. There was a brief, but awkward, pause that Jess would dearly have liked to break, but the housekeeper disappeared back into the house without a word.

Inexplicably disappointed not to have learned more about Monsieur Dupont's son, David, Jess exchanged glances with Hope once more.

'What a balls-up.'

'You can say that again. Thank goodness the housekeeper was here. Otherwise we might well still be sitting outside the gate. Fancy forgetting to tell her…!'

Less than a minute later, Antoinette reappeared.

'If you'd like to come with me, you'll be staying down here.'

She pointed down a gravel path that led towards an old brick wall – all but concealed beneath a magnificent purple bougainvillea.

'We can leave your things in the car for now. Come and let me show you the guest house. My apologies once more. You're going to find it in a bit of a state, I'm afraid.' She turned towards Jess. 'Did you say you were staying for a while?'

'Well, hopefully a month or so, maybe more. Until our money runs out.'

Antoinette smiled at her – this time looking more relaxed. 'And it *will* run out pretty fast in St-Tropez if you go to the wrong places. I'll have to tell you where to go and where to avoid.'

'That would be very, very useful.'

Jess and Hope followed Antoinette down the path and through an archway in the brick wall. Brutus trotted alongside them. It was probably just a side effect of spending two days in a car, but he appeared unusually full of beans and Jess hoped that maybe his new diet was beginning to give him a bit more energy.

The archway led into a walled garden. The first sensations upon entering the garden were the wonderful scent of flowers and the persistent buzzing of bees. The gravel path split and fanned out into three separate paths, one to the left, one to the right and one straight on. Each of the paths was bordered by overgrown box hedges. The flower beds themselves were full of roses of all colours, as well as bright blue lavender and taller purple flowers that Jess didn't recognise. Alas, they were also full of weeds and brambles and clearly hadn't been cared for in a good while. In the middle of the garden was a little wooden arbour, submerged beneath a mass of pink flowers, with a bench set inside, in the shade. The whole place smelt and looked delightful, if a bit unkempt.

'What a lovely garden.' Jess nodded at Hope.

'Yes, indeed. And what a fabulous scent in the air.' Hope smiled back, her eyes misty. 'I've never been anywhere like this.'

'It's terribly neglected, I'm afraid. Monsieur Dupont used to do it all himself, but he's hardly been out of his room for months now. Luckily, there's no shortage of water here. We have three wells at *Les Romarins* and an automatic watering system, so the plants are still surviving amidst the weeds.'

They walked past the arbour to the far corner of the garden, where a wooden door was set in another arch.

'Your house is through here.'

Pushing the door open, Antoinette led them through into what would become their home for the next few weeks, maybe months.

In front of them was a patch of what had once no doubt been lawn, but which was now an unruly mixture of weeds and long grass. Beyond this was a charming building that stopped Jess in her tracks. It was totally different from the villa itself. Gone was the rustic, Provençal look of the main house. Here they suddenly found themselves in ancient Greece. The building was a single-storey, all-white affair, with a flat roof. A line of Doric columns ran along the front, beneath which was a delightful shady terrace. In the middle of the lawn, directly in front of the entrance, was a white marble statue of a naked goddess in classic Greek style, her robe just preserving her modesty, her long hair coiled up on her head with a few locks hanging to her shoulders.

'Aphrodite herself! What a place!' Jess turned to Antoinette. 'Is this old?'

Antoinette shook her head. 'Not *very* old – just a hundred years or so. I believe it was built in the nineteen-twenties. In fact, I remember hearing that the Germans used it for storing ammunition before the invasion.'

'Invasion?'

'Yes, in 1944, just after the Normandy landings, when the Allies came up from Italy and invaded, right here and along the coast.'

This was news to Jess. 'So, there was fighting here in St-Tropez?'

'Yes, indeed. The original villa was badly damaged by shelling and rebuilt after the war. But this little house was untouched.'

It was like walking into an ancient Greek temple. The house was bigger than it looked, with a little internal court-yard ringed with more columns, in the centre of which was another beautiful statue on a plinth – this time of a completely naked woman bearing a vase in her hands. There were two bedrooms – each with its own marble-clad bath-room – a fine modern kitchen, and a large open-plan living area opening onto the courtyard. In here there was a dining table with seating for eight, and a pair of leather sofas facing a huge TV screen. There was also a thriving colony of spiders, whose webs were all over the place. As Jess walked into the kitchen, something caught in her hair and she shook it off. In her profession, spiders were commonplace, but she still didn't really like them.

'I'm so sorry I didn't know you were coming. I would have cleaned it up for you.' Antoinette sounded mortified and Jess was quick to reassure her.

'Don't worry about it. Please. We'll soon have it tidied up. We've got nothing else to do apart from feeding and walking the dog. Leave it to us. Really.' Jess glanced at Hope, whose eyes were wide with appreciation – spiders or no spiders. 'What a fantastic place.'

'I've never been anywhere like this in my life.' Hope repeated her mantra as she glanced down at her feet where the Labrador was rolling happily on the cool marble slabs, raising a cloud of dust as he did so. 'And I get the feeling Brutus approves.'

Antoinette was opening doors and checking cupboards.

'I've turned the fridge on and it should be cold in an hour or two. There are bottles of water and wine in the cupboards, but I wouldn't touch anything else – or at least check the expiry dates first. The last time anybody stayed here must be at least a year ago and it'll all be stale.'

She glanced at her watch.

'I'm sure the last thing you want to do is to go shopping tonight. Leave it to me. I'll pop back up to the house and fetch fresh sheets and towels for you and, while I'm at it, I'll bring you something to eat tonight and for breakfast tomorrow.'

'Please don't go to any bother on our account, Antoinette. We can cope.'

'That's very sweet of you, Jess, but you must think we're absolutely awful. Fancy Mr Dupont not telling me you were coming!'

'Really, it's okay.'

Antoinette disappeared back to the villa to get their linen, leaving the two girls standing in the kitchen.

'This is one hell of a place! Cheer up, Jess. All right, it's a bit dusty, but we'll get that sorted.' Hope was sounding upbeat.

'Of course. Sorry, I didn't mean to look miserable, but it's not quite the start I was hoping for.'

'We all make mistakes, Jess. So he forgot, it doesn't matter. We'll soon have the place shipshape.'

'I know, Hope. And you're right. We'll soon get this place tidied up. Now, let's see if we can find a vacuum and a few mops and brushes.'

By the time Antoinette returned with an armful of linen, they had located the cleaning utensils and had made a start.

The housekeeper, still looking apologetic, deposited the sheets and towels and returned to the villa for a second load. When she came back, she was carrying two hefty shopping baskets. From these, she produced veritable cornucopia of delicacies, ranging from olives to eggs, pâté and local cheese. She also brought fruit, bread and a couple of packets of biscuits. As she stocked the fridge, she kept apologising.

'I'm so, so sorry. Anyway, listen – tomorrow morning, I'll go to the shops and get in a load of food for you.' She waved away Jess and Hope's protests. 'It's what Mrs Dupont would have wanted me to do. That'll keep you going for a few days and then I can explain where to buy more food.'

'There's really no need.'

'Oh yes, there is. I'll go and make up your beds now and I can come and change the sheets whenever you want. And I can do any laundry for you, too. Just tell me.'

Jess shook her head decisively. 'Absolutely not. We certainly don't want to make extra work for you. We can make our own beds and we'll do our own laundry – and that includes sheets and towels. I can see there's a washing machine. Is there an iron and an ironing board?'

'Well… yes, but I'm very happy to do the sheets, really.'

Jess thanked Antoinette again and politely refused her help. A bit of laundry was the least they could do. Finally, Antoinette agreed and Jess could see she was secretly rather pleased.

'Well, if you're sure. Thank you. Now, there's a swimming pool over to the east of the villa. If you go back into the rose garden and take the path to the left, it'll lead you there. If you want to swim in the sea, you'll need to take the right path and just follow it round the other side of the villa and down. But the water's still a bit cold at this time of year.'

Hope smiled. 'Don't forget, we're English. We don't feel the cold! I'll give it a try.'

Jess shivered. 'Speak for yourself. I'll come with you and stick my toe in the water, but you might be on your own after that.'

Antoinette smiled. 'You'd probably do better in the pool, Jess. It's heated all year round.' She glanced at her watch. 'Anyway, I'm afraid I have to dash off and prepare dinner for Mr Dupont and then go home and look after my husband. Here's my phone number if you need anything. I'm at the villa from eight in the morning to seven or later, most days, with a few hours off in the afternoon. Anything you want, just call.'

She glanced down at the dog who was lying stretched out on the floor, looking as if he belonged here.

'What about the dog? What's his name again?'

'Brutus. He can stay here with us unless Monsieur Dupont prefers to take him. We've brought his bed and some food. He'll be fine.'

Antoinette looked relieved.

'Very good. I'll make sure Monsieur Dupont knows you've arrived, but I have no doubt he'll be very happy to know that you'll look after the dog. I'm sorry he's not feeling very sociable today, and I'm even sorrier he didn't tell me you were coming, but he'll be in contact with you before long. Would you like me to give you a hand with your things, bringing them from the car?'

'That's very kind, but there's no need, thanks. We haven't got a lot of stuff.'

'Well, *au revoir,* and remember to tell me if you need anything.'

Once they had emptied the car, Jess and Hope spent an hour cleaning the house and making their beds. In fact, apart from a bit of dust and a whole legion of dead flies, along with some disgruntled spiders that Hope painstakingly caught in a glass and released a good long way from the house, there wasn't an awful lot to do, and the place was soon quite habitable. Jess sat down and had a long phone conversation with Mrs Dupont in London, while Hope made them some tea. She made no mention of the fact that Mrs Dupont's son hadn't thought to inform his housekeeper of their imminent arrival – preferring to let her go off on her cruise without worries.

The old lady was very pleased to hear that they had got there safely and that Brutus hadn't found the journey too stressful. As she talked, Jess glanced down to the black shape sprawled at her feet, grunting happily to himself, and was able to assure her that Brutus was in fine form. She also decided it best to omit any reference to the incidents in the hotel or his change of diet. Time would tell as far as that was concerned.

'And have you met George?'

'Your son? Um, no, not yet.'

Jess went on to tell her what Antoinette had said about him not feeling very sociable and she heard concern in Mrs Dupont's voice as she responded.

'Oh dear. I'm so sorry. The thing is – I should really have told you, but his wife died last year and he's been suffering from depression. Will you try to cheer him up, please, Jess? I'm sure you'll be able to do that.'

'I'll do my very best. I promise.' She hesitated a moment. 'And I saw his son, David, but only briefly.'

'Poor David.'

Jess waited for more, but it wasn't forthcoming. Finally she tried a bit of prodding.

'He didn't look very happy either.'

'No, I'm afraid he and his father have both been quite miserable. He's had a hard time. Next time you see him, give him a big hug from me, will you?'

Chance, Jess thought to herself, would be a fine thing.

'Anyway, Jess, tell me all about Brutus. Is he eating properly?'

Properly wasn't really the adverb Jess would have chosen for Brutus's diet – at least not up to the previous day. She made no mention of his flabbiness, flatulence or unfitness and just told Mrs Dupont how happy he looked, here on the Côte d'Azur.

'And he's not the only one. Hope and I have been blown away by the beauty of this place.'

'I'm so glad you like *Les Romarins*. I have very fond memories of the years I spent there. I hope you both have a wonderful time. Do stay in touch. I'm off to Southampton tomorrow and we sail the morning after. I imagine there'll be telephone connections and internet on board – although I don't really get involved with all that computer business.'

'Of course I'll stay in touch, and thanks again, Mrs Dupont.'

'Goodbye my dear. You have a wonderful time and re-member – I'm counting on you to cheer George and David up.'

Jess had no idea how she was supposed to do this, but she answered positively all the same.

'I'll do my very best.'

Chapter 6

The little house was equipped with air conditioning, but they found they didn't need it. No doubt when summer arrived in full force it would prove a godsend, but for now, the evening air temperature was warm but very pleasant, and they sat outside in the little courtyard to have their evening meal, to the accompaniment of a chorus of cicadas. The food Antoinette had brought was mouth-watering, and there was more than enough to feed several hungry families.

The last serious meal for either of them had been in the hotel where Brutus had come close to wrecking the place, and by now they were both hungry. Their appetites grew as they unloaded some of the wonders that Antoinette had produced for them.

There was an amazing selection of sliced ham and salami. To their amazement, they found a dish containing four thick slices of foie gras, accompanied by what tasted like pear compote. Along with this were hard boiled quail's eggs and huge green olives. There was half an asparagus quiche – clearly homemade – and they made themselves a salad out of two enormous tomatoes, which smelt and tasted as if they had been picked only a few minutes earlier. They added a selection of different lettuce leaves, dressing them with local olive oil and wine vinegar.

There were no fewer than four different cheeses, wrapped in anonymous paper, varying in form from hard, yellow exteriors to soft, creamy interiors, none of them familiar, but all excellent. Antoinette had also supplied them with a long fresh baguette, and Jess found herself wondering if the occupants of the villa would be eating dry biscuits tonight as a result.

The meal was delightful and the bottle of very pale, almost grey, rosé wine they opened to accompany it was spectacular, even if the label was new to both of them. They finished the meal with a bowl of wonderful fresh black cherries and finally sat back, replete, smiles on their faces, feeling decidedly drowsy. As the sky darkened, the swallows shooting overhead were replaced by bats, and all around them was silent. They couldn't even hear a car. It was wonderful.

'Blimey, Jess, this is the life.'

Jess couldn't agree more.

'Too true. Mind you, if we carry on eating as well as this, it'll be Brutus who has to put us on a diet.'

They both slept like logs that night and Jess was particularly pleased not to be bothered by mosquitoes. Next morning, she was woken by a cold, wet nose prodding her bare arm. She opened her eyes and saw Brutus standing beside the bed, wagging his tail.

'Morning, Brutus. Sleep well?'

In reply, he stretched luxuriously, producing his trademark half-howl, half-whine.

'Want to go out?'

Jess slipped on shorts, a T-shirt and flip-flops and led him through to the front door. A glance at the clock told her it was just before eight o'clock and there was no sound from Hope's bedroom, so she didn't disturb her. She and the dog stepped out onto the terrace and looked around. Brutus wasted no time in locating an appealing tree, while Jess wandered across the lawn to the wooden door leading to the walled garden. In there, she was initially surprised to see puddles on the paths and to hear running water, although the sky was once again cloudless. Then she found that the water was coming in the form of a fine spray emanating from a network of black hoses laid between the plants. Clearly, this was courtesy of the precious wells beneath the property. Droplets covered the leaves and flowers, and the early morning sunshine sparkled on the petals like jewels. It was refreshing, beautiful and tranquil. Apart from the sound of the water and the buzzing of bees, it was still completely quiet in there – no rumble of traffic, no planes overhead and no voices, not even in the far distance. She took a deep breath, relishing the peaceful atmosphere.

She felt a warm body touch her legs and glanced down to find Brutus standing beside her, his tail still wagging.

'Want a little walk, Brutus?'

She tried to remember which door led to the pool and which to the sea. In the end she opted for the left-hand door and pushed it cautiously open, finding herself on a path that wound its way around the side of the villa. As she and Brutus followed it, she saw no signs of life from the villa, but she did notice the silver sports car now parked on the gravel outside the front door. Instinctively, she glanced up at the windows in the roof of the house, but the shutters were all closed, and there was no sign of the car's enigmatic driver.

As they passed the side of the villa, it immediately became clear that she had taken the wrong path. Instead of heading for the sea, she found herself in a charming spot, rather lower than the surrounding ground, surrounded by a tall, impenetrable hedge of meticulously-trimmed rosemary. The bushes were covered in a mass of little blue flowers and the scent was almost overpowering. Once again, legions of bees were hard at work. In the middle of this sheltered area was a delightful swimming pool, the water absolutely motionless in the still early morning.

Or at least it was for a few seconds.

There was a sudden splash that made Jess jump, and the next thing she saw was a very happy Labrador surfacing after flopping in. He shook the water off his head and looked up at her. It didn't take much imagination to see a broad smile on his face.

'I'm not sure you're supposed to be in here, Brutus.' She had a feeling the other inhabitants of the villa might object to finding dog hair in their pristine pool. 'I think you'd better come back out again.'

Brutus clearly had other ideas, and he set off on a tour of the pool, nose just lifted above the water, tail streaming out behind him. Apart from her fear that dogs and pools maybe shouldn't mix, Jess was sure of one thing. Even though Brutus didn't appear to display any great interest in walking far at the moment, if he could get into the habit of going for a good swim every day, his weight problem would soon be resolved. She walked across to the shallow end, where four steps led down into the pool, slipped off her shoes and put her feet in the water.

It wasn't hot, but it definitely wasn't cold. Enjoying the sensation of the water on her legs, she vowed to come back for a swim later on. She stood in the shallows and watched Brutus for a few minutes, enjoying the warm morning sun on her shoulders. The thick hedges would offer excellent protection on a windy day and they almost completely hid the pool from sight. Glancing up, she saw that it was only overlooked by three shuttered windows on the upper floor of the villa, but, otherwise, occupants of the pool would be assured of their privacy. For a moment, a rather naughty thought occurred to her. She had never tried skinny-dipping in her life. Maybe this was the place to try. No sooner had the thought come than she dismissed it. She and Hope were here as guests, and it would be wise to behave responsibly.

After a while, she called Brutus, feeling that the time had come for the two of them to head back to their little house. Obligingly, he swam back towards her, but then encountered a problem. In his current unathletic state, he appeared unable to pull himself out of the water onto the bottom step. Seeing him struggle, Jess tucked her shorts up as high as she could and went down the steps to help. By the time she had tugged him out of the water, she was almost as wet as the Labrador.

As Brutus finally climbed heavily up the steps and went off to shake himself, Jess glanced down and saw, to her dismay, that her white T-shirt was now soaked. It was plastered tightly to her body and had become almost transparent. Having just climbed out of bed, she was naked underneath. She grabbed the bottom of the T-shirt and started flapping it desperately, trying to dry it at least sufficiently to allow her to make her way back to the house without looking too obscene.

Then, for some reason, she looked upwards.

The shutters were now no longer all closed. The shutters either side of one of the windows overlooking the pool were open, as was the window itself. And unmistakably, in the shadows inside the window, his head just visible over the sill, was the driver of the silver sports car – David Dupont. For a second their eyes met and then, as her hands flew up to cover herself, he pulled back and disappeared from view. Jess blushed red, splashed up the steps, turned and fled, her arms firmly crossed in front of her.

Fortunately she met nobody on her way back to the house and she was able to get safely inside, accompanied by Brutus, without further embarrassment. The embarrassment started the moment she walked in the door.

'Miss Wet T-shirt, I presume.' Hope was giggling.

'Bloody hell, Hope, you don't know the half of it. I've just inadvertently put on a show for David Dupont, who was peeking out at me from his bedroom window.'

'Well, I wouldn't worry too much. The way you and Brutus smell at the moment, I doubt if he'd be thinking too many lustful thoughts.' She looked down at the dog, who had rolled onto his back and was scooting himself around on the marble floor tiles, grunting happily, leaving a slippery trail in his wake. 'I think I'd better dig out the mop again – and an old towel.'

Jess went through to her bathroom and stripped off her wet clothes. As she stood under the jet of warm water, she found herself analysing her feelings. Yes, there was embarrassment, but there had also been a moment back there when, even in the midst of her discomfort, she had felt a shiver of desire. Although the idea of him peeking at her from the shadows while she walked around as good as topless should have been creepy, it had in fact been stimulating. What on earth was going on inside her head?

She was still mulling it over when she emerged from her room, dressed in fresh, dry clothes. Hope was quick to reassure her.

'As far as you showing your boobs to David Dupont is concerned, I wouldn't worry. Don't forget, we're in St-Tropez. As far as I remember, this is pretty much the place where topless sunbathing took off. He's probably lost count of how many naked or half-naked women he's seen.'

Jess grimaced. 'I've never sunbathed topless in my life, and I have no intention of starting now, thank you very much.'

'What? Not even if all the other girls on the beach were topless? I wouldn't mind.' Hope gave Jess a grin. 'It's not as if you or I are built differently from all the others.'

Jess shook her head uncertainly, still puzzled by the emotions the sight of David had stirred in her. Surely, for somebody as adamant as she was about not wanting to parade her nakedness in public, she should have been mortified. But, although she had been embarrassed, there was no getting away from the fact that she had rather enjoyed the sensation of feeling his eyes upon her. And considering she was so determined to avoid any contact with men – particularly wealthy men – this was unexpected, to say the least.

Hope, in the meantime, had worked out how to make them each a pretty convincing-looking cappuccino, using the amazing coffee machine in the extremely well-equipped kitchen. Jess took a sip and pronounced it excellent.

Brutus, having disposed of his breakfast handful of biscuits, came trotting over and sat down beside her, resting his head on her knee. Hope must have found an old towel and dried him, because he was now just a bit damp, rather than wet. He still smelt a bit doggy, but at least he was now clean. Jess rested her hand on his head and scratched his ears as she looked across at Hope.

'So, day one of our holiday. What would you like to do?'

'Whatever you like, although if I don't have to get back into a car again for a few days, I won't be sorry.'

'Me neither, although we're going to need to do some shopping before too long. Looking at the map, we're only a mile or so away from St-Tropez, so why don't we walk in and take a look round? I seem to remember reading that there's a coastal footpath.'

'Sounds good to me. Maybe we can leave Brutus at the villa while we're away. Until he loses a good bit of weight, I don't see him walking a mile there and a mile back again, do you?'

Just then, there was a tap at the door and Brutus raised his head from Jess's knee, clearly involved in an internal debate as to whether he should adopt his usual guard dog ways and bark the house down, or do nothing. In the end he must have decided he was on holiday and he just followed Jess out to the door, wagging his tail amiably.

'Jess, *bonjour.*'

It was Antoinette, laden down with bags. Jess rushed to help her, relieving her of the two heaviest ones.

'Good morning, Antoinette. But you've bought half of St-Tropez! There was no need for all this, honestly.'

A long baguette protruded from one of the bags. From the smell of it, the bread was fresh out of the oven.

'This is all so very kind. How much do I owe you?'

'Nothing at all.' Antoinette made a dismissive gesture. 'I got a phone call from Madame Dupont just as I was going home last night, and she told me to look after you both and get you anything you need.' She caught Jess's eye. 'Just one thing – to be honest, I didn't mention that Monsieur Dupont hadn't passed on the message that you were coming. I hope you don't mind. I didn't want to cause trouble between them.' She hesitated. 'I'm afraid it doesn't take much to make him grumpy these days.' She shook her head sadly.

Jess nodded. 'I spoke to her last night as well and I didn't mention it either. Let's leave it like that.'

Antoinette looked relieved. She handed over another couple of bags, from which a wonderful aroma was making not only the dog, but Jess, salivate. By this time they were back in the kitchen and Antoinette noticed a different smell. She wrinkled up her nose. 'Have you given the dog a bath?'

Jess and Hope exchanged glances.

'Yes, but not deliberately. He jumped into the swimming pool. I'm very sorry. I took him for a short walk earlier on and I turned left instead of right and ended up at the pool. Before I could stop him, he'd splashed in. I'm sorry about that. I'll make sure he doesn't do it again – not least because he couldn't get out again and I ended up getting soaked.'

'I wouldn't think it matters if he goes in the pool, but it'll be easier for him in the sea. There's a little beach just below the villa where he can just walk in and out and you won't even need to get your feet wet. Just take the other door out of the walled garden and follow the path. Coming from here, it's the one on the right you need.'

'That's terrific, thank you, Antoinette. Hope and I were thinking of walking into St-Tropez this morning. It's so close, there's no point taking the car, and I imagine there's nowhere to park if we do.'

'Actually, there's a pretty big car park, and at this time of year you should be able to find space. In the summer, though, it's normally packed.'

'To be honest, we've both had enough of driving for a while. And with all this lovely food you've bought us, we don't need to go to the shops for a few days.'

'Well, if you don't want to take the car, there's the little local bus, the *navette*, but it only runs a few times a day. I'll look you up the timetable. Otherwise, you can walk back up the road you drove down or, of course, there's the path round the coast.'

Jess and Hope exchanged glances.

'I think we'll go for the coastal path. I imagine it's going to be very scenic.'

'The views are super, but it's not the best path in the world. I'm not sure if Brutus here will be able to scramble over the rocks too easily.'

'Until we can get him weighing a good bit less and feeling a bit more energetic, it's too far for him anyway, I think. Could we leave him with you for a few hours this morning?'

'Of course. Just bring him up to the villa when you set off. Either ring the front doorbell or come round the side. You'll easily find the kitchen door. It's the opposite end of the house from the swimming pool, so you'll walk right past it on the way to the beach.'

'Wonderful, thanks.'

Jess opened a paper bag protruding from one of the carriers and her eyes opened wide. In it were fresh croissants and pains aux raisins, and the aroma that wafted up from the bag was irresistible. She raised her eyes towards Antoinette again. 'Will you join us for breakfast, Antoinette? These look amazing. Thank you so much. Hope's already an expert with the coffee machine.'

'Cappuccino or espresso?' Hope was already at the machine.

'Thank you, but I'd better go back and prepare breakfast for Monsieur Dupont. He normally surfaces about now.'

Jess glanced at her watch and saw that it was now almost nine o'clock. She hesitated for a moment. She was honest enough to admit to herself, if not to the other two, that it was the other occupant of the house that interested her more.

'And David? Is he an early riser?'

Antoinette shrugged. 'Who knows? Some days I don't see him until lunchtime. Other days his car's already gone when I arrive. The car's still here today, so maybe he's already up, or maybe he's still closed in his room.'

'I spoke to Mrs Dupont last night and she told me they've both been depressed. Are they still suffering?'

Antoinette instinctively glanced over her shoulder and lowered her voice. 'I'm afraid so. I try, but I just can't seem to get through to either of them.'

'Mrs Dupont asked me to try to cheer them both up. Do you think it can be done?'

Antoinette shrugged again.

'It won't be easy, but please do try.'

Chapter 7

They walked up to the villa at just after ten and left Brutus with Antoinette. The back door to the kitchen was open and easy to spot and the dog, nostrils flared, needed no persuading to trot in and station himself alongside Antoinette, who was busy preparing food.

Hope nodded towards him. 'No treats for Brutus, please. He needs to lose a good bit of weight. We'll be back by two and we'll feed him then. Is that all right?'

'Of course.' Antoinette smiled down at the dog. 'My cousins had a Labrador and he was always hungry. They say it's a gene thing. He was always begging, but we had to harden our hearts – for his own good. So you can rely on me. By the time you take him back to England, let's see if, between us, we can get him looking slim and fit.'

Both Jess and Hope agreed that one of their priorities was going to be to get the Labrador back into shape, and that would involve getting him walking and swimming. As they emerged at the end of the path from the villa to the sea, they immediately found the little bay that Antoinette had described. The gravel beach shelved gently into the clear water and they felt sure Brutus would find it easy to get in and out. That, at least, would be a start to his rehabilitation.

The coastal footpath was, as Antoinette had said, quite sketchy in places and they had to take it slow. Certainly, in his present corpulent state, Brutus wouldn't have stood a chance of scrambling along it. In fact, Jess and Hope would have taken their time even if the path had been wide, flat and perfect. The views were a delight and they were forever slowing or stopping as something caught their attention. The coastline was rocky – low cliffs punctuated by narrow creeks and occasional beaches. The water was crystal clear and they regularly spotted fish – sometimes quite big fish – in the shallows.

There was little or no wind and the sea was flat calm. A handful of yachts of differing sizes dotted the mouth of the bay, their sails hanging hopefully, but limply, from their masts – going nowhere fast. An open fishing boat was close in to the coast and they could clearly see the fisherman on board as he pulled up lobster or crab pots, many of them containing valuable crustaceans that would, no doubt, appear in the local fish shops later that morning.

The vegetation on the hillside behind them was mainly just low scrub with an occasional pine tree, but it was punctuated by flowers of all colours, ranging from swathes of bright red poppies to clumps of big yellow daisies and different exotic flowers right down by the water's edge. It was an idyllic scene and they both drank it in appreciatively.

There were very few houses to be seen. On a low headland, surrounded by overgrown bushes and shaded by an enormous umbrella pine, Jess's attention was drawn to what looked like a tumbledown farmhouse. It was made of stone and looked as if it had been there for centuries. To an architect like Jess, this represented perfection – a house in a wonderful position, with an amazing view, packed with history and needing complete restoration. She had no illusions as to the number of millions of euros a place like this had to be worth and she sighed at the thought of it ending up in the hands of a barbarian like Drugoi, or worse – if that was possible.

It took them twenty minutes or so before the rocky part of the path finished and they found themselves at the start of a gently-curving beach. At the end of it was a beach bar, complete with colourful umbrellas and reggae music coming from a series of speakers. The two girls looked at each other.

'This would appear to be our local.' Jess glanced at her watch. 'Coffee time?'

'Sounds good to me.'

They sat down at a table and relaxed under an umbrella. The air was already hot and it felt good to get into the shade, stretch their legs, shrugging off their sandals and pushing their feet into the warm sand. A black girl with blonde dreadlocks came across and gave them a smile.

'Hi, I'm Thérèse – everybody calls me Terri. Can I get you anything?' She spoke in English, with just a hint of a French accent lurking in the background.

'Hi, could we have two cappuccinos please?' Jess caught her eye. 'So, how did you know we spoke English? How could you tell?'

The waitress grinned. 'You look like you're on holiday, so I thought it was likely you'd be foreign. We get visitors here from all over the world and most speak English, rather than French. Where do you come from? England?' Both girls nodded. 'Staying long?'

'Hopefully at least a month, maybe longer.' It was on the tip of Jess's tongue to tell her they were staying at Mr Dupont's villa, but decided against it. It was pretty clear from what Antoinette had said that he and his son were keeping themselves to themselves, so it was probably best not to name names.

Terri smiled. 'Then I hope you come and see us often. If you come around sundown on Fridays and Saturdays, there's rum punch and dancing.'

As she went off to get the drinks, Hope settled back in her chair, a contented expression on her face, and glanced across at Jess. 'Ever tried rum punch?'

'Oh, yes… Tastes like a fruit salad, kicks like a mule.'

'What about dancing on sand?'

'Could be fun.'

'Could be hard work. We'll have to give it a try.'

Jess looked along the beach. It was almost empty. It took her a few moments to work out that today was Tuesday, the second or third of June. Presumably the place would get busier when July and August came along. The only people she could see for the moment were an elderly couple walking along the water's edge, a family with little children playing in the shallows, and a girl sunbathing at the far end of a wooden jetty. There were only two other people sitting under the shade of the umbrellas of the beach bar, both deeply engrossed in their phones.

As Jess and Hope sipped their coffees, they chatted and made plans for the next few days.

'I don't know about you, Hope, but I get bored very easily when I'm on holiday. I think I might have a go at the garden by the house. It's such a shame it's been neglected. The least I can do is to cut the grass and do a bit of weeding.'

'Sounds like a good idea. I'll help. We'd better just make sure we recognise the weeds from the good stuff. It wouldn't do to start pulling up Mr Dupont's prize specimens.'

After their coffee, they carried on round the last headland, past the waterside cemetery, until they arrived at St-Tropez proper. They threaded their way down through the narrow streets between lovely ochre townhouses – many covered with creepers, rambling roses and brightly-coloured bougainvillea – until they reached the harbour. After the peace and quiet of the coastal walk, this came as quite a shock to the senses.

Hope suddenly stopped dead, turned and grabbed Jess by the arm and then enveloped her in a warm hug.

'Thank you so very, very much, Jess. I really don't know how to thank you enough. I've been dreaming about this place for so long, I was starting to think it would never happen. And, without you, it wouldn't have.' She released her and grinned. 'Now that I'm here, the next thing on my agenda is that millionaire I've been searching for. Keep your eyes peeled.'

The harbour itself was packed with boats, and the quay-side was crowded with people. Cars threaded their way through tourists on the road that ran along the water's edge, while a couple of serious-looking policemen, carrying pistols in holsters, directed the traffic.

Hope turned her attention to the boats moored, stern-first, up against the quayside. 'Blimey, take a look at these, would you? It all looks like my poster, but the boats have got even bigger. I shudder to think what one of these costs.'

Jess nodded. The unbroken row of massive luxury yachts – what her father would have called 'gin palaces' – was certainly impressive. Some were two storeys high, and with a bridge on top – absolutely huge. Further out, moored along the side of the long stone breakwater, were even bigger yachts – one even with its own swimming pool.

Some boasted masts and sails, but the majority were quite clearly powered by engines, rather than the wind. As the girls walked along the waterside, trying not to trip over the hefty mooring ropes looped over iron bollards, they read the names of the boats and, unsurprisingly, the names of the tax havens where most were registered.

'So what *does* one of these cost?'

It so happened that Hope asked the question as they were walking past a particularly big specimen, named *Helios IV*, registered in the British Virgin Islands. Her question was overheard by a man sitting on one of the mooring bollards. He looked up and provided the answer.

'Three million dollars, give or take a few thou.' His accent might have been Australian or maybe South African. He grinned up at Hope, who was now looking embarrassed. 'They don't come cheap.'

Jess took a better look at him. He was a good-looking guy, probably about their age, or maybe early thirties at most. He was wearing deck shoes, shorts and a dark blue T-shirt bearing the name of the yacht on his left breast. His shoulder-length hair was bleached – presumably by the sun, although Jess wasn't going to rule out chemical intervention. He looked suntanned, fit and healthy, and she couldn't miss the fact that his eyes were still trained on Hope. Clearly he had seen something he liked. Jess wondered if his interest was going to be reciprocated and waited for Hope's response.

'I'm sorry, I didn't mean to sound nosey. I was just talking to my friend.'

The man stood up and held out his hand, first to Hope and then, as an afterthought, to Jess. 'No problem. Hi, my name's Max, and this is my yacht – *Helios*.'

Jess did a double-take. Surely a young guy like this couldn't be the owner of a boat worth millions. She saw Hope's jaw drop as she also took in the ramifications of what she had just heard.

'Your yacht?'

Max nodded. 'That's right. Want to come aboard and take a look?' He glanced at Jess, once again as an apparent afterthought. 'Of course you're both very welcome.'

Hope's eyes were by now wide open in amazement. She gave Max a big smile and introduced herself in return. 'Hi, Max. I'm Hope and this is my friend, Jess. We're here on holiday and I've never been on anything like this before.' She exchanged glances with Jess for a moment. 'We'd love to look over your yacht. Wouldn't we, Jess?'

Jess nodded, although she still wasn't totally convinced. Max looked way too young to own something like this. Still, at any rate, she knew she owed it to Hope to come along as company, at least for now, and she was quite interested at the idea of taking a look inside. Rafael had chartered one in Greece a few years before, but that had been nothing like as huge as this.

'Is it all right to go aboard the boat in these shoes?' She pointed down at her sandals and saw Max nod.

'Of course. We just don't like high heels. They tend to make a bit of a mess of the teak. Come aboard.'

He led them both over a polished wooden gangplank with stainless steel handrails on either side of it and onto the boat. Jess noticed that he offered Hope his hand as they reached the end of the plank and Hope demonstrated no hesitation in accepting his help. As for Jess, she had to make her own way across the plank and onto the low stern deck, barely a foot or two above the waterline.

They followed Max on a tour of the vessel, which confirmed Jess's expectations. It was quite simply the lap of luxury. In fact, inside the main lounge – he referred to it as the saloon – you could have been forgiven for thinking you were in a prestigious apartment somewhere on dry land. There were fitted carpets, luxurious sofas, even a cocktail bar in one corner, and real windows, rather than portholes. There were paintings on the walls and French windows leading out onto a patio with no fewer than three little palm trees in pots. Max led the girls out and invited them to sit down on the smart rattan furniture.

'Can I get you ladies a drink? It's noon so I could break out the gin and tonic if you like. Or how about a glass of champagne?'

Jess was just about to refuse politely when she heard Hope's voice.

'I'd love a glass of champagne, please, Max.' From the expression on her face and her tone of voice, Jess definitely got the impression Hope liked Max. A lot. After all, Jess thought to herself, one of Hope's stated aims in coming to St-Tropez had been to find herself a millionaire. It looked as though she might have achieved this on her very first day. Not bad going. Not bad at all.

Max disappeared back into the saloon to fetch the champagne, allowing the girls time to exchange a few words.

'Nice boat, Hope. How about the captain?'

'Dreamy.' Hope looked as though she meant it. 'Both of them.'

'Are you going to be all right on your own if I go back and feed Brutus in an hour or so?'

'Definitely.'

'Make sure you behave yourself. You don't know anything about the guy.'

'Yes, Mum.' Hope grinned. 'It's all right, I'll be a good girl.'

'And if you're going to be late, send me a text.'

'Yes, Mum.'

'Here we are: a bottle of shampoo.' Max appeared with a champagne bottle, ice bucket, and three glasses hanging upside down from his fingers. Expertly, he opened the bottle and filled their glasses, handing them across with a smile. 'Cheers, and welcome to the *Helios*.'

'Cheers, Max, and thanks for inviting us aboard.' Hope reached across and clinked her glass against his, treating him to a beaming smile.

They had a pleasant chat, learning about the yacht and the coastline around St-Tropez. Hope told Max how they were doggy-sitting, and likely to be staying for a month or more, and Jess could see that the idea of having Hope around for a while appealed to him. He told them a bit about himself, but gave no indication as to the origins of his considerable wealth. Presumably a generous daddy, Jess thought to herself, but at least in comparison to somebody like Drugoi, Max was pleasant, attentive, and seemed like a nice guy. Clearly, Hope shared her opinion of him.

They had just finished the bottle of champagne between them and Max was asking if they wanted more, when Jess glanced at her watch and saw that it was already past one o'clock. She stood up, gave Hope a little wave, and made her apologies. Neither Max nor Hope looked sorry to see her go, although he gallantly accompanied her to the gangplank and even offered her his hand as she climbed up onto it.

'Goodbye, Jess. I hope to see you again.'

'Bye, Max. I'm sure we'll meet up again very soon. Thanks for the champagne.'

Chapter 8

Almost directly opposite the yacht, on the other side of the road, was the local tourist information office. Although it was closed for lunch, there was a big map of the town on display and Jess saw from it that the most direct route back home was through the streets and over the hill. It wouldn't be as picturesque as the coastal path, but, having told Antoinette she would be back to feed the dog by two, she didn't want to start off by being late, so she decided to go for it.

Excluding their stop at the beach bar, it had taken them the better part of an hour to get there along the coastal footpath and Jess was interested to find that by taking the direct route back she made it in barely forty minutes. At one point she was overtaken by a sweet little boxy-looking bus, like something out of a kiddies' storybook, and realised that this had to be the *navette* that Antoinette had mentioned. Clearly, this would be the fastest way back another time. It was hot walking, although there was a surprising amount of shade to be found under the trees as she left the crowded town streets and found herself on the wider avenues flanked by swish villas. As an architect, it was interesting to study the different building styles through gaps in the hedges as she walked past. Apart from the White House look-alike she had spotted the previous day, there was quite a variety of other styles, including one whose design looked as if it owed much to the Taj Mahal. Clearly, there was a lot of money in these streets.

When she got to the gates of the villa, she pulled out the keys Antoinette had given her and pressed the remote control. The yellow light started flashing and the gates opened. As they did so, she was reminded of David in his silver car. For a moment she found herself thinking of Rafael. He, too, was very wealthy, although in his case, he had worked for it. He, too, liked sexy sports cars – although his were always new, not classic old cars. He, too, had a swanky house. She had broken up with him as much over his lifestyle as anything else. This made her reaction to David Dupont even more inexplicable. Surely the parallels were all too clear, so how was it she still managed to feel attraction towards somebody so apparently similar? Had she no sense at all?

Closing the gates behind her, she walked up the drive to the villa to collect the dog. As she reached the gravelled parking area she noted that the silver Jaguar was still parked alongside the Range Rover. Presumably this meant that David was around, unless he'd gone out on foot. Instinctively her eyes checked out the upstairs windows, but the closed shutters gave nothing away. She went round to the kitchen door and received a rapturous welcome from Brutus and a friendly reception from Antoinette.

'I hope you didn't spend too much money. I must take the pair of you into town one of these days and show you the best places to shop, and the cafés and restaurants where you won't get overcharged.'

'We found a little beach bar which was super, but it would be great if you could pass on a bit of your local knowledge sometime. How's Brutus been?'

'He's been very well behaved. He didn't beg for food, but his eyes never left my hands when I was getting lunch ready. In the end, I gave him a raw carrot and he ate it all in a matter of seconds.'

'That's great, thanks. I'll take him for a quick walk and then we can go home and I'll feed him. Brutus, how about a walk?' The dog started to wag his tail. 'Or maybe a swim?'

They walked down the path to the tiny secluded beach – tucked between two rocky promontories and little wider than the Range Rover – and the dog wasted no time before wading in. Jess sat down on a rock and watched as he doggy-paddled his way out into deeper water, clearly delighted to be in the sea. She decided to see if his Labrador DNA was up to retrieving something. After hunting round, she found a smooth piece of driftwood and picked it up. She called Brutus, who turned obligingly towards her. As he came swimming back to shore, she threw the stick out past him and was gratified to see him turn and head out after it. Once he had collected it in his mouth, she tried calling again. It worked. He returned to the beach and dropped the stick proudly at her feet.

'Good dog, Brutus.' She patted his head, jumping back to avoid being soaked as he shook himself. 'Now, go fetch.' She picked up the stick, threw it back out again, and was delighted to see him turn and plunge back in. They did this quite a few times before he started to look a bit weary, and so they then walked back up the path, past the villa, to home. She was well pleased. This was more exercise than she had ever seen the dog take.

She gave him his lunch and then made herself a sandwich. After the champagne at lunchtime, she avoided any more wine and just drank some water, sitting out in the courtyard where the temperature in the shade was just perfect. Probably because of the alcohol she had drunk, as well as the walk and the after-effects of the previous days in the car, she felt her eyelids grow heavy and she dozed off.

When she woke up, the dog was still snoring at her feet and she saw that it was almost four o'clock. She had slept for well over an hour. She made herself a coffee and decided the time had come to check out the swimming pool. Although the dog opened one eye as she emerged from her room in her bikini with a towel wrapped around her, he showed no sign of wanting to accompany her, which was probably just as well. She let herself out quietly and left him to his dreams.

When she got to the pool, however, she was in for a surprise. As she rounded the rosemary hedge, she found that she was not alone. There was a figure already in the pool and a quick glance immediately told her who it was. Inexplicably her heart quickened as she saw that it was David. For a moment she hesitated, before deciding that, having come this far, it would look funny if she were to turn and run off, so she made her way across to where he was floating. She slipped off her sandals, but kept the towel wrapped around herself as she greeted him.

'David? We met briefly yesterday. I'm Jess.'

Reluctantly, or so it seemed, he propelled himself slowly across to where she was standing and caught hold of the side of the pool with one hand. Jess found herself looking down at his muscular, tanned shoulders and there was no hiding the fact that she liked what she saw. His face, on the other hand, remained impassive – far from welcoming. His blue eyes were bright, but the dark rings beneath them were testimony to internal troubles.

'Hello. Yes, I'm David. Antoinette tells me you know my grandmother.'

'Yes, that's right. She asked me to come over with her dog while she goes on a cruise.'

'Aha.'

It wasn't the most enthusiastic of responses, but Jess did her best not to be disheartened.

'I'm here with my friend, Hope.'

'Aha.'

'We're staying in the guest house for a while.'

'Aha.'

By now, Jess was beginning to get a bit fed up of his terse replies, but she remembered what Mrs Dupont had told her about how both David and his father were suffering from depression, so she made one more attempt to kick-start the conversation.

'Have you met Brutus, the dog?'

'Yes, I have. I saw him in the kitchen at lunchtime.' At least he sounded a bit more forthcoming. 'I understand he's on a diet.'

'That's right. He's terribly unfit.' Jess hesitated. 'Is it all right if I have a swim? It's absolutely boiling in the sun.'

'Yes, of course.'

His expression was less welcoming than his words, but Jess decided to go for it anyway. She peeled off her towel and laid it on a sun bed along with her sunglasses, feeling very self-conscious stripping to her fairly minimal bikini in front of him. Hurriedly, she went along to the far end and walked into the pool down the steps. Ducking her shoulders under water, she felt a sensation of relief to be away from his gaze.

She remembered him spying on her earlier when she had inadvertently done her Miss Wet T-shirt impression and that same mixture of feelings struck her – part embarrassment, part arousal, as a result of his gaze.

The water was a wonderful temperature and she sank into it gratefully. Although quite a strong swimmer, she stayed around the shallow end for a while, criss-crossing the pool from side to side. David remained at the far end and made no attempt to come down and join her. After a while she swam up the pool and back again a few times, passing close to where he was idly floating, but he didn't try to engage her in conversation, and his blank expression remained in place, definitely not inviting any approach.

After another couple of lengths, she decided to call it a day. It was pretty clear that she wasn't wanted here, so she mustered a final smile as she passed him.

'I'd better get back to Brutus – the dog.'

'Aha.'

'Well, goodbye then, David.'

'Goodbye.'

She swam back to the shallow end and climbed out up the steps. She didn't turn round, but she was sure she could feel his eyes on her as she did so. She would have rather liked to stretch out in the sunshine by the pool to dry off, but she knew when she wasn't wanted. Regretfully, she came back round to where she had left her towel, retrieved it along with her sunglasses, and made her exit, all without making any further eye contact with him.

As she walked back through the walled garden, she did her best to analyse her feelings. There was annoyance at his less-than-welcoming attitude towards somebody who, after all, had been asked to come here by his grandmother.

There was regret that this handsome man, to whom she felt an inexplicable attraction, clearly didn't appear to feel the same attraction towards her. But, above all, the strongest sensation going through her head was one of pity. Clearly David wasn't a happy man – for whatever reasons – and it saddened her to see a fellow human being who was so evidently depressed. Pretty clearly, trying to fulfil Mrs Dupont's request that she try to cheer David up wasn't going to be easy. Antoinette had been dead right about that.

When she got back to the guest house, she pulled a sun bed out onto the overgrown lawn and stretched out in the sun to dry. A few seconds later she felt the touch of a cold wet nose against her thigh as Brutus, roused from his sleep, trotted out to greet her.

'Hello, dog. At least you're pleased to see me.'

She gave his head a pat. By now, after his snooze in the sun, he was bone dry again in spite of his lunchtime swim. She felt his tongue against her palm and then a heavy thud as he sat back down again and busied himself scratching his ear with his back leg.

She lay back and soon dried out in her turn. As she lay there, she reflected upon the events of the last few weeks and months. After splitting up with Rafael she had genuinely buried herself in her work and she had enjoyed herself. She knew she was good at her job and she knew she wanted to continue to be an architect. The problem now was just where she wanted this to be. If only she could manage to find herself a job down here, it would be fantastic. There was something about this place, the weather, the food, the stunning beauty of the Côte d'Azur that attracted her, just as it had attracted so many people. The almost magical blue light that enveloped the landscape gave the impression of living in a dream. Of course there was the language problem and Brexit looming but, even so, it was a wonderful dream. But dreams, she knew, didn't always come true.

After a while, bored of doing nothing, she got up and investigated the shed tucked away in the far corner of their bit of garden, immediately finding what she wanted. A virtually brand new electric lawn mower was in there, along with a collection of gardening tools. Their garden was completely private, well away from the villa and any prying eyes, so she set about mowing the lawn, just as she was, in her bikini, feeling rather licentious as she did so. For a moment she even flirted with the idea of removing her top half, so as to achieve an overall tan, but she couldn't bring herself to do it. St-Tropez might – as Hope had said – have been the birthplace of topless sunbathing, but this was definitely a step too far for Jess.

As it turned out, it was just as well she kept her top on. She had just finished mowing the lawn and was standing back, admiring the immediate improvement this had brought about, when she heard a man's voice. Turning towards the sound, she saw a figure standing at the gate leading from the walled garden. The sun was behind him and for a second, she wondered if it was David Dupont, but when the voice came again, she realised it wasn't, and an inexplicable feeling of disappointment struck her.

'Hello. Are you Jessica?' He sounded rather hesitant and looked a bit embarrassed at the sight of a girl in a bikini.

'Yes, I am. Are you Mr Dupont?'

The man walked across the freshly-mowed lawn towards her, looking around appreciatively as he did so. He was carrying what appeared to be a heavy bag.

'Hello, yes, I'm George Dupont. Thank you so much for mowing the lawn. You're on holiday – you shouldn't have. I'm afraid I've let the garden go a bit.'

As he emerged from the direct sunshine, Jess saw that he was probably in his early sixties. He was a good-looking man and the resemblance to his son was unmistakable, although his hair was now grey. She could also see a resemblance to old Mrs Dupont, particularly around the eyes, but the black rings under them were, however, very similar to those on his son's face. Evidently the depression Mrs Dupont had mentioned was still present in father as well as son.

He put the bag down and they shook hands a bit awkwardly. By now she was wishing she had opted for a T-shirt and shorts for her gardening exploits, and from the expression of embarrassment on his face, so did he.

'Here's Brutus. Have you two been formally introduced yet?'

George Dupont knelt down beside the dog, a smile appearing on his face that transformed him in an instant, so that Jess caught a glimpse of the real man beneath the grief.

'Hello, Brutus. I've heard a lot about you.' He glanced up as Jess. 'My mother must trust you a lot to let you look after her beloved dog. She's forever talking about this old fellow as if he was my little brother.' He studied the Labrador critically. 'I see she still insists on stuffing her dogs full of food. You should have seen the last one. He could barely get through the door.'

After stroking Brutus for a few moments, he straightened up again.

'Antoinette tells me you've got him on a strict diet. Good for you.' His expression changed to one of contrition.

'Look, Jessica, I really must apologise. You must think I'm awful. Mum told me weeks ago that you and your friend were coming to stay and it's inexcusable of me not to have passed the message on to Antoinette. I just forgot, I'm afraid. I seem to be forgetting more and more these days. I'm so very sorry.'

'Really, Mr Dupont, it's fine. Everything's fine. Hope and I are both just so grateful to have the chance of staying here for a few weeks. It's such a wonderful place.'

'Hope – that's a nice name. But just a few weeks? Mum told me her cruise is going to last for three months. Can't you stay here until she gets back? It'll be nice to have some young company here again, Jessica.'

Jess smiled back at him. 'I hope we can stay as long as possible – and it's Jess. Everybody calls me Jess.' She glanced at her watch. 'Can I offer you a tea or a coffee? A glass of wine, maybe?'

'A cup of tea would be lovely.'

'I'll just go and put the kettle on.'

'While you do that, I'll stick these bottles in the fridge for you. I thought you might like a few bottles of good white wine – and it's my attempt to say sorry again for forgetting to pass on Mum's message.'

'Please don't give it a thought. And thank you so much, but there's absolutely no need, you know.'

'It's the least I can do.'

Jess went back into the house, filled the kettle and then went through to her room to pull on a T-shirt and shorts, blessing the instinct that had prevented her from mowing the lawn topless. When she came back out again, she found George Dupont on the kitchen floor playing tug-of-war with Brutus, who had got hold of a hefty piece of driftwood from somewhere. It was good to see the Labrador looking friskier – and his playmate was looking cheerier as well.

'Do you take milk and sugar, Mr Dupont?'

'George, please. Call me George. No sugar, just milk please.' He stood up, looking less embarrassed now that she was properly dressed again, and rested against the worktop as she prepared the tea. 'Have you got everything you want here? Does everything work? It's been a while since the place was used.'

'It's fabulous and we've got absolutely everything we need. And I just love the style of the place. It's the first time on my life I've stayed in a house with Doric columns and a statue of Aphrodite outside the door.'

'Doric columns, eh? Well spotted. Of course... my mother told me you're an architect. You'll have to come and take a look at the villa. It was rebuilt after the war by a loony architect. I've forgotten his name, which is probably just as well. Although the outside's fairly traditional Provençal style, it's a bit quirky inside.' He smiled again. 'When I say quirky, I mean a bit idiosyncratic. I don't know what the guy was smoking at the time – it was all done in the sixties, right in the middle of Flower Power and all that – and I reckon he was stoned out of his head most of the time. At least, I hope so. Anyway, that's what I wanted to say – would you and Hope like to come for dinner today or tomorrow? I'd enjoy your company and maybe my son might join us.'

Jess noticed the smile fade as he mentioned David. Clearly, there were issues there. She did a little bit of gentle probing.

'We'd love to, thank you, if you're sure it's no trouble. Um... I saw David at the pool earlier this afternoon. Does he live here with you?'

George nodded his head. 'For the moment. He's been with me for a few months, recuperating.' He caught Jess's eye and she read the sadness within. 'He maybe told you, he had a bad accident back in the winter, and he's staying here while he tries to get over it.'

'Oh dear, I'm sorry.' This, at least, went some way towards explaining David's obvious unhappiness. 'I hope he gets better soon.'

George made no reply so Jess hastily passed him his tea and returned to more mundane matters.

'Would you like a biscuit, or one of the lovely pains aux raisins Antoinette brought us?'

'Thank you, no. I'd better not.' He seemed grateful for the change of subject and sipped his tea silently for a few moments before returning to his invitation. 'So, if you two would like to come for dinner, would tonight, tomorrow or another night be better for you?'

Jess had been thinking about this. 'If it's all the same to you, I think tomorrow might be better. I left Hope down by the harbour in St-Tropez a few hours ago and I'm not sure what time she'll be back, nor what state she'll be in.' She gave him a smile. 'We were drinking champagne on a yacht at lunchtime. I left before the second bottle got opened.'

'Tomorrow it is. I'll tell Antoinette. And you'd better warn your friend that those sailor boys can be a handful – you know, a girl in every port and all that. Anyway, are you two omnivorous, or is there some food we should avoid?'

'We eat anything, but please tell Antoinette not to go to a lot of trouble for us. Now that I've dug my bikini out, I'd better follow the dog's example and go on a diet.'

'Don't be so silly. You can't come to France and diet. Just make sure you get lots of exercise – and Brutus here will help with that.' He swallowed the last of his tea and stood up. 'Right, I must go and tell Antoinette you're coming tomorrow, before I forget again.' He gave her a smile. 'My apologies once more.'

'It's absolutely fine. Don't give it a thought. And thank you so much for that wine… and everything.'

He reached down to give Brutus a pat before leaving. 'Do you know what I think I might do one of these days? If you don't mind, I think I might start taking our furry friend here for a walk every now and then.' He caught Jess's eye and shook his head soberly. 'I need to get out. Would you believe I've hardly left the house for almost a year?'

Jess gave him an encouraging smile in return. 'Yes, please. Brutus needs all the exercise we can give him. Just come over any time. And you can tell David he's very welcome to take him out as well, if he likes.'

A very distinct shadow fell across George's face and Jess immediately regretted mentioning his son. They exchanged farewells and phone numbers and she stood at the door, watching him make his way back over the freshly-mown grass and disappear through the gate. She was pleased to find him far more natural and normal than she had feared and to have seen a smile on his face from time to time, but not, alas, when speaking of his son. Whatever the accident had been, its impact on the family, coming soon after the death of George's wife, had clearly been considerable.

Hope arrived back home with a silly smile on her face just after six and the silly smile remained firmly fixed across her face for the rest of the evening. Jess recounted the events of that afternoon, George's invitation, and passed on his warning not to trust sailors. She saw Hope grin.

'Max was a perfect gentleman.' She giggled into her mineral water. 'Which is probably just as well seeing as I must have drunk at least a bottle of champagne all by myself.'

'So nothing happened?'

Hope shook her head. 'Nope. Like I said, he behaved impeccably. All right… he did give me a tour of the cabins in the afternoon, including his cabin – he called it the state-room. It was absolutely enormous, with a king size bed and all the trimmings. Jess, have you ever lain on a bed with a mirror on the ceiling above you?'

Jess shook her head decisively. 'No I haven't, Hope, and I thought you said nothing happened.'

'Nothing much happened. All right, we did fool around a bit, but, like I told you, he didn't try to have sex with me.' There was what sounded suspiciously like a note of regret in Hope's voice. 'So I've got that to look forward to next time.'

'There's going to be a next time?'

Hope nodded. 'You bet. He's going to be based here all summer. He charters the boat out to rich people like himself, though he says most of them are happy just to stay moored up in the harbour, rather than brave the open sea. So I'm hoping to see quite a lot of him.' She giggled again. 'And he can see as much of me as he likes, any time.'

'So you've found your millionaire?' Jess was really happy for her. 'That was pretty fast work.'

'I told you St-Tropez would be full of them, Jess. Now all we've got to do is to find one for you.'

'I've tried one of those and it didn't work. I'm just fine as I am, Hope.'

'Keep telling yourself that, Jess.'

Chapter 9

Next day, they both took the dog for his morning swim and Hope bravely joined him in the water. Jess was quite content to sit and watch as the two of them splashed about happily – Hope claiming that the water was 'like a warm bath'. Jess had had warm baths many times in her life and one thing was certain: inviting as the clear Mediterranean looked, it felt absolutely freezing to the touch. She determined to go for a swim later on in the definitely warmer water of the pool – just so long as David wasn't in there at the time. Trying to strike up a conversation with him the previous day had been very hard work and she had felt very embarrassed. She preferred not to have to go through that again, particularly if she was going to be having dinner with him that night anyway.

After Brutus's swim, they took him for a short walk along the coast, in the course of which they were surprised to come across two elderly ladies, sunning themselves stark naked on a secluded beach. Even the dog looked taken aback. Jess and Hope hurried past and, once they were a safe distance away, Hope voiced what Jess was thinking.

'Do you think those two are relics of the Swinging Sixties? Peace, love and take your top off?'

'Not just your top.' Jess shook her head with a bewildered grin. 'I don't know what these old people are coming to. It was never like this in my day.'

After a while, they spotted a path leading inland. This led through rough scrub and onto an unspoiled hillside. The previous night she had read up about St-Tropez on the internet and had discovered that this whole area, right up to and including the distant hills way back inland of them, had been designated an area of special natural beauty, with the protected status of a national park. This, too, was far from what she had been expecting.

Back at the house, she and Hope had a mid-morning coffee, and then Jess went down to the pool for a swim, casting an eye at the shutters in the villa above her to see that they were all closed, and tip-toeing the last few feet around the rosemary bushes to check whether David was already in there. This time the coast was clear and she enjoyed a good long swim, counting thirty lengths of the pool. When she began to feel tired, she climbed out of the water and stretched out on one of the sun beds, feeling the hot sun make short work of drying her body and her bikini. After a while, she turned over onto her front and was dozing happily when she heard a noise from above. Rolling back over again she glanced up and saw the same shutters and window open once again. This time, David was leaning on his elbows on the window ledge, making no pretence of concealment. Jess found herself blushing at the directness of his gaze and did her best to affect nonchalance as she called up to him.

'Hello, David. Good morning.'

'Good morning.' Had he forgotten her name?

'Are you coming for a swim?'

'No.'

Jess made a mental note to try to avoid straight yes/no questions with him from now on.

'Your father's invited us for dinner tonight. What's Antoinette preparing?'

'I don't know.'

A three-word answer was progress, but it could hardly be called a conversation. Jess tried again.

'What time should we come along?'

'You'd better ask Antoinette.'

Four words.

'Are you going to be there?' Jess was conscious of the hope in her voice. She needn't have bothered.

'No.'

'No?'

This time he appeared to register that some sort of fuller explanation was demanded.

'I can't, I'm afraid. I've got a thing.'

He didn't elaborate and Jess didn't press him. Although pleased she had managed to squeeze a seven-word answer out of him, Jess felt a twinge of disappointment that he wouldn't be joining them after all.

'That's a pity. Some other time, maybe.'

'Maybe.'

With the slightest wave of the hand, he retreated into his room again and Jess lost sight of him. She lay back down on her front again, her head turned away from the house, seriously questioning her own sanity. How could it possibly be that she could feel attraction for such a morose, taciturn, some might say downright rude, man? She sighed in frustration. Just what was going on inside her head?

Dinner that evening with David's father proved to be very good and very pleasant. As it turned out, it wasn't all cooked by Antoinette. She had prepared a lovely cold potato, egg and black olive salad, and an open fruit tart for dessert, but the main part of the menu was cooked by George on the barbecue. But it was the location of the barbecue that fascinated the girls – particularly Jess. It wasn't outside, but indoors. It was built against the dining room wall, right alongside the table. George spotted the expression on her face.

'You know I said this place was a bit quirky?'

The girls, accompanied by a very excited Brutus, were standing alongside George as he cooked three lobsters, split down the middle into halves, on the gas barbecue. All around the stainless steel grill were vents, leading to powerful fans that sucked the smoke and smell away to the outside as soon as it was produced. Just four or five feet from the flames, Jess couldn't smell a thing. It was amazing and she told George so. He laughed.

'If you think an indoor barbecue's strange, wait till you see the bath in the lounge.'

'The bath…?'

'Go through those glass doors and take a look. I'd better concentrate on my cooking.'

Jess and Hope wandered through into the large lounge and gawped. Sure enough, there, in the middle of the room, was a glossy white bathtub, sunk into the floor. The weirdness didn't stop there. There was a pizza oven set into the far wall, startling yellow and purple tiles covered the floor, a mirrored disco-ball was suspended from the ceiling, and a series of triangular windows ran along one side of the room to complete the wacky feel of the place. Hope turned to Jess and raised her eyebrows.

'Did you ever…?'

'Nope, never.' Jess looked back over her shoulder towards the dining room and called to George. 'What did you say the name of the architect was?'

'I still can't remember. I believe my father found him down at the port one day. I think he said he was Finnish or Danish or something Nordic. He was bonkers, but they were all a bit crazy in those days.'

In spite of the cooking having taken place inside, they sat outside on the terrace to eat. This wide paved area extended along the full length of the villa and looked directly out over the sea. The temperature was perfect, the breeze so light it barely ruffled the napkins, and the scent of rosemary was in the air. Jess glanced across at Hope, thinking of her long-standing dream of visiting St-Tropez and reflecting that it hadn't been such a bad idea after all. Certainly, the reality was just like her poster and her dreams: blue sky, deeper blue sea, palm trees and umbrella pines, purple bougainvillea growing up the wall, fresh lobster on the plate in front of her, and ice-cold white wine in her glass.

'George, you're a very lucky man.' Jess raised her glass towards him. 'You live in one of the most fabulous places on earth.'

'I often try telling myself that, but nature has a way of compensating. Yes, I have the great good fortune to live here, but life hasn't exactly been kind to me.'

He caught Jess's eye and she saw his eyes glistening. Silently kicking herself for broaching the topic, she was about to try to steer the conversation into safer waters when he continued.

'My mother probably told you about Babette – my wife, David's mother. She died just over a year ago.' His voice dropped to almost a whisper. 'It was cancer. There was nothing they could do to save her.'

'I'm so sorry.' Jess kept her voice low as well. George didn't seem to notice she had spoken.

'And then David's accident. I keep asking myself what my family's done to deserve so much bad luck. Yes, it's a wonderful place to live, but only if you're happy. And happiness doesn't come from money or beautiful views, it comes from good health, and being surrounded by people who love you.'

Jess took a big mouthful of wine, wondering what she could possibly say to help cheer him up. Hope got there first, sounding almost as emotional as he did.

'My mum died two years ago. At first, I thought I'd never get over it, but it gets easier. It's true, you know, what they say – time really is a great healer.' In spite of her words, Jess saw her wipe away a tear. 'I know my mum wouldn't have wanted me or my dad to spend our lives mourning her loss, and I'm sure your wife would have felt the same way.' Jess saw her reach across, catch hold of George's arm and give it a squeeze. 'It'll pass, but I know it's terribly, terribly tough.'

Just then, Brutus, maybe sensing something in the atmosphere, hauled himself to his feet from the position he had taken up under the table and pushed between Jess and George, resting his big hairy head on George's thigh. Jess saw the Labrador's soulful brown eyes gaze up at George as he added his own canine encouragement. Nobody moved for a few moments and then finally George stirred, reached gently down with both hands to catch hold of the dog's head, and spoke to him so quietly his words were almost inaudible.

'You know something, Brutus, you're a very good dog.' He raised his eyes towards Hope and then across to Jess.

'Thanks, girls. I'm so very glad you've come, and thanks for bringing this chap.'

Releasing his grip on the dog, he wiped the back of his hand across his eyes and took a deep breath.

'I know he's on a diet, but do you think I could give Brutus the head of my lobster? Our old dog used to love that.'

'I'm sure this one would love it as well.' Jess suppressed a sigh of relief at the lightening of the mood. 'Besides, lobster's supposed to be low-calorie.' She wasn't too sure that this was true, but a little treat under the circumstances seemed totally appropriate.

After dinner, George gave them a brief tour of the ground floor and Jess saw more examples of the Scandinavian architect's eccentricities – from the rectangular toilet and matching bidet in the cloakroom, to the study which was clad from floor to ceiling in lime green glass tiles. Working in there would surely be like trying to write inside a lettuce! There was a lift to the upstairs bedrooms, completely lined with mirrors, even the floor and ceiling. Jess stood in it for a moment and it felt weirdly disconcerting. To an architect, it was a fascinating trip back in time, and an insight into how the psychedelic sixties had striven to turn traditional artistic values upside down. Practicality had been a far lower priority back in those days when what counted was the ability to shock.

By the time she and Hope left the villa and walked back to the guest house with the dog, it was dark and the sky was full of stars. The moon hadn't risen yet, but the starlight produced more than enough illumination for them to find their way. There was very little light pollution here and the stars felt close enough to reach out and touch. Jess glanced across at Hope.

'One thing's for sure – we're immensely lucky to be here, aren't we?'

'You said it. And, Jess, one way or another we're going to do our very best to help George get over his loss, and David get over his accident. Right?'

'Right… but it isn't going to be easy.'

Chapter 10

Over the next few days, their walks with Brutus gradually increased in length and the dog started to shed a few pounds and gain energy. Antoinette ran Jess and Brutus into the town centre one afternoon in her little car and walked them through the streets, pointing out the best shops for bread and other food, cheaper restaurants and good value cafés. The dog trotted along with them quite willingly, which was definite progress. It was while they were down at the harbourside, however, that Jess had her first embarrassing moment in St-Tropez.

They had stopped for ice tea in one of the less expensive pavement cafés and Jess hooked Brutus's lead around the leg of the table. Antoinette was exchanging a few words with an elderly lady at the next table while Jess was idly studying the hordes of people who came strolling past. Among these were a mother and child, the little girl holding an ice cream cone. The little girl stopped to pet the friendly Labrador, but made the mistake of letting her ice cream come too close to the ever-hungry dog. Before Jess could stop him, with a move like a striking cobra, Brutus suddenly jerked his head forward and vacuumed the ice cream out of the cone and down his throat. It disappeared without touching the sides.

As his long pink tongue licked his lips in appreciation, the little girl stared uncomprehendingly at the empty cone for a few seconds before looking up at her mother, tears gathering in the corners of her eyes. Keen to avoid an international incident, Jess leapt to her feet, pressed the lead into Antoinette's hand and apologised to the mother, who was still trying to work out what had happened.

'*Excusez-moi, Madame. Le chien mange tout.*' She was relieved her A-level French proved to be up to the task.

To her surprise, the lady laughed and replied in English.

'Don't worry. I keep telling Holly she should eat more quickly. It's a good lesson to her.' Her accent was unmistakably Scottish.

'I'm so sorry. Do let me get her another one. Please.'

'It's all right. She was losing interest anyway. Thank you, but there's no need.' She glanced down at her daughter. 'Want another ice cream, sweetie?'

The little girl thought for a moment and then shook her head, returning to stroking Brutus. After a second or two she hesitantly held the empty cone out to him and he took it very gently from her fingers and crunched it up. The mother smiled again.

'That's good. We don't need to look for a litter bin. Enjoy St-Tropez.'

As she and her daughter set off again, Jess sat back down again and addressed the dog sternly.

'You are a naughty, greedy dog, Brutus. No more stealing food, all right?'

She wagged her finger at him and he leant forward and licked it – totally without any signs of remorse.

Antoinette handed Jess the lead back and grinned.

'They were British, too, weren't they? I bet if you asked everybody in a fifty-metre radius of us now where they came from, you'd have a dozen different nationalities, and more foreigners than French people. St-Tropez really is multilingual and truly cosmopolitan.'

Apart from having coffee or tea with Antoinette from time to time over the days that followed, Jess and Hope made a point of meeting up with George as often as possible – for coffee in the kitchen of their house, or for a drink on his terrace – and did their best to put, and keep, a smile on his face. Jess was very pleased to find him starting to spend time in the walled garden, beginning the laborious process of removing the weeds. Considering that he had told her he had barely been outside for a year, she took this as a very positive sign and she and Hope joined in to give him a hand.

Hope disappeared for a few hours most days to be with her sailor, and the grin on her face when she returned from her visits to the *Helios* grew ever wider. Jess spent an hour or so most evenings weeding the flower beds around the guest house. Pretty soon, the place began to look really rather smart.

The weather remained very warm, although the forecast for the weekend wasn't so good. Hope and Brutus swam in the sea every day and Jess got up to forty lengths of the pool each time she went. Her skin gradually began to turn a golden brown in the sunshine and she felt fit and relaxed. This holiday was definitely doing her good. She saw nothing more of David – either in the pool or at his window – although his car was still parked beside the Range Rover most of the time. She wondered if he maybe went out on foot or even in a boat, but there was no sign of him.

On Saturday morning the sky was overcast, but it was still very warm, although the humidity had definitely increased. Jess had decided that the time had come to buy herself a new bikini. The one she had been using was a few years old and regular daily wear was beginning to take its toll. After her Miss Wet T-shirt moment earlier in the week, she decided she really couldn't run the risk of a wardrobe malfunction while at the pool – particularly if David or his father were around. She asked Antoinette where she should go to buy a replacement and received the suggestion that they take the ferry across the bay to Ste-Maxime, where shops were likely to be a bit more affordable than the very expensive ones they had spotted in St-Tropez.

They left Brutus at the villa – George had promised to take him for a gentle stroll –and walked round the coastal footpath once more, stopping off for a coffee at the beach bar. The friendly waitress, Terri, welcomed them.

'So, how's it going, girls? Having a good time?'

Hope answered for both of them. 'Amazing, thanks, Terri. St-Tropez's a wonderful place.'

'And have you started to make friends?'

Hope grinned. 'I have – very definitely.'

Terri smiled and glanced across at Jess. 'And what about you, have you been making friends?'

'Yes, I've been making friends.' Antoinette and George surely qualified. 'Although Hope has been friendlier than me.' She winked across at her friend.

'There are some rather good-looking men in St-Tropez... very good-looking.' Hope sounded as if she knew what she was talking about.

Terri grinned and then looked back at Jess. 'You should come along this evening to try our rum punch – do a bit of dancing maybe. You'll find a lot of good-looking men here – take your pick. Any time after eight. Come and see me and I'll give you a drink on the house.'

When Terri had gone off to get their coffees, Hope looked across at Jess. 'Max has got a bunch of bankers on the yacht for the weekend, so I'm at a loose end tonight. Shall we give it a go?'

Jess didn't really feel in the least bit interested in hooking up with some random man, but she said yes anyway. It would be good to meet some new people. She wondered if David ever came along to the beach bar, and the idea of bumping into him rather appealed, even if she had a pretty good idea what his sullen reaction to seeing her would be. Why oh why, she demanded of her subconscious, was she still thinking about him when he was patently not interested? Annoyingly, her subconscious refused, yet again, to provide an answer.

The fast ferry across the bay took barely fifteen minutes. Jess reflected that in the car they had taken three times as long to crawl through the queue of traffic. Clearly, here in the gulf of St-Tropez, the best way to travel was by boat.

Ste-Maxime was bigger, noisier and more modern than its more famous neighbour back across the water. There was a marina and a promenade with palm trees, meticulously-manicured lawns, and people everywhere. They found numerous restaurants, most with tables outside, as well as ice cream shops and cafés. There were also lots and lots of cars, with a busy road running along the seafront. When Jess commented on the traffic noise to one waiter, he told them they were lucky they hadn't been there a few weeks earlier. Every year in May, apparently, thousands of Harley Davidson motorbikes descended upon the area en masse and the noise levels were 'enough to make the fillings fall out of your teeth'.

Jess and Hope each bought themselves not one, but two, new bikinis. Somehow they got the feeling they were going to get a lot of use. They weren't cheap by any means, but Jess felt confident she would have paid even more on the other side of the bay. She also bought a couple of new tops – a bit skimpier than her normal stuff, but now that she was getting a decent tan, she felt she could show off a bit. After a sandwich lunch in one of the narrow streets in the pedestrian area – where they could no longer hear the traffic – they took the ferry back across the bay. As they did so, Hope got very excited as she spotted the *Helios* come past, heading out to sea. Max's mop of yellow hair was clearly visible on the high bridge but, in spite of Hope's shouts and waves, he didn't notice her among the other passengers on board the ferry.

As it was getting even more hot and humid, in spite of the now total cloud cover, they took the little bus back to the villa. There were only half a dozen people on board apart from themselves and it appeared that everybody knew everybody else, including the driver. He evidently knew the addresses of some of the older ladies and delivered them right to their doors. It was rather sweet in a Trumpton sort of way and added to the very homely feel she was beginning to get from St-Tropez. Very different from Jess's notion of the place as some sort of international jet-set hangout, peopled exclusively by Latin lovers and dyed blondes. She was pleasantly surprised – and impressed.

After dinner that evening they walked back to the beach bar just as dusk descended. The air felt clammy and both of them were wearing their lightest clothes. Jess, ever prudent, had checked out on the internet the best way to go home afterwards along roads, having decided against using the coastal footpath for their return. The cloudy sky would mean no starlight to guide them and the rocky stretch was likely to be dangerous in the dark. She had even considered driving, but the sheer bulk of the Range Rover in the narrow roads was a bit off-putting, particularly when it came to finding a parking space.

The party was in full swing by the time they arrived at the beach bar. Terri the waitress spotted them as they walked in and called them over to the bar, where a huge glass bowl contained the rum punch. She ladled them each a generous serving, complete with chunks of fruit and little paper umbrellas, and led them to a spare table.

A few people were dancing, but most were sitting around, chatting and drinking. The dance floor was, of course, just sand, and Jess was relieved to see that her choice of shorts and flip-flops was what most people were wearing. It was lovely to sit back and relax, watching the lights of the disco reflect out across the water, the little waves sparkling as they rolled into the beach. She raised her glass and clinked it against Hope's.

'Sitting on a beach in St-Tropez drinking rum punch takes a bit of beating, doesn't it? Good old Mrs Dupont. Here, a toast to her and her faithful hound.'

Hope nodded contentedly and held up her glass, a blissful expression on her face. They tried the punch and agreed that it was very good, very fruity, and probably lethal. Just then Hope's phone whistled and she checked the incoming text message.

'It's Max.' Jess could see her friend's eyes sparkling. 'He's coming round to join us, bringing some of his bankers.' She grinned. 'Only, he spells it with a W. He did say they were a bit hard going.'

The last thing Jess wanted was to meet up with a bunch of objectionable rich boys – and probably drunk ones as well – but she couldn't really say anything, seeing as they would be with her best friend's boyfriend. If the worst came to the worst, she knew she could always go home early and leave Hope with Max. Her thoughts were interrupted.

'Hi, did I hear you speaking English?'

They both looked up. There was a man standing by their table, looking down at them. The light from behind hid most of his face, but his outline was unmistakable. This guy was either the Incredible Hulk, or in the later stages of a cataclysmic allergic reaction to peanuts. Alternatively, he had been working out – very seriously indeed. As Hope put it later, he had muscles in places where other people didn't have places.

'Yes. Are you from England, too?'

The Hulk moved slightly to one side and Jess found she could now see his face. She could also see at least some of the tattoos on his bare arms. His T-shirt had had the arms ripped off – quite possibly with his teeth – and his biceps bulged alarmingly. Jess had never been a fan of body-builders, but she had to give him credit for the effort he must have put into getting to this state – and no doubt the dodgy substances he had ingested in the search for what he deemed to be physical perfection.

'Yeh, but I work here now.' His accent was indefinable, with just a hint of American in there somewhere.

'Really?' Jess remembered that Hope's boyfriend until last year had spent every spare hour in the gym, but without achieving the monumental results of this man-mountain standing in front of them. 'What do you do?'

'I'm a minder.' The Hulk glanced round and dropped his voice dramatically. 'There are some very important people who live here or visit here. I work for an agency that provides protection for them. My name's Pete. What're yours?'

'I'm Hope, and this is Jess.'

He held out a massive hand and Jess saw Hope take it, shake it, and retrieve her hand uncrushed afterwards, so she did the same. She was grateful to receive only the lightest squeeze from him.

'Can I get you two ladies a drink?'

Jess pointed to her punch. The glass was still nearly full. 'Thanks, but we've only just got these.'

He nodded. 'Do you mind if I sit down?'

'Do, by all means.' Hope pointed to a spare chair and Pete lowered himself onto it. Jess distinctly heard a creaking sound as he did so – presumably from the chair, rather than Pete's knees.

'So, are you here on holiday?'

Jess sat back and let Hope do the talking. She listened idly as Pete spoke of his time in the Marines, his sporting achievements, but not about his work. Clearly this was a taboo subject. As he talked, she was mildly surprised to hear that he didn't appear to be hitting on either of them. Maybe, she wondered to herself, there was a Mrs Hulk somewhere nearby. He was still chatting when Hope spotted an inflatable boat, coasting in to the shore, and she jumped to her feet.

'Here's Max.'

As he watched her rush off to the water's edge, Pete glanced across at Jess.

'Max?'

'Hope's new boyfriend. He's got a yacht.'

'Got a yacht or works on a yacht?' Pete sounded as dubious as Jess had been.

'Both, I think. He owns a yacht that he charters to rich folk. I think he still goes along as skipper, though.'

'Well, there's no shortage of rich folk around here. Some of them keep yachts that they only use three or four times a year.'

'All right for some...'

She left the rest unsaid as Max appeared.

'Hi, Jess, I've brought you some company.'

Jess stood up to greet Max and his party.

'Hi, Max. Come and have a rum punch. This is Pete.'

There were three men with Max. Jess took a good look at them as they came into the light and suppressed a sigh. She knew the type. Pale skin, immaculate hair, manicured nails, and branded clothes that implied a familiarity with water sports that they most probably didn't deserve. She didn't need the wave of alcoholic breath that accompanied them to tell her they had already started on the booze. Still, Max was Hope's friend, so she summoned a bright smile.

'Hi, guys. Welcome to the beach bar.'

'And hello to you, darling.' The tallest of the three came across and offered her his hand, squeezing it a damn sight harder than the Hulk. Jess recoiled, surreptitiously rubbing her hand behind her back to restore the circulation as he introduced himself. 'I'm Monty.' He was wearing a T-shirt, on the front of which was the slogan: *Second Place isn't an Option*. She sighed again.

The other two also shook hands and Monty made a point of sitting down right beside her, in the seat where Hope had been.

In fact, the evening didn't turn out to be as bad as she had feared. The other two bankers – with or without a W – were fairly normal and spent most of their time talking to Pete and Max. Monty was evidently very interested in Jess, but she managed to keep him at arm's length. The rum punches flowed and the music was equally intoxicating. At one point a strange contraption, like a jump from a gymkhana, was produced and a limbo competition ensued. Jess had never been particularly good at this sort of thing – with her long legs her centre of gravity was too high up – but Pete the Hulk turned out to be an expert, easily winning the first prize.

First prize turned out to be a local delicacy – *Tarte Tropézienne* – a large round sponge cake filled with a mass of soft cream. Jess and Hope had already spotted these on sale in the town, but had decided to give them a miss as they probably contained more calories than an average family needed in a whole day. It was all right for Pete. No doubt he would be able to work them off in the gym.

As Jess stood in the crowd, watching the final stages of the limbo competition, she felt a hand tap her on the arm. She looked up to see a tall, good-looking man at her side, who greeted her in French.

Although they were in France, Jess was almost surprised to hear French being spoken. Up to now, most of the people she had met had spoken English – apart from the bus driver and a few of the old ladies on board. She had had just about enough rum punch by now to be prepared to risk running out her rusty A-level French, so she took a deep breath and had a go.

'*Bonsoir. Je m'appelle Jess.*'

'And my name's Olivier. I'm very pleased to meet you.' He had correctly worked out that his English was considerably better than her French. She heaved a silent sigh of relief as she shook hands with him.

'That's great. You speak English. I'm afraid my French is pretty rusty.'

'It sounded pretty good to me, but I need to practice my English, if you don't mind.'

Jess nodded happily and took a good look at him. He was probably around her age, dark-haired, with a friendly face. He was wearing jeans and a blue T-shirt with *AMU* across the front. His face and arms were tanned and he looked fit.

'So, Olivier, what brings you here? Do you work in St-Tropez?'

He shook his head. 'No, my parents live here, but I work in Aix-en-Provence.' He tapped the logo on his T-shirt. 'At the university – Aix-Marseille Université.'

'Oh, so do you teach at the university?'

'Yes, I do. My subject's twentieth-century history.'

Jess pricked up her ears. 'That's really interesting. You sound like the perfect person to tell me what happened here during the Second World War. I only heard about the fighting recently.'

'Whatever you want to know. My doctoral thesis was on that very subject. As a *Tropézien*, I have a particular interest in what happened here. Several members of my family were killed in the bombardment.'

Jess and he returned to the table and she was fascinated to learn more about the events of August 1944. Much of the port of St-Tropez, along with buildings further inland, had been blasted to bits by allied bombs and shelling. Allied forces had streamed ashore from landing craft, and men had fought and died in this very place.

While Olivier was telling her all about the landings in his impeccable English – learnt, apparently, over the course of a year working in Brighton – Monty the banker parked himself right up against her other side. He was constantly offering her drinks, and it wasn't long before the pressure of his knee against her leg began to annoy her. Taking advantage of a moment when Olivier had disappeared up to the bar, she turned to Monty and asked him, very politely, to leave her alone. Unfortunately this appeared to have no effect and a bit later, after Monty had swallowed another couple of rum punches, she started to feel his fingers on her thigh. Enough was definitely enough. She was about to round on him when fate took a hand.

Pete reappeared at the table with his limbo prize *Tarte Tropézienne,* now cut into slices. He passed these around the table, refusing to take no for an answer. Jess nibbled a corner of her huge slice and received the confirmation that this was a very, very rich and fattening mixture. As a visibly very drunk Monty staggered off to the bar to replenish his glass, she had an idea of how she might be able to kill two birds with one stone. She waited for him to come back and, once again, he sat down almost on her lap. She put her plan into operation.

'Stand up a minute, Monty, would you? I think I saw something on your chair.'

Reluctantly and unsteadily he pulled himself to his feet and looked down suspiciously at his seat.

'Can't see anything.' He tried, and failed, to stifle a belch.

Then, just as he was slumping back down again, Jess slipped her slice of cake onto the seat beneath him and waited for his reaction. For a moment, she caught Olivier's eye and saw him choke back a giggle.

Monty's reaction was delayed. In fact, it was not until several minutes later, as he had almost finished his drink, that Jess observed him starting to wriggle uncomfortably. Gradually his alcohol-sozzled brain must have begun to register that all was not as it should be down below. She saw him slide his hand underneath his bottom and then whip it out again in alarm. He looked up and called across the table to Max.

'Hey, Max, could we head back to the boat?'

Max raised his head in surprise. 'Yes of course, Monty, but it's still early. Is something wrong?'

'Um, I'm not sure.' The banker's face was a picture of embarrassment. 'I think maybe there might be.'

While Max rounded up the others, Hope came over to where Jess was sitting.

'Jess, Max wants me to go back with him and the bankers. I'll probably stay the night with him on the yacht if that's all right with you. Will you be OK getting home on your own? He says it's going to rain later, so do be careful.'

'I'll be fine. Go and enjoy yourself. Just make sure you don't let Monty sit down on the good sofa.'

Hope's eyes opened wide. 'Why, has he wet himself?'

'Something like that.'

After Max and his group had left, Jess explained to Olivier what had prompted her to sacrifice her slice of cream sponge and he laughed.

'Remind me not to make you angry.'

'I wasn't angry, just fed up with rich bastards like Monty who think their money will get them whatever, and whoever, they like. That doesn't work with me.'

'How about a dance? That'll take your mind off him.'

Olivier turned out to be a very good dancer and Jess had a great time with him, although dancing on sand was definitely an acquired art and remarkably tiring. Their evening was interrupted a little while later by a lightning flash that lit up the sky, followed by a deafening clap of thunder. Along with the thunder came the rain that Max had predicted.

This wasn't ordinary English-style rain. This was torrential, monsoon-like rain. Within seconds, everybody was sheltering under the umbrellas, but the rain was falling so hard a fine spray came through the material and started to soak them all. Jess glanced down. It seemed very likely she was going to repeat her Miss Wet T-shirt look once again although, thankfully, this time she wasn't naked underneath. One thing was for sure – walking home in this would result in her being drenched.

Another lightning flash, accompanied almost immediately by an even louder thunderclap and even harder rain, brought the soirée to an end. She saw Louis, the DJ, abandon his post and start to turn off the lights. In the sudden silence – apart from the drumming of the rain on the umbrellas – she heard Olivier's voice at her ear.

'I think we'd all better head for home. Where are you living?'

'It's a twenty-minute walk that way.' Jess pointed back over her shoulder.

'Walk? You'll be drowned. Can I give you a lift?'

Jess gave a sigh of relief. 'Thank you so much, Olivier. That would be absolutely great.'

Jess saw Pete loom up in front of her. His T-shirt was now plastered onto his chest and his abs looked like a sheet of corrugated iron. He didn't appear to notice the rain.

'I was going to offer you lift as well, Jess, but I'm on the Harley tonight. You're probably better off in a car.' Pete sounded quite disappointed. 'But I'll see you here again, I'm sure.'

'Of course. It's been good to meet you, Pete.'

Jess kissed him goodbye on the cheeks, French-style, and then made a run for it with Olivier. His car, a little Renault, was parked barely a hundred yards away, but Jess was pretty well soaked by the time she reached it.

They leapt in and she explained where she was living, directing him along the now near-flooded roads until she spotted the track leading off to the left.

'It'll be terribly muddy up there. It's not far from here to where I'm staying, so maybe it's best if you leave me down here.'

'Of course not. I know this road pretty well. An old school friend of mine used to live up here. It's uphill, so we'll see how far we can get. If I start slipping and sliding, I know I can always run back down to the road.'

The little car managed to make it up the slope without too much trouble, but they both decided it wouldn't be a good idea for him to risk driving down the other side towards the villa for fear of not being able to get back up again. The track to the gates was now a stream of muddy water and looked virtually impassable. Jess thanked him profusely and was just kissing him on the cheeks when bright headlights from behind illuminated the car. As the other vehicle came past, she saw it was David's silver Jaguar. She distinctly saw him look across at the two of them and then accelerate down the streaming wet hillside, the car snaking from side to side in the mud. In the split second when their eyes had met, the expression on his face had been even less welcoming than ever.

'That was David Dupont.' Olivier was watching the sports car's tail lights slewing wildly from side to side as it headed down the hillside. 'He's that school friend I was talking about. Is that where you're staying?'

'Yes, so do you know him well?' Jess was surprised.

'Since we were little boys. We went to school together until they sent him off to school in England, but he came back every summer. He's a good guy. It's good to see him out and about again after his accident.'

Jess would have liked to stay and ask him more about David, but she could feel the water seeping down her back and into her underwear. It was an uncomfortable feeling so she decided to head for home. It was a pity David hadn't stopped. A lift in his car down to the villa would have meant she might have got home not totally soaked.

'Anyway, Olivier, thank you so much. Will I see you at the beach bar again?'

'I certainly hope so. I'm off back to Aix tomorrow, so why don't we try to meet at the same time next Saturday?'

'It's a date.' She gave him a final smile, jumped out of the car and slipped and slid her way down the slope – surprising herself by managing it without falling over. Olivier very kindly stayed at the top with his headlights on until she reached the bottom. Once there, she pressed the remote to open the gates, gave a final wave towards Olivier, and went inside.

When she got back to the guest house, she was so wet, it made very little difference, so she took Brutus for a walk without bothering to search for a waterproof. By the time they got back again, both of them were absolutely drenched.

Jess grabbed the old towel and set about drying the dog, but not before he had shaken himself all over her and the kitchen. She left him there and went off to have a shower, dry her hair, and change into fresh clothes, and then spent half an hour cleaning the kitchen until it was spotless once more. Finally dumping the cloth in the sink, she looked down at the dog, wagging her finger at him.

'Next time, Brutus, shake yourself outside. Got it?'

He looked unapologetic and settled down at her feet as she made herself a mug of tea. As she sipped it, she reflected upon the people she had seen that evening. Pete wasn't her type, but he certainly was a character, and a nice guy beneath the hard man exterior. Monty most definitely had not been her type, and she wished him the hangover of the century the next day. Olivier, under other circumstances, could have been her type but, annoyingly, the face that lingered in her mind was still the grim, unfriendly face of David Dupont. Not for the first time, she seriously questioned her sanity. What on earth was going on?

Chapter 11

After a wet and windy weekend, the weather cleared again by Monday and within a few days, the paths and beach were bone dry once more. Jess and Hope continued to take regular walks with the dog, gradually extending his range and getting to know their surroundings well as they did so. Daily swims for the Labrador also helped and they both began to see a reduction in his tummy measurement along with an increase in energy from him.

George came along most days to take the dog for walks and he often stayed for a coffee. Jess also found him in the garden more and more and she and he often sat under the overgrown gazebo together. As Hope was spending much of her time with Max on the *Helios*, Jess and George were often together like this and they talked a lot. Gradually, as the days went by, she began to sense a lightening in his mood as his spirits slowly began to lift. Whether this was down to her presence, or the company of the Labrador for walks, was hard to tell. Certainly, the dog was getting him out and changing his monotonous routine – that had to be a good thing.

After an initial attempt to find out more about David's state of mind, which immediately brought a cloud of gloom down upon his father, Jess avoided any further mention of him or the accident he had suffered.

As for David, she saw little or nothing of him. His car was often absent when she walked past so, at least, it appeared he was getting out and about. There was no further sign of him, either in the pool or at his window, the shutters of which remained firmly closed at all times. She continued to swim regularly and felt all the better for it, but deep down, she rather regretted no longer seeing him.

At the end of the week, she and Hope decided to invite George for dinner at the guest house – along with David if he could be persuaded to come. When she broached the subject with George, he appeared genuinely pleased at the invitation and, after a bit of prodding from Jess, he promised to do his best to persuade his son to come as well. Max was away for another long weekend on the boat with clients and so Hope and Jess set about preparing a really good meal for Friday night, in the hope that both father and son would come along.

Jess got hold of some fresh dressed crab from the fish shop and prepared one of her mum's specialities, consisting of crabmeat and grated apple, served with sliced avocados. Hope decided to christen the barbecue they had found in the shed, and had bought two enormous steaks that she intended to grill and serve with roasted vegetables.

Once everything was ready on Friday afternoon, Hope took Brutus down to the sea for a swim while Jess headed for the pool. This time, as she walked down through the rosemary hedges, she heard splashing. Rounding the corner, she found that she was going to have company. David was already there, swimming lazily across the pool and back again. Jess stripped off her towel and waded into the water, secretly rather glad she was wearing one of the new bikinis.

She swam slowly down the pool until she was alongside him and slowed, treading water.

'Hi, David. All well?'

'Yes, thanks… Jess.' So he did know her name.

'That's good. And are you coming along for dinner tonight with your dad? We've got the biggest steaks I've ever seen in my life.' Jess actually found herself crossing her fingers on one hand as she spoke.

There was a pause. 'My father was very insistent I should come.'

This didn't answer Jess's question, so she awaited what else he might have to say with keen anticipation. For the first time she spotted an emotion on his face that wasn't annoyance or gloom. This time she felt sure she saw regret.

'I don't do much socialising these days.'

'Really? I often see you out in the car.'

'Yes, I do go out in the car, but I haven't been for a meal, or even a drink, with anybody for months now.' For just a second his eyes met hers, before dropping just as quickly. 'I'm afraid I'm not very good company these days.'

Jess was acutely aware that he still hadn't answered her question and she feared that all this might be the preamble to a refusal, so she desperately searched for some way of persuading him to change his mind. The best solution she could think of was to involve his father.

'I do hope you can come. I've been spending time with your dad recently and I know he's worried about you – although he really looks much more relaxed since Brutus arrived.' Crossing her fingers even harder, she baited the hook. 'I know it would mean a lot to him if you were to come along. Please do. I would love it if you could, and so would he.'

David didn't reply immediately. Jess kept her eyes on him, waiting for him to make his decision. As she did so, she registered yet again how strong and muscular his arms and shoulders were, and noticed how his piercing blue eyes had the ability to reach deep inside her on the rare occasions when he raised them towards her.

'All right, if you really think it'll help him, I'll come.' Apparently remembering his manners – for the first time since she had met him – he continued as an afterthought. 'And thank you for inviting us. You're very kind.'

'Not at all. It's the very least we can do to try to repay at least a tiny bit of your hospitality.'

'You're welcome… Jess.'

'See you later, David.'

Before he could change his mind, Jess turned and swam off, limiting herself to a few widths of the shallow end before heading back to the house. As she picked up her towel and dried herself off, she surreptitiously crossed her fingers again and hoped he wouldn't change his mind.

She and Hope had invited the two men for seven o'clock and they had bottles of beer and wine in the fridge in readiness. Jess had chosen to wear a light summer dress for the occasion. It was very short, but she felt her brown legs looked pretty good in it, and she found herself wondering if David would notice.

At just after seven, they heard the crunch of gravel outside and Brutus raised his head towards the door and gave a very restrained, neighbourly woof. Jess called out to the courtyard where Hope was lighting the barbecue.

'They're here, Hope. I'll go and let them in.'

Jess, accompanied by the Labrador, went over to the door and opened it to find George standing there. Alongside him was David. In a wheelchair.

'Good evening, Jess. Here we are. David, you did remember the champagne, didn't you?'

From his wheelchair, David held up a bag from which two bottles protruded, the gold foil reflecting in the evening sunlight. He wasn't smiling, but at least he wasn't glowering either.

'Good evening. Here's the champagne.'

Jess suddenly felt an overwhelming urge to reach down and give him the biggest, warmest hug she had ever given anybody in her whole life. In an instant the depression, the moodiness, the downright hostility became explicable and she felt desperately sorry for him. Little wonder he had been depressed by his accident. For a few seconds she felt a burning sensation in the corners of her eyes, but she fought back the urge to burst into tears.

'Good evening, gentlemen. I'm so glad you've come.' She did her best to act as if she had been expecting one of her guests to be a man in a wheelchair, as she took the bottles from him and waved the two of them inside the house. 'You really shouldn't have brought anything. We've got loads of stuff in the fridge.'

She led them through to the courtyard where she and Hope had set up a table and four chairs, with the barbecue in one corner. Jess hurried over to remove one of the chairs, but David's voice stopped her.

'It's all right, Jess. I can manage.'

As she looked on, he reached over his right shoulder and removed a pair of metal crutches from a holder and rested them against the table beside him. Using his strong arms, he pushed himself up and onto his feet, holding onto the wheelchair for support. He then cautiously reached across and grabbed first one and then both crutches and transferred his weight across. His father pulled the wheelchair out of his way and David took a few hesitant steps across the courtyard until he could sink down onto one of the seats at the table.

'Shall I take the crutches?' Jess could hardly trust her voice after witnessing this laboured scene.

'Thank you.' David held them out to her and she rested them against one of the pillars. His father sat down opposite him just as Hope came across to say hello, before returning to the barbecue. For a second the two girls' eyes met and just as quickly dropped again. As surprises went, this was one of the biggest of Jess's life and she felt pretty sure Hope would be feeling the same way.

'I'm so very glad you've both agreed to join us tonight.' Jess glanced down at the bottles in the bag she was still holding. 'Should I open the champagne?'

'You choose, girls. We're in your house.' George was busy stroking the dog's head, while David appeared to be more interested in the ground at his feet.

Jess glanced across the courtyard. 'What do you think, Hope? Champagne?'

'Absolutely!'

'Then champagne it is. We can celebrate the fact that Brutus has lost a kilo or two this week.' Jess was determined to stay upbeat and to do her best to coax at least a smile out of David before the night was out.

She hurried back to the kitchen and opened one of the bottles, putting the other in the fridge. She picked up four glasses and came back out again to find that Hope had managed to get George talking, although his son was just sitting silently, staring out over the courtyard. Jess filled the glasses, passed them round, and then took a seat alongside David, resolved to get him involved in the conversation. She would dearly have liked to ask him about his accident, but she felt this was neither the time nor the place. Instead, she stuck to the banal. Picking up her glass, she clinked it softly against his.

'Cheers, David.'

David returned his attention from wherever it had been and glanced at her briefly.

'Cheers, Jess.'

Jess took a mouthful of wine and murmured appreciatively.

'What amazing wine. Thank you again.' She searched for a possible ice-breaker. 'Tell me, do you know the beach bar just around the coast from here on the way to St-Tropez?'

He nodded. 'Yes, I know it.'

'Have you been there recently?'

'No, but I used to.'

'We went there last weekend, but then we got rained out. What a storm!'

'Yes it was.'

Jess felt as if she was trying to get blood out of a stone, but she gritted her teeth and tried again, taking refuge in the old English staple in these situations: the weather.

'I've never seen rain like it. It just bucketed down. I was lucky. A man I met there gave me a lift home, otherwise I think I might have drowned.'

Was that a spark of interest in his eyes when she mentioned Olivier?

'Yes, when it rains here, it really rains.' Talk of the weather had at least produced an eight-word sentence from him – the longest of the evening so far.

'I saw you out in it as well. I thought your beautiful car was going to slide off the track as you went down the hill.'

'Yes. It certainly was slippery.'

For some reason, Jess felt she wanted to tell him that Olivier was just a friend, nothing more, but she couldn't think of any way of saying it without sounding a bit pathetic so, instead, she tried another topic of conversation. This time she made a point of choosing a question that had to elicit more than just 'yes' as an answer.

'So what sort of places do you go to when you go out in the car?'

'Nowhere special.' He hesitated and she could see he was deciding whether to go into any more detail. In the end, to her relief, he did. 'The thing is, getting in and out isn't so easy, and, as you've seen, I'm still not very good on crutches. So, like I say, I just drive.'

Jess could feel her heart bleeding for him as he spoke. If all he was doing was going out for long drives, little wonder he was depressed – however sleek and sexy the silver car was. Still trying to keep the conversation upbeat, she concentrated on the car.

'Is it easy to drive – you know, seeing as you've got trouble with your legs?' As she asked the question, she regretted alluding to his injuries, but he answered without any apparent difficulty.

'It's got hand controls. I don't need to use my feet.'

Jess gave a silent sigh of relief.

'Well, it's a gorgeous car. It looks like something out of a Bond film.'

'One of the very first Bond films. It was built when Sean Connery was still a youngster.'

'Jess, I've been meaning to ask you something.' Jess looked up as their nascent conversation was interrupted by George's voice. 'You're an architect, aren't you?'

'That's right – although I'm an architect without a job at the moment.'

'Of course. My mother said you lost your job for thumping a Russian. Is that right?'

In spite of the emotions aroused in her by the realisation of the seriousness of David's injuries, Jess couldn't help smiling. As she did so, she caught David's eye and, just for a moment, she saw what might have been a spark there. Encouraged, she set about putting the record straight.

'I didn't thump anybody, although I came close to it.' She went on to recount her run-in with Drugoi and she saw both men shake their heads in disbelief. When she reached the end of the tale, to her delight, David was the first to react.

'What a bastard.'

Only three words, but they were just about the first she hadn't had to prise out of him. She gave him a big smile, but he had already looked away.

'And your boss doesn't emerge from the episode with any great credit, does he?' George took a mouthful of his drink and carried on. 'Anyway, I was wondering if, maybe, you might like to take a look at the villa for me. You know – cast your architect's eye over it and give me your honest opinion.' He took another mouthful of wine. 'My wife always said she wanted to make some changes – it *is* pretty dated as you must have seen. We never did anything about it and then, of course, there was her illness.'

There was an awkward silence as Jess saw him begin to retreat into himself again, so she hastened to reply before she lost him.

'I'd love to take a look, George. What sort of thing were you thinking of doing? Just cosmetic changes inside, or something more structural?'

She was relieved to see his eyes lift and focus on her once more. A few weeks ago, that would have been much more of a struggle. This was definitely progress.

'I wouldn't want to change the character of the place too much. It's a pretty idiosyncratic house, but that's how it was built, and I'd like to keep that. But there are a few things I'd like changed – mainly practical things. Next time you've got a spare minute, why don't you come up for a glass of wine and tell me what you think?'

'I'd love to.'

The meal turned out to be very good, and both men complimented them on the food. Hope sliced the huge steaks vertically into strips, Chateaubriand-style, and served the meat with leaves of fresh rocket and slivers of parmesan. The result was excellent and Brutus wasn't the only one who thought it smelt wonderful. The champagne bottle was emptied pretty quickly and Jess brought out the red Burgundy she and Hope had found in the big supermarket. By the time they reached the fruit salad and ice cream, Jess felt the evening had gone really well, at least as far as George was concerned. As for David, it was hard to judge. He remained fairly taciturn, but she thought she glimpsed a hint of a smile at one point when the dog did his best to climb onto Hope's lap as she was serving the meat. However, no sooner had he finished his dessert than he made his apologies.

'I'm afraid I have to get back to my computer. I've got a pretty important online meeting with some guys in California.' He caught Jess's eye for a moment. 'I'm sorry.'

Jess felt a pang of disappointment. Somehow, after the food and the wine, she had been hoping he would maybe have mellowed enough to start talking a bit more. Instead, she watched as he laboriously returned himself to the wheelchair. Once he was settled and the crutches returned to their holder, she accompanied him to the door. She wondered if she should offer to push the wheelchair, but he didn't ask and he seemed competent, negotiating the little step at the door without difficulty. As she looked down at him, she could see that his powerful shoulders and arms were more than strong enough to propel himself along. Once outside in the starlight, he half-turned the chair towards her and looked up.

'Thanks again, Jess. That was very kind of you and Hope. Sorry I wasn't very good company. I did warn you.'

'For somebody who claims not to have been out socially for a while, I thought you were great. I wish you could have stayed on. I'm sure there's lots you and I could talk about.'

'Well, hopefully you'll be staying here for a good while. I'm sure we'll have other opportunities to talk.'

Jess was still wondering whether to shake his hand or even maybe kiss him on the cheeks when he spun the chair round again and headed back across the lawn to the gate. She saw him lift the latch and then turn his head briefly.

'Good night, Jess, and thanks again.'

It was hard to tell in just the light of the stars, but she had the impression his face might just have broken into a hint of a smile. Then the chair disappeared from sight and she walked slowly back into the house.

George looked up as she came back to the table.

'Thank you for inviting David.' He sounded pleased.

'Thank you for persuading him to come.'

'That's down to you, Jess. As recently as lunchtime he told me in no uncertain terms that he wasn't coming. Clearly, you're more persuasive than me.'

'George… can I ask you something?' Jess saw him nod, the expression on his face indicating that he probably knew what was coming. 'David's injury… how bad is it? Is he going to get better?'

She saw George shake his head uncertainly and a wave of sadness swept through her.

'Nobody knows, I'm afraid. The accident was six months ago now, and progress has been slow. All his fractures have healed well, but it's the nerve damage that's the big unknown. The nerves are controlled by the brain, so it's the brain that's the problem now.' He looked across the table at the two of them. 'He's seen some of the best surgeons in the world and the consensus is that it's unlikely he'll ever walk properly again unless there's some miraculous improvement in his nervous system. If not, then hobbling with a stick is about as good as it might get.'

'How awful.' Hope's face mirrored Jess's. 'What was it? A car accident?'

George shook his head slowly. 'No. A boat.'

'A boat? How did he break his legs in a boat?'

'It was a powerboat, a racer. It flipped over and crashed at high speed. He was into all those high-octane sports – hang gliding, climbing, skiing, motor racing, powerboat racing. You name it, he did it.' He looked up slowly. 'He knew the risks, but that never stopped him. It's tragic, really tragic.'

His voice tailed off and Jess dived in to rescue the evening from descending into a case of what the French call *vin triste*.

'He's young, he's strong, he's fit. I'm sure he'll be able to progress.'

'I'm not sure he wants to, Jess.'

'What do you mean?'

'He's always been an all or nothing sort of boy. Now that he finds himself in a wheelchair, it's as if his life's finished. It's a vicious circle. Until he decides he wants to try to get better, and that means intensive physiotherapy, he won't be able to improve. At least for now, he's still clinically depressed and he says he can't be bothered to do as the doctors say. And that means that any physical improvement just isn't happening as it should. The doctors say it's got to come from him and, so far, it hasn't.'

'How awful. So he just doesn't want to help himself?'

'Something like that. Mind you, I haven't been much help since Babette's death. I'm afraid my depressed state hasn't made me much of a role model for him.'

'But you're sounding more positive now, even compared to just last week. You're definitely improving, so maybe he can.'

Jess and Hope between them managed to turn the conversation away from this morbid subject, mainly by getting George to talk about his work in the garden and the sort of changes he had in mind for the villa. When he finally left half an hour later, he managed a big smile to both of them as they kissed him on the cheeks. They watched him as he walked over to the little gate and disappeared.

Jess turned to Hope and directed a finger towards the dog who was standing at the door, his tail wagging hopefully.

'Shall we take Brutus out for a walk?'

They decided to avoid the beach and headed inland, up a path they had discovered through the scrub that looped round before returning to the villa. As they walked, they discussed the evening's events. Uppermost in both their minds was David and his wheelchair. As ever, Hope lived up to her name.

'The fact that he's able to walk with sticks, crutches, that's good, isn't it? At least that means he can get out of the chair and move about.'

'But his dad says he doesn't want to. It's as if he doesn't want to get better.'

'It must have been a terrible shock to the system, specially if he was such an adrenaline junkie before. And don't forget – his mum died just last year. What he needs, Jess, is for you to help him regain the will to live.'

'Me, why me?'

'Because it's obvious he fancies you, that's why.'

'It's obvious… what?'

'He fancies you. And it's as plain as the nose on your face that you fancy him. You need to step in and get involved.'

Jess was speechless. First, she had had no idea that her attraction towards David – which she was honest enough to acknowledge at least to herself – had been so apparent. But second and more puzzling was how Hope could possibly think that David found her attractive. He had barely looked at her all evening and his responses to her attempts at conversation had been little more than monosyllabic.

'I don't see it, Hope. Besides, I'm no medical practitioner. I don't know the first thing about depression – or broken legs for that matter.'

'You heard his dad. David's got medical practitioners coming out of his ears, but he isn't listening to them. What he needs is somebody to get his spirits up – and you're the girl for the job.'

They walked in silence for a little while before Jess came to a decision. And this decision – she told herself – had nothing to do with any possible attraction either she or David might feel for the other. David's grandmother in London had asked her to do her best to help both men. So far, David's father seemed to be doing better – whether as a result of her presence or quite possibly the arrival of the dog. Now it was the son's turn. She glanced across at Hope's shadow beside her.

'If I can help, I will.'

Chapter 12

The next night they walked round to the beach bar again. This time there was no risk of rain and the sky was clear and cloudless as the sun slipped towards the horizon. The air temperature was still high and both of them had opted for their lightest clothes. Jess even let Hope persuade her to walk along the beach to the bar with her feet in the water and she had to admit that the sea temperature was now a good bit warmer. Maybe she would be joining Hope and Brutus in the sea before long.

They got there early, before too many people had appeared. Jess looked around but saw no sign of Olivier yet and hoped he would keep his promise of coming to meet her. She was looking forward to seeing the handsome, cultured Frenchman again. This relative calm gave her the opportunity to talk to Terri as she sipped a glass of cold mineral water. After the champagne and red wine the previous night, she had decided to give it a little while before starting on the rum punch.

'Terri, do you know a guy called David? David Dupont?'

A shadow fell across the waitress's face. 'Of course I know him. We all know him. You've heard about the accident?'

'I heard he crashed a powerboat.'

Terri nodded. 'It was right out here.' She pointed out into the shadows of the gulf. 'He had this amazing power-boat. He used to race it and he used to win a lot of races.'

'And the accident was during a race?'

'Yes, but he didn't hit another boat. He hit something under the water – a container, I think they said it was.'

'Wow!'

'You know Pete, the muscleman? You should ask him. He was racing in another boat and he saw the whole thing.'

A few seconds later, Hope joined in the conversation.

'Terri, there's something else we were wondering...'

Jess looked across at Hope, wondering what she was going to ask. She took a sip of mineral water and let the ice cube rest on her tongue, melting in her mouth.

'Did he, does he, have a wife or girlfriend?'

Jess jerked upright, appalled. As she did so, she choked, coughed, and the ice cube shot across the table into Hope's lap. Blushing, she hastily apologised. Hope struggled masterfully not to giggle out loud. Fortunately, Terri had been looking over her shoulder and had noticed nothing. She turned back and answered Hope's question as Jess mopped her face and did her best to stop her cheeks from burning.

'No wife, but lots and lots of girlfriends. You've met him, have you?' Hope nodded as Terri went on. 'Well, you've seen how handsome he is and, of course, he's absolutely loaded as well.'

'They're a wealthy family. So, lots of girlfriends?' Hope was still fighting what she supposed to be Jess's corner. 'Any special girlfriend?'

'Not that I can think of, but there was always a queue of women around him wherever he went.' Terri laughed.

'I should know. I was in the queue myself for a good long while until I met Louis. Anyway, if you see him, give him my love. We all hope he gets better soon.'

After she had walked off, Jess gave Hope an accusing look. 'Just exactly what were you doing, asking Terri all those questions?'

'Just testing the water. A bit like you paddling along this beach.' Hope gave her a grin. 'At least now you know the coast is clear.'

'Why should that be of interest to me? What do you mean?'

'You know exactly what I mean.'

Jess shook her head in mock annoyance. 'Hope, I've said it before and I'll say it again. You may have come here to find yourself a man, but I'm quite happy as I am. And I'm certainly not looking for another rich guy.'

'Of course you aren't.'

Jess snorted. She would have preferred an argument from her friend, rather than just this condescension. But before she could retort, a familiar, bulky, form appeared.

'Hello, girls. How are you both?'

'Hi, Pete. We're fine. All well in the world of personal security?' Hope gave him a kiss on each cheek and a big grin.

'Nobody's taken a shot at me this week, so that's good.' He glanced across at Jess. 'How about you, Jess? All well?'

'Yes, thanks.' She stood up and kissed him as well, then hesitated for a moment. 'Pete... Terri said you saw the accident when David Dupont crashed his powerboat. Is that so?'

He nodded. 'You know David?'

'Yes, a little.'

'How's he doing? Nobody's seen him for months. I even heard a rumour a while back that he'd died.'

'No, I'm pleased to report that he's very much alive.'

'Well that's good news. And his legs? They were really badly crushed. I know – I was one of the first on the scene. I've seen some bad stuff in my time and his legs were in an awful state. Is he getting better?'

'Still a work in progress, I think. So, Pete, tell us what happened.'

They both listened to Pete's account of what sounded like a horrific accident. The boat had hit a container lying just below the surface and had flipped into the air, cartwheeling end over end for a hundred metres. It sounded as if it was a miracle he hadn't been killed.

Pete had just finished his tale when Jess felt fingers tap her bare shoulder. She looked up to find Olivier standing there. She jumped to her feet and kissed him on both cheeks, delighted to see him.

'Hi, Olivier. Great to see you.'

'Hi Jess. How long did it take you to dry out last Saturday?'

'I couldn't have been any wetter if I'd jumped in the sea. Thanks again for the lift home. Without you I probably would have drowned.'

Olivier went over and greeted Hope and Pete. To Jess's surprise, Pete replied to his greeting in fluent French. Clearly, the big man wasn't just all bone and muscle.

They had a lovely evening. Gradually, other people arrived and Jess recognised a number of faces from the previous week. By the end of the evening, she had danced with quite a few people, including Pete, Hope and, of course, Olivier, and she had had a whale of a time. Finally, around two o'clock in the morning, the music stopped and they all started to make their way home. Both Pete and Olivier offered Jess a lift home, but she opted to walk back around the coast with Hope, rather than leave her by herself. She kissed both of the men and exchanged phone numbers with Olivier before setting off.

Now that the music had stopped, it was a wonderful, still night, with very little noise apart from the rhythmic movement of the waves against the rocky shoreline and the usual background chirping of cicadas. There was enough light from the near full moon for them to be able to make their way along the coastal footpath without too much trouble. The only lights they saw were across the bay in Ste-Maxime, along the coast beyond, and what might have been a cruise ship out at sea. The hillside behind them was pitch black, either because all the occupants of the villas were asleep or because they only used the houses as second homes for a few weeks in August – and it was still the month of June.

There was one light, though. As they reached George's villa, Jess saw a light burning in one of the upstairs bedrooms. She quickly worked out that it was coming from David's room and felt a little pang of sadness for him, still awake at this time of night.

Brutus was very pleased to see them and actually broke into a run as they took him for a walk up the hillside behind the villa as usual. Hope was impressed.

'Our four-legged friend seems to be getting his energy back, which is good. So, Jess, talking of friends, how come you didn't take Olivier up on his offer of a lift home? I could have walked or taken a ride on the back of Pete's Harley, you know.'

'I thought I'd rather walk home with you.'

'I'd have been OK. For another time, you go ahead. Don't worry about me.'

'Of course, Hope, but it was fine.' Her voice tailed off.

'So, what about Olivier? Are you interested?'

'Olivier? Yes, he's a really nice guy.'

'Nice? Just nice? Does that mean you don't fancy him? I think he's gorgeous.'

Jess gave it some thought – not for the first time that night. Yes, he was a good-looking man. He was intelligent, friendly, and he had a great sense of humour. Under other circumstances, she could have easily seen things developing with him. But something, or someone, was holding her back. Hope wasn't her best friend for nothing. She had clearly been reading her mind.

'Still thinking about David?'

'Yes, I suppose so. Oh, I don't know, Hope. There's just something about him.'

'Like the fact that he looks like a movie star and he's apparently loaded?'

'No, not that.' She reached over and tapped Hope on the wrist. 'I really mean that. The last thing I want is another man like Rafael. But there's something about David. Yes, he's grumpy, he's suffering, he's depressed, but there was something else.' She hesitated, searching her own mind for the answer. 'It's just that underneath it all, I think he's a genuinely nice guy and I think he needs somebody.'

'We all need somebody, Jess. So what're you going to do about it?'

'Well the first thing I've got to do is to try to cheer him up, get him interested in life again.'

'And how do you propose to do that?'

'I wish I knew.'

Sunday was a lazy day and Jess and Hope stayed around the house, doing the laundry and pottering in the garden. Just before lunchtime, they took the dog down to the beach and Jess finally let herself be persuaded to try swimming in the sea. She was happy to find that, after the initial shock, the temperature was really quite pleasant. Certainly, it was warmer than any seaside holiday she had ever had in Britain. And, once she had got used to the water, the swim itself turned out to be a lot of fun.

Brutus was clearly delighted to have two swimming companions and he splashed happily between the two of them as they threw an old tennis ball about. After a while, Hope set off on a longer swim out into deep water, but Jess chose to stay with the dog. It was then that disaster struck. Jess had chosen to wear her old bikini and it was while she was locked in a scramble with Brutus for the ball that the wardrobe malfunction she had been dreading happened. A scrabbling paw caught on the top of her bikini and something gave. Seconds later – to her horror – she saw a triumphant Brutus swim shoreward bearing her red bra in his mouth.

'Brutus, you little bugger, come back here.'

By this time, Brutus had reached the beach and he clearly had no intention of returning the purloined article. Instead, he settled down at the top of the beach by the footpath with her bra between his front paws and a wide canine smile on his face.

'Brutus, give that back... Brutus, come! Come here! Come!'

Brutus was essentially an obedient dog, and Jess's command worked remarkably well. She was gratified to see him stand up, trot back down into the water, and start swimming towards her. Unfortunately, she hadn't been explicit enough with her instructions, and he left her bra lying on the beach alongside the coastal footpath.

As the Labrador arrived at her shoulder and she felt his cold wet nose against her, she pondered what to do. A glance out to sea showed her that Hope was a good hundred yards away by now, head down, swimming strongly. A close inspection of the footpath revealed no signs of life and there was nobody on the terrace up at the villa, so, apprehensively, she decided to swim back in and retrieve the missing article herself. Accompanied by the dog, she headed back until she was in only a couple of feet of water and then, after one more nervous look in both directions, splashed out of the water and ran up the beach to grab it.

She waded hastily back into the water, sat down on a rock and slipped the bra back on with considerable relief, noting that the clip was looking a bit bent. Clearly this particular bikini's days were numbered. She had only just clipped herself up again and was beginning to recover from her embarrassment when she heard a voice, directly behind her.

'Jess... and Brutus... how good to see you.'

Antoinette's voice made her jump. She turned her head and saw the housekeeper standing at the little wooden gate where the private path led up from the beach to the villa.

'Hi, Antoinette. All well?'

Hearing a familiar voice, Brutus came charging out of the water and up the beach to greet his friend.

'Yes, fine, thanks.' Antoinette sounded relaxed. 'Is that Hope out there in the sea? Brutus! Go and shake yourself somewhere else, would you? Here, go fetch.'

Jess saw her pick up a chunk of wood and throw it out to sea. The Labrador plunged after it with considerable enthusiasm.

'He's looking a lot more energetic, isn't he?'

Antoinette slipped off her sandals, waded into the water and sat down on a rock a few feet away from where Jess was sitting. They both sat in silence for a few moments, enjoying the warmth of the sun. It was all very still and the only noise came from a cluster of seagulls fighting over some tasty titbit a little further around the coast. Apart from the two of them, the only other living being to be seen was Hope, now swimming back towards the shore. Jess found herself smiling.

'I still can't quite believe we're on the Côte d'Azur and yet it's so quiet. You're the first person I've seen since I came down to the beach.'

'We're very fortunate here. The masses tend to stay on the bigger beaches.'

'Do you ever come down here for a swim yourself?'

'I do sometimes, when it gets really hot. You wait – August down here can be absolutely boiling.'

'What about the others – George and David?'

'George never swims in the sea – in fact he rarely uses the pool. His wife, Babette, used to be a great swimmer and David when he was younger used to do a lot of swimming and underwater fishing. He often used to bring me octopus and even an occasional lobster for the kitchen.'

Jess sighed for him. 'I wonder if he'll ever be able to do that again.'

'I don't know, but I'll tell you one thing, Jess. Since you and Hope arrived, he and his father are so much more cheerful, and that's got to mean something.'

At that moment, Hope arrived back and splashed towards them, fighting off the joyous welcome provided by Brutus.

'Hi, Antoinette. Coming for a swim?'

Antoinette shook her head.

'No, I've just popped down for a few minutes on an errand. George wanted me to ask Jess if she felt like coming round for a glass of wine this evening and taking a look at the house. And Hope, of course you're very welcome as well.'

Jess gave her an answering smile.

'Of course. Do tell him I'd be delighted to come round and take a look at the villa. Hope, are you here this evening?'

'Max said he'd be back around five, so, if George doesn't mind, Antoinette, I promised I'd go over and join him in the harbour.'

'Of course. *Vive l'amour*. So, Jess, if you're sure, would six o'clock be all right for you?'

'Perfect. Tell him I look forward to seeing him then.'

As she stood up and waded back to the beach, Hope caught Jess's eye and winked.

'And his son, hopefully, eh, Jess?'

Jess didn't reply.

Chapter 13

Jess and Brutus went over to the villa at six o'clock as arranged. She brought her laptop, pad and measure with her, in readiness for her survey, and she found George waiting for her with a bottle of cold Chablis. He told her he had just spent an hour working in the garden and there was welcome colour in his cheeks as a result. There was, however, no sign of David. Jess, while not surprised, couldn't help but be disappointed.

She and George sat on the terrace and chatted for a while before starting their inspection of the house. As usual on these occasions, Jess the architect did her best to find out what the client wanted, before making any proposals of her own. In essence, it was pretty simple. George wanted to retain the quirky character of the building, while making it a bit more practical and bringing it up to date.

'I wouldn't want it changed too much. Babette and I had so many good times here, I wouldn't want to lose those memories.'

Jess was delighted to hear him managing to speak about his dearly beloved wife in matter-of-fact tones.

'And do those memories extend to, for example, the bath in the lounge?'

He managed a smile. 'Well now you come to mention it… I think that's maybe one of the changes that need to be made. And another thing…' His smile broadened into a grin. 'I think it's time I got myself a toilet that's the same shape as my bottom.'

'And what about bigger changes? Like this terrace, for example, are you happy with it like it is?'

'I love it, although I suppose it might be good to get some sort of windbreak. It can get a bit nippy here in the autumn and winter.'

Once she had got a clearer idea of his thoughts, Jess got George to give her a tour of the building, leaving the Labrador dozing on the terrace. Using her clever little Leica laser measure, she measured the rooms and quickly sketched the floor plan on her pad as they went round. Once they had finished on the ground floor, he took her upstairs. To get there, they used the mirrored lift and she quickly realised one of the main disadvantages of having mirrors everywhere was that it probably hadn't been such a good idea to wear a short skirt. For the second time that day she felt her cheeks burn as she glanced down and got a clear view up her skirt to her pants, reflected back at her from the floor. Fortunately, George gallantly kept his eyes straight ahead, but when they stepped out, she resolved to use the stairs in future.

'Of course the lift has been a godsend with David in his chair.' George kept his voice low and Jess wondered whether his son was nearby.

There were three bedrooms on the upper floor, all equipped with ensuite bathrooms and all, in Jess's view, desperately in need of a revamp. One bathroom was chocolate brown, one avocado green, and the last one a lurid yellowy orange. She glanced at George.

'Any emotional attachment to the bathroom décor? How would you feel about changing the colour schemes?'

'I would be delighted. And I know Antoinette would be, as well. She keeps telling me it's getting harder and harder to tell what's clean and what's dirty. What were you thinking of? White?'

'Whatever you like, George, but, personally, I'm for white in bathrooms. Let's give it some thought.'

There was a fourth room on the upper floor and it was here that Jess found David. A quick calculation had already told her that this had to be the room from where he had been watching her, and it turned out not to be a bedroom, but a study. In there she found a battery of state-of-the-art computers on a glass and steel trestle table and, in front of them, David in his wheelchair, surrounded by files and piles of paper. Unless he was engaged in several complicated videogames at the same time, it looked very much as if he was working. Somehow, the idea that he might have a job, rather than just be living off inherited wealth, served to increase his appeal to Jess.

'Hi, David.'

'Hello, Jess.' He spun the chair round so that he was facing her and, just for a second, she got the impression that his expression looked welcoming, before it returned to its normal blankness. 'You're here in your professional capacity, I believe.'

'That's right.' She decided to try to keep him talking. 'So, as this is evidently your study, what changes, if any, would you like to see in here?'

She saw him think for a moment before pointing down to the floor beneath the long work surface.

'If you could do something about all this, I'd be pleased. I'm afraid it's going to burst into flames one of these days.'

Jess looked down and immediately saw what he meant. The floor was a mass of cables, extension leads and multiple adaptors. It looked like a plate of spaghetti – only a lot more dangerous.

'Ouch. Yes, I see what you mean.'

Turning to George, she asked him one of the questions she had written on her list earlier.

'Would I be right in thinking that the electrical wiring is the original wiring from fifty years ago?'

'Some bits of the downstairs have been rewired, but I'm afraid this is all old stuff upstairs.'

Jess added an exclamation mark alongside that particular bullet point. David hadn't been too far off the mark when he had mentioned a possible fire hazard. She looked back at him.

'I saw your light on last night on the way home from the beach bar. It must have been two or three in the morning. Were you still working?'

David nodded. 'That's the problem with having business connections in the USA. They're up and running when the rest of us would rather be in bed.' Jess wondered what sort of business he was in, but decided it would be rude to pry at this stage. He paused and then she was surprised, and pleased, to hear him ask an unprompted question.

'Did you have a good time at the beach bar? Did you get to practice your French with the people there?'

Jess shook her head. 'I'm afraid my French is still very much schoolgirl French. Luckily everybody round here seems to speak English. And yes, thanks, I had a good time and I bring you good wishes from Terri. She sends her love. You remember her?'

'Yes, of course. Is she still with Louis?'

Jess was delighted at his interest, and she sensed his father's surprise.

'Yes, and Louis says hi as well. Oh yes, and big Pete.' She took a deep breath and decided to go for it. 'He was telling me all about your accident. It sounded horrific.'

She heard what sounded like a sharp intake of breath from George, and saw David's eyes fall. But, to her great satisfaction, he didn't clam up.

'It must have been. I don't really remember much about it, except for a sensation of spinning, falling.'

Jess did her best to keep the conversation going.

'Pete told me your boat cartwheeled for a hundred metres.'

'It must have been something like that.'

'All because of a shipping container.'

'That's right.' He hesitated for a moment and then looked up blankly. 'So bloody stupid, isn't it? All this just because somebody on a freighter miles away didn't tie a container on tight enough.'

His voice was strained and, as he spoke, his hands waved helplessly towards his legs. Jess immediately felt a wave of sympathy for him. Nevertheless, she was delighted she had managed to involve him in a real conversation for once. She glanced across at his father, who was looking stunned.

'Is there some of that lovely Chablis left, George?' She saw him nod, so she returned her attention to his son. 'David, can you spare a few minutes to come down and join us to talk about things that need doing here in the villa? It would be very useful for me if you could.'

'All right.' Her spirits soared. 'Just give me a few minutes to finish what I'm doing and I'll be down.'

As she and George walked back down the stairs, he surprised her by catching hold of her hand giving it a squeeze.

'That was amazing, Jess. Have you any idea what just happened up there?'

'Am I right in thinking he hasn't spoken much about the accident?'

He squeezed her hand again before releasing it. 'He's *never* spoken about the accident. That's just about the first time he's even acknowledged it happened. Jess, I could hug you.'

Jess saved him the trouble. As they reached the bottom of the stairs, she stopped and looked across at him. His eyes were welling up, so she stretched her arms around his waist and gave him a warm hug, feeling him shake with emotion as she did so. Then she kissed him softly on the cheek and stepped back.

'He's doing well, George. And so are you.'

'Jess, I really, really hope so.'

David was true to his word and came down to join them less than five minutes later. Jess was impressed to see that he appeared on his crutches, rather than in the wheelchair, and she sensed that this was also progress. Brutus got up and gave him a warm welcome while his father poured the drinks and they settled down, looking out over the sea. The sun was setting off to the right of them and the palm trees in the garden already cast long shadows. It was a delightful warm – but not suffocatingly hot – evening and Jess felt relaxed and very, very satisfied that her gamble appeared to have paid off. She decided to get down to business.

'So, I've got a list of suggestions. Would you like me to read them out to you?'

Both men nodded, so she started with something she hoped would make them laugh. She was determined to keep the tone light.

'If it was my house, I'd lay a bit of carpet or linoleum on the floor of the lift. I got a good view of my knickers as we came up in the lift and I imagine any other woman using it would have the same problem.'

George smiled and, just for a second, a flash of something appeared on David's face. Encouraged, Jess continued with her list, running through major works like rewiring the whole house, to less invasive jobs like removing the bathtub from the lounge and constructing a glass barrier as a wind-break on the terrace. She opened her laptop and showed them a number of photographs of renovated bathrooms, so they could see the various colours she had chosen for the bathroom furniture in the past, as well as the floors and tiles. Last of all, she came to the kitchen and made a practical suggestion.

'The kitchen could definitely do with a revamp, maybe even an extension, but I suggest we have a word with Antoinette first. She's the person who uses it every day and we need to make sure we give her what she needs.' She closed her laptop and set down her pencil and pad. 'Give me a day or two and I'll draw you up some plans, so you've got something to work from, but tell me, gentlemen, any initial thoughts?'

She saw George exchange glances with David before replying.

'Thank you very much, Jess. I don't disagree with any of it and I especially like the sound of the windbreak outside. That way I might even be able to have my Christmas dinner on the terrace. I've only done that a few times in my life.

It's often warm enough in December, but we can get a cold wind off the sea or down off the mountains.'

George glanced at David again.

'What do you think, David? Anything to add?'

Jess saw him shake his head.

'All sound like great ideas.' He paused as something struck him. 'Will this work mean us having to move out, or could it be done around us?'

'The only really disruptive job will be the rewiring. If you get a good contractor, I see no reason why it couldn't be done pretty quickly, though. I had a quick look behind a couple of plugs and it would appear that your father's architect had the good sense to put the wires in conduits, so it shouldn't be necessary to rip out too many great chunks of plaster from the walls. Anyway, you could always move into the guest house for a couple of weeks while it's going on.'

'But where would you go?' George sounded concerned.

'Depending on how soon an electrician could start, I'll most probably be back in the UK and out of your hair by then.'

Jess saw clear regret on George's face, but his son's expression remained inscrutable. Undeterred, she carried on.

'Have you got a trusty electrician by any chance? Maybe Antoinette knows somebody?'

George beamed at her.

'Even better. Antoinette's husband *is* an electrician, and a very good one. He's the chap who did the few bits of rewiring downstairs. I can ask her to ask him.'

'Excellent. See if he can come and give you an estimate. Remember, you need three things from him: how much it's going to cost, how long it's going to take, and when he might be able to start.'

'And isn't his cousin or his uncle a plumber?' David was thinking aloud. 'He could probably do the bathrooms for us.'

Jess was delighted to hear David join in and take an active part in the conversation. Seeing him so animated, she decided to try a little bit of positive reinforcement, although she sensed she was on thin ice. Affecting a nonchalance she didn't feel, she made an observation.

'I was wondering while we were walking round whether we should take the opportunity to make this place more wheelchair-friendly – you know, ironing out a few steps, putting in a ramp or two. But then I thought to myself, that's not really necessary, is it? David, you're looking pretty good on crutches, so I imagine you'll be out of the chair for good before long.'

Her words were followed by silence. In reality it probably only lasted a few seconds, but to Jess, it felt like an age. Then, to her infinite relief, David answered. His voice was strong, even if he didn't look up and meet her eyes.

'I really hope so.'

Jess caught George's eye and Jess felt she could read hope, and maybe respect, in them. Encouraged by the reactions of both men, she made a show of rubbing out one of her bullet points and observed, 'Fine, that's one less thing to be done.'

Reaching for her glass, she took a big mouthful of the ice-cold wine and breathed a silent sigh of relief.

Chapter 14

The next few days passed quietly. The weather remained very pleasant and Jess settled into a routine of swimming, sunbathing, walking the dog, working in the garden, wandering into St-Tropez for a coffee or to do some shopping and – whenever she could – chatting to George. Alas, David was conspicuous by his absence most of the time. Still, Jess remained hopeful that the first stirrings of recovery she had noticed in him on Sunday evening might continue to develop.

On Thursday Jess got a text message from Olivier, inviting her out for dinner the following night. This immediately made her stop and think. She did her best to explain it to Hope over a cup of coffee and a fresh croissant in their kitchen.

'He's a really nice guy. I'm sure if I go out with him I'll have a good time, but I'm not feeling any real attraction.'

'Because of the attraction you feel for somebody else.' Hope sounded quite confident of the truth of her assertion.

'Maybe… I don't know, Hope.' Jess took a sip of coffee to give her time to marshal her thoughts. 'It's a funny thing. Somehow, I feel a real link to this place and to George and David. Both of them. Whether my feelings for David go beyond the friendship stage, I really can't say.'

'From what I've seen, they do. I've known you for years and years, Jess, and I don't think I've ever seen that look in your eye before.'

Jess looked across in surprise. 'What look in my eye?'

'Lust, Jess.' Hope gave her a knowing look and a wink and Jess felt herself blushing. 'That feeling that you'd like to tear his clothes off and ravish him. The feeling I get every time I see Max – but then, you see, that's what I do.'

'Hope, please, not in front of Brutus!'

Jess glanced down at the dog, stretched out on the cool floor. Hearing his name, he opened one eye, checked that no food was forthcoming and relapsed into his comatose state. His interest in the opposite sex had been surgically removed by the vet some years previously, so at least he was spared these concerns. Jess smiled down at him and did her best to respond to her friend's observation.

'I will admit that when I saw David in the pool, before I knew about his accident, I did think he was pretty hunky. And the day I inadvertently gave him my Miss Wet T-shirt show, it actually did feel rather good, in a naughty sort of way.' She glanced at Hope, who was nodding. 'But the thing is, now that I know the extent of his injuries – that's both physical and mental I'm talking about – I really don't know what my feelings for him are, after all.'

'What do you mean?' Hope sounded as puzzled as Jess herself was feeling.

Jess tried again.

'The overriding feeling I have towards David is one of pity. I feel really, really sorry for him. For such an active, energetic man to be cut down like this and reduced to crutches and even a wheelchair is so tragic. I look at him and I feel like crying.'

'He's still the same hunky, handsome guy, Jess.' Hope's voice was encouraging. 'So, he's a bit less mobile. He'll get better, or he'll come to terms with it, and you've got to do the same thing. Otherwise, what are you saying? That seeing him in a wheelchair stopped you fancying him?'

'God, Hope, that makes me sound like such an awful person. It's not that, I'm sure. It's not that I don't still find him attractive, it's just that the first thing that springs into my head, and my heart, when I see him is this feeling of pity.'

Hope tactfully got up and went over to the sink to wash the coffee cups, leaving Jess to her thoughts. Hope was right about the lust thing. From the very first time she had seen David, she had found him very attractive, physically attractive. Of that there was no doubt in her mind. And now, could it really be that his injuries had somehow made him less appealing? If that was the case, what did that make her? Superficial? Callous? It was an uncomfortable thought. But then something else occurred to her.

'Besides, Hope, it's all very well me trying to work out if I'd like to rip David's clothes off and jump all over him. The simple fact is that he hasn't shown the slightest interest in me. What's the point of me doing all this soul-searching when the relationship isn't going to go anywhere, anyway?'

'Of course he fancies you. Are you blind, Jess?'

Jess shook her head slowly. 'You heard what Terri said. There must be a queue a mile long for his affections – wheelchair or no wheelchair. He's handsome, he's rich – he's bound to have somebody else already.'

'So where is she, this other woman? We've been here over two weeks now and, to my knowledge, nobody's come to see David. Doesn't that strike you as a bit odd if he's already got somebody?'

'He told me he's got business connections in the States. Maybe she's over there.'

'Rubbish. If she loved him, she'd be here, at his side. No, take it from me, Jess, you're the one for David. I'd lay good money on it. In fact, I will. A hundred euros says you and he end up together.'

'You might as well pay me now. It isn't going to happen.'

'Because of you, or because of him?'

Seeing that Jess wasn't going to answer that one – mainly because she didn't know how – Hope reverted to the original question.

'So, what about Olivier, then, Jess?'

Jess looked down at the phone still in her hand. Slowly, she made up her mind.

'I enjoy his company. I think I'll say yes and go out for dinner with him – as a friend. That isn't going to affect the way I think about David, is it? And, who knows? Maybe Olivier's the man for me after all.'

The expression on Hope's face made clear what she felt about this.

–

Olivier offered to come and collect Jess from the villa the following night, but she arranged to meet him at the beach bar instead. Looking back on it as she waited for him down on the beach, she realised that this decision had been motivated by a desire to avoid being seen by David in the company of another man. Whether this was just to spare his feelings because he was unable to go out, or for some deeper reason, was something she was still contemplating when she saw Olivier coming across the sand towards her.

'Hi, Jess.'

'*Bonsoir, Olivier.*' Jess felt a wave of pleasure at the sight of him and gave him a hug and a kiss on both cheeks. 'It's very good to see you. Had a busy week?'

He shook his head. 'Not really. Tuition's stopped for the summer and most of the exams have finished. I've mostly been doing my own research.'

'Still Second World War stuff?'

'Yes. I've just got hold of records belonging to the German defenders – not just the Allied attackers. I'll bore you with the details some other time. Anyway, if you feel like it, I thought we could maybe go up to the village of Ramatuelle for dinner. It's up in the hills above St-Trop. Traffic permitting, it's only about twenty minutes away. How does that sound?'

'That sounds great, Olivier. Do you realise, Hope and I have been here for weeks now and we haven't been out of St-Tropez even once!'

They drove out of town along the main road on which Jess and Hope had arrived, but then turned sharply to the left and were soon climbing into the wooded hills on increasingly narrow roads, negotiating a series of sharp bends. As they climbed, so the views down to the coast got better and better. Olivier was a good driver and Jess settled back comfortably in her seat, doing her best to remember, as he pointed out a number of spots where he assured her she and the Labrador would be able to go for lovely long walks. She had already told him all about Brutus and the fact that she and Hope were doggy-sitting here this summer and trying to get him fit again. One walk, in particular, sounded particularly interesting.

'While you're in this part of the woods, keep your eyes peeled for any vestiges of the war.'

'What, like bombs and things?'

He shook his head. 'No, I imagine all that stuff got cleared up years ago – at least I hope so – but there used to be a number of gun positions and bunkers up here in the hills. See that track there? Try walking down it and then cutting up to the right. You'll soon find some interesting relics. I enjoy coming across the ruins and imagining what it must have been like back then.'

Ramatuelle was a delight. They parked alongside a monument to the Resistance, a few hundred metres outside the village, and walked up along a tree-lined road to the centre. They came to a little square with a simple church, surrounded by a jumble of sun-bleached pink terracotta roofs. A lone olive tree, its leaves grey and dusty, stood at one end of the square, and from there a narrow road curled downhill, flanked by little restaurants. Olivier led Jess to one of these and they were shown to a table outside on the terrace in front of the restaurant.

The road continued to drop away from there and Jess could see out over the wooded hills right down to the Mediterranean, shimmering almost purple in the evening light. A light breeze blowing up from the sea just took the edge off the heat and the temperature was perfect.

'Wow, what a super place. Thank you for bringing me here, Olivier. I must remember the way and bring Hope up here some time. And, like you say, we could give the dog a good walk while we're in the hills.'

The menu was written on a blackboard that the friendly waitress brought over to them and propped on a neighbouring chair. Jess read through what was on offer and then waited to hear what Olivier was having, before deciding to have the same. They chose mixed salad with grilled goat's cheese as a starter, followed by mussels. Instead of the traditional *moules marinière*, Olivier suggested they try the restaurant's speciality, which was mussels with curry sauce. Always prepared for a challenge, Jess said yes and she didn't regret it, although when they appeared, they were a rather off-putting lurid greenish colour. The taste, however, was excellent.

As they drank cold rosé and ate their food, they chatted, and Jess found that she was definitely enjoying Olivier's company. He was very bright, as well as being good-looking, and it was a lovely way to spend the evening.

He told her more about the war and the part played in preparing for the landings by the local Resistance, supported by OSS operatives, parachuted in or smuggled ashore from submarines. It was fascinating, but he soon turned the conversation to her, asking her how she was finding life in the place he and the locals all called St-Trop. She was quick to sing the town's praises.

'It's an amazing place. I freely admit that I came here expecting the worst. I thought it was going to be full of brash, selfish, rich people and, instead, I've found it full of some lovely, really normal people.'

'That's good to hear. Yes, there are a lot of very rich people around, but that doesn't automatically make them bad people. And there are enough ordinary folk about to dilute them.' He took a sip of wine. 'Like the Duponts, where you're staying. Yes, they're rich, but David's always been approachable. He's a good guy. I was really glad to see him up and about again after his awful accident.'

'Not so up and about.' Jess told Olivier about the shock she had received at seeing David in the wheelchair.

'Poor guy.' Olivier sounded really sorry for him. 'And he was so active. I do hope he manages to recover.'

'I'm not sure full recovery's on the cards. If he's lucky, he might get some improvement, but he's pretty knocked about.'

The thought of David was sobering, but Jess did her best to relegate him and his problems to the back of her mind, at least for now, and concentrate on her current friendly, handsome, and knowledgeable companion.

It was barely ten o'clock when they finished eating so Olivier suggested going down to the beach bar for a dance and Jess agreed happily.

They found the bar humming, with more people there than the previous week. Clearly, as summer approached, more and more people were heading for the Côte d'Azur. Jess and Olivier struggled through the crowd to the bar and found Terri, as ever, at the rum punch bowl.

'Hi you two. Rum punch?'

Olivier shook his head and waved his car keys. 'Just mineral water for me, I'm afraid.'

'Make that two, Terri, please.'

Jess leant against the bar and looked around, spotting a few familiar faces and a lot of new ones. Then she got a shock. Among the new faces was a very unwelcome one. Very unwelcome indeed. She shrank back against Olivier and felt his arm catch her shoulders supportively.

'You all right, Jess?'

'I'm all right, but I've just seen somebody who isn't. Look – that chubby guy over there. Ever seen him before?'

'No, never. He doesn't look French. Who is he?'

'His name's Drugoi – or at least that's what he calls himself. He's Russian.' Jess could hardly believe her eyes. 'And he's an arsehole.'

Olivier grinned. 'So I take it you don't like him very much?'

At that moment the two mineral waters appeared on the bar. Grabbing both little plastic bottles, Jess led Olivier round to the back of the bar and they perched on a pile of beer crates while she told him the story of how she had lost her job.

'So what's he doing here?' Olivier sounded as surprised as Jess herself.

'God knows. Do you mind if I take another peek at him?'

'Not at all. I'll come with you.'

Together, they tiptoed – no mean feat in sand – to the end of the bar and peered surreptitiously across the throng of drinkers and dancers to the other side. Drugoi was still standing where Jess had seen him, and near him were three other figures – two she recognised and one she didn't. At his side, wearing a figure-hugging pair of very short shorts and a skimpy top, was a very beautiful blonde. For a moment Jess thought it might be the same one she had met in London, but then realised that this was a different 'companion'. This girl, like her predecessor, was probably a good few years younger than Jess herself – and that would make her less than half the oligarch's age. Jess wasn't close enough to see her eyes, but she felt pretty sure she would recognise the same lifeless expression in them.

The figure on the other side, however, was familiar. Clearly Drugoi brought his interpreter with him wherever he went. Dmitri was wearing what looked like the same white shirt he had been wearing with his suit in London, but, incongruously, this was accompanied by a pair of garish orange shorts. His frighteningly white legs protruded from the shorts like sticks of celery and finished in dark socks and black leather shoes. If he had been hoping his ensemble would allow him to blend into the St-Tropez scene, he was sadly unsuccessful.

Behind him, standing a few paces back – in the shadows – was another familiar face, and this time it came as a bigger surprise to Jess. It was none other than Pete – muscleman Pete, the minder. So, presumably, his current client was none other than Drugoi. She turned to Olivier, trying to make sense of what she had seen.

'I wonder what Drugoi's doing here at St-Tropez. Of all the people to meet, he's definitely not one I would have chosen.'

'And Pete's working for him while he's here, I guess.'

'Certainly looks that way.'

'Shall we go somewhere else? We can head back into town and find another place to go dancing.'

Jess shook her head. 'I like it here. You like it here. I left my job because of that bastard. I don't see why I should have to leave my favourite bar as well.'

'Hi Jess. Hi Olivier.'

It was Hope.

'Hi, Hope, you'll never guess who I've just seen.'

Jess went on to point Drugoi out to Hope. She then had to restrain her friend from going across and throwing her drink in his face.

'Leave it, Hope. He's an arsehole and that's all there is to it. Where's Max?'

'He's back in the harbour with his latest guests. But at least this lot are only here for the weekend, so I'll get to spend most of next week with him.'

'More bankers?'

'No, this lot are foreign – all men. Very serious and a bit scary, apparently. They just sit round drinking vodka and speaking Russian.'

'Russians, here?' As she spoke, Jess realised that there were probably many more Russians than she had imagined here in St-Tropez. It really was a very cosmopolitan place.

'Well, Jess, if we're staying, how about dancing?' Jess felt Olivier's hand on her bare shoulder.

'Why not?'

Jess danced with Olivier and began to feel a bit better after the shock of seeing her old nemesis again. From time to time she spotted Drugoi, still accompanied by the blonde, with Pete standing in the shadows behind him. When she began to feel a bit weary, she returned to the bar and handed Olivier over to Hope. As she watched them dance together, she sipped her mineral water and reflected on the evening so far.

It had been a lovely meal and she had thoroughly enjoyed Olivier's company. He was a good dancer and his caring attitude over the Drugoi affair had endeared him to her. But the truth was that, while she enjoyed his company, she knew that she couldn't see the relationship developing. And the reason – she just had to accept it – was David. She kept thinking about him, as she had been since trying to rationalise her feelings towards him when speaking to Hope the previous day.

She knew she liked David a lot. The simple fact, though, was that getting together with him – assuming that he had any interest in her, which was still far from proven – would bring so many problems, practical problems, to overcome. Coming here tonight, for example, would be impossible. The beach was inaccessible to a wheelchair, and, most probably, crutches. Even if he managed to make it down here, he wouldn't be able to dance or move about. But that was only the tip of the iceberg.

There was the whole question of his mental state. His father had made it clear that David's depression was deep-seated and intractable. Jess had absolutely no experience of depression and she was terrified of doing something wrong and making matters worse. Was she prepared to take on somebody like him? Yes, she liked him, felt sorry for him, but did she feel deeply enough about him to assume the responsibility of getting involved with somebody as troubled as David?

But, even more important was the effect this might have on him. What if she did start a relationship with him and it didn't last? He was so very vulnerable at the moment – not just physically. What if she found herself unable to cope with the demands of looking after a disabled person? If she managed to get him to love her, only for her to then abandon him, what would that do to his already grievously wounded psyche? Given the depth of his depression at the moment, for all she knew, it could send him toppling over the edge. The ramifications were too terrible to contemplate. Was she strong enough to take on this sort of responsibility?

'Hi, Jess.'

She was roused from her reverie by a familiar voice. She looked up and gave him a smile and a kiss on the cheek.

'Hi, Pete. I see you're on duty tonight.'

He glanced sideways and lowered his voice. 'Yup. You've probably seen my man over there, but I can't tell you his name.'

'I don't know what his real name is, but with me he used the name Drugoi – and his little friend is Dmitri. Not sure about the blonde, though.'

Pete's face was a picture.

'You know him? You've met him? Nobody's supposed to know who he is. And you're right about Drugoi being a pseudonym.'

Jess gave him a three-line précis of her previous dealings with Drugoi and she saw Pete nod as she finished. 'So, Pete, you can probably imagine that he isn't exactly my favourite person at the moment.'

'Doesn't surprise me. I only just met him yesterday, but he doesn't strike me as particularly loveable.' He dropped his voice to little more than a whisper. 'Mind you, that's what I'm here for. He's probably made himself a lot of enemies over the years. Some of them, unlike you, would probably be more than happy to stick a knife in his back.'

'Just hand me the knife…'

'I'm not joking, Jess. Some of my clients are marked men.'

'Well I can't say I feel too sorry for him.' Jess took a deep breath. 'Anyway, just promise me you won't go stopping any bullets aimed at him. Whatever he's done to deserve it, you haven't. You just be careful.'

At that moment, Hope and Olivier returned, flushed from their exertions.

While Pete greeted the two of them, Jess found herself turning over in her head what Hope had said earlier. She reached over and caught her by the arm.

'Hope, you know you said there are Russians on the yacht tonight?' Hope nodded. 'Tell me a bit more about them.'

'I don't know very much, really. Max gets all sorts of different people coming along to charter the *Helios* – mostly through an agency – and he knows very little about them in advance. He says this lot look like gangsters and it's all a bit tense, like they're waiting for somebody or something. It's all very mysterious. He said they're going off somewhere tomorrow, so I'm out of it for now.'

'Waiting for somebody...?' Jess turned to Pete, who was chatting to Olivier. 'Pete, this is probably going to sound paranoid, but you know Hope's boyfriend, Max, don't you?'

'Yes, I saw him here last week.'

'It's just that Hope said he's got a bunch of foreigners, all men, on board the yacht this weekend. Max says they look like gangsters. Tell him, Hope.'

'He said they're a bit scary. All they do is drink vodka and speak Russian, and it's as if they're waiting for something or somebody.'

Jess saw the interest in Pete's eyes.

'You don't think there could be any connection, do you, Pete? Only it seems a bit of a coincidence, seeing as Drugoi's just arrived, doesn't it...?'

Pete's expression hardened and she glimpsed the steel beneath the jovial exterior. 'What's the name of the yacht?'

'*Helios*, or more precisely, *Helios IV*. She's moored down at the harbour. I mean, it's probably nothing, but it just occurred to me. Oh, and Hope, didn't Max say they're sailing off somewhere tomorrow?'

'Yes, but he didn't say where.'

'Thanks, girls, I'll get it checked out. Like you say, it's probably nothing.'

'You just take care.'

The easy smile returned to his face.

'If they couldn't kill me in Iraq or Afghanistan, I don't see them managing it in St-Tropez.'

Drugoi must have disappeared at some point, along with Pete, Dmitri, and the blonde girl, and, as the evening progressed, Jess had a pleasant time, dancing and chatting with Olivier, Hope, and a few other people she was getting to know. Finally, at just before one o'clock, Olivier apologised and told Jess he had to go back home.

'I promised I'd take my mum and dad to Grenoble for lunch with my sister and her husband in the morning. It's their wedding anniversary. It's a fair old drive, so we'll need to get away pretty early and I'd better get a few hours' sleep. I hope you don't mind.'

'Of course not. I tell you what. Seeing as Hope's here, why don't you leave us here and we'll walk home around the coast? That'll save you a bit of time. It's a full moon tonight so we'll easily find our way.'

'It's no trouble to give you a lift. Both of you...'

In the end, Jess managed to convince him that she was happy to walk home and she accompanied him to his car, where she gave him a warm farewell hug. She was fully prepared to give him an equally warm kiss but, to her surprise, he just pecked her on the cheeks. As she walked back to where Hope was sitting, she reflected that it would appear that Olivier was quite happy to just be her friend and that, she told herself, was exactly what she had set out to accomplish. Wasn't it?

'So, did you let him down easy?' Hope looked up as she returned and Jess saw that she was smiling. 'Seeing as your heart already belongs to another...'

'For your information, Olivier was the one who didn't want to get physical.'

Hope didn't look particularly surprised.

'Is that so? Well, he is a very good dancer, after all.'

'What's that supposed to mean?'

'A little bird told me that Olivier might be less interested in the contents of your pants than, for instance, Pete's.'

Jess looked up suspiciously. 'And just which little bird might that have been, then?'

'Olivier himself.' Hope was grinning now. 'He told me he rather fancies Pete. He's got a thing for muscular men apparently.'

'Blimey… I'm really not very good at reading the signs, am I?' A sudden thought occurred to her. 'So, does this mean I may be wrong about David as well?'

'What do you think?' Hope was grinning.

Jess didn't reply. She just shook her head. She was quite sure she knew the answer to this one.

Chapter 15

Jess was woken by Brutus's cold wet nose nudging her bare shoulder. She glanced at the clock and saw that it was already almost nine o'clock, so she climbed out of bed, slipped on a T-shirt and shorts, and took him out for his morning walk. After walking up through the fields behind the villa, they dropped down onto the coastal footpath and made their way along to Brutus's beach. As he plunged happily into the sea, she sat down on her usual rock with her feet in the water. She had only been there for a few minutes when she was joined by George.

'Good morning, Jess. I saw you from the window. I hope you don't mind if I join you.'

She turned and gave him a big smile.

'Hi, George. Of course not. And how are you this gorgeous sunny morning?'

'Feeling pretty sunny myself, to be honest.' He smiled back. 'I'm still in awe at how you managed to get David talking the other night. And he's been doing more talking to me since then – not a lot, but he's definitely started to open up.'

'That's terrific news. I'm so pleased.'

Brutus came swimming back to greet George and was then clearly delighted to have a stick thrown out into the deep water for him to fetch. As George sat down again after throwing it, he turned back to Jess.

'I even called Mum to tell her all about it. By the way, she sends her love. They're in the Caribbean at the moment, en route to the Panama canal.'

'And all going well?'

'All going brilliantly – even the weather. She says she'll give you a ring one of these days to catch up.'

'That'll be nice, and I'm so pleased to hear everything's going well for her. So, David's started talking… that's great news.'

'Isn't it? And it's all down to you, Jess.'

'Of course not. I just must have pitched up at the right time. So, tell me George, what's he talking about?'

'The accident and its repercussions. For the first time he's actually starting to talk about how he feels.' His expression became more serious. 'It won't surprise you to hear that there's a long history of depression in our family.' He pointed ruefully towards his own face. 'Take exhibit A here, for example. I've been afraid he'd never come out of the cloud he's been under, but now, hearing him start to articulate his feelings, I'm really hopeful once more.'

'That's such great news, George.'

'And the other bit of good news is that Antoinette's husband, Jean-Pierre, is more than happy to rewire the house. He's calling in this morning to take a look and give me a price. That's the other reason I wanted to talk to you. I was wondering, if you aren't busy, if you might like to come along at half past eleven to see him? That way you could discuss all the technical things with him. Would that be possible?'

'Of course, George, I'll see you then.'

Jess and the electrician arrived at the villa together. He parked his van alongside the Range Rover and Jess noticed that David's lovely old Jaguar was absent. Presumably he was out for a drive, and she felt a little stab of regret that she wasn't going to see him.

Jean-Pierre had clearly been briefed by his wife and he knew her name.

'*Bonjour, Jess.*' He held out his hand in greeting.

'*Bonjour, Jean-Pierre. Excusez mon français. Je ne parle pas très bien.*' Since talking to George, Jess had been wondering whether her French was going to be up to discussing technical matters. Luckily George appeared at the door just then and accompanied them round the house. He was able to translate where necessary, but Jess surprised herself – and probably the two men – by managing to understand and make herself understood pretty well. Even so, by the time Jean-Pierre had refused a second glass of cold rosé and made his exit, she felt exhausted.

'Very impressive.'

She looked up at the sound of his voice. It was David, once again on crutches, rather than in the wheelchair. He looked tanned, his shoulders and arms strong, and she felt a distinct shot of what Hope had diagnosed as good old-fashioned lust at the sight of him. She even found herself blushing a bit as she looked up at him.

'Impressive? My French?'

'I thought you said you could hardly say a word. That sounded pretty good to me.'

There was no doubt about it. David was smiling. And talking to her!

'I'm glad you thought so. It was a struggle, but I think communication was achieved.'

'Very definitely.' George came back from the front door, after seeing the electrician out. 'Jean-Pierre was also very impressed, both by your command of his language and your knowledge of the intricacies of electrical installations.'

'Well I can assure you that I definitely know more about electrics than French.'

George produced another glass and emptied the bottle of rosé into the three glasses.

'Cheers. So, David, where've you been?'

For a moment, Jess got the feeling he was debating whether to reply, but then she distinctly saw him make an effort. 'I went up to Ramatuelle for a change. I'd forgotten how lovely it is up there.'

Jess nodded enthusiastically, keen to keep him talking.

'I went there last night for dinner. I loved the place.' Feeling that she should clarify matters, she was quick to add. 'I was with Olivier. He's the guy who gave me a lift home the other night in the rain. I don't know his surname, but he teaches at the university in Aix.'

'Olivier Masson. I thought I recognised him in the car with you last week. I went to elementary school with him.' David sounded quite unexpectedly animated. 'Was he good company?'

'Very. He told me all about the fighting round here during the war.'

'That's his subject, I think. I haven't seen him for a year or two. Is he well?'

Jess could see that George was clearly delighted to hear his son sounding so interested. She did her best to keep the conversation going.

'He's fine, I think. We went to the beach bar later on and he did a lot of dancing.'

'Olivier always was a good dancer.'

The way he said it, just like Hope had done, Jess felt pretty sure he also knew of Olivier's sexual orientation. Was that even a look of relief on David's face?

Then David surprised them by reaching for the remote control for the TV.

'Do you mind?'

He flicked through the channels until he came to the local news station.

'The quayside was crawling with CRS when I came back through town. I wonder what was going on.'

George noted Jess's incomprehension and explained. 'Have you heard of the CRS? They're the paramilitary police.'

They didn't have long to wait. A slick-haired reporter standing on the quayside was soon describing the events that had closed the harbour. Jess managed to understand enough of what he was saying to discover that the events had taken place early that morning. Then, to her amazement, the camera zoomed in on a close-up of the stern of none other than Max's boat, *Helios IV*. She sat in stunned silence, still trying to digest this, as she watched shots of lots of burly men in uniforms, flashing blue lights, and panoramic shots of the waterfront, losing track of what the reporter was saying. After a while, George turned down the volume and looked across at Jess.

'Well, well, well. Gang warfare would appear to have reached St-Tropez now.' Then a look of concern crossed his face. 'Are you all right, Jess? You look as if you've just had a shock.'

'I *have* just had a shock. That boat, the *Helios*, is the boat owned by the guy Hope's been seeing for the past few weeks.'

She saw George and David exchange glances.

'Did you understand what they were saying on TV, Jess?' George's voice was supportive.

'Some, but not a lot.'

'The reporter said the CRS were called in first thing this morning. They raided the boat and they've arrested four men.'

'But, why? What for?'

'They got an anonymous tip-off.'

George was looking concerned, as was David.

'Something about a bunch of Chechen hitmen sent to assassinate somebody.' George had a sudden thought. 'Where's Hope now? She wasn't on board, was she?'

Jess stood up, shaking her head. 'No, thank goodness. She's here, but her boyfriend owns the boat and he must have been on board. Did they mention anything about the boat's owner being arrested?' Both men shook their heads. 'Would you mind if I dash off? I'd better go and break the news to her.'

'Of course. If there's anything you want us to do, just say. All right, Jess?'

Jess gave them both a grateful smile.

'Thank you so much. Hopefully it'll all get sorted out soon. Thanks for the wine, George.'

'Thank you for talking things through with the electrician.'

Jess hurried back to the guest house and felt an acute sense of relief when she spotted Hope sunbathing on the lawn, with the dog stretched out beside her.

'Hi Jess, how did it go with the electrician?'

'Fine, thanks, but you'd better come inside. There's something I've got to show you on the TV.'

They spent the next half hour glued to the television screen and, gradually, they managed to work out exactly what had happened. The boat had been raided in the early hours and, as George had said, four arrests had been made. A small arsenal of weaponry had been discovered in their possession and the boat was now being subjected to a detailed search. There was no mention of Max by name, and there was no sign of him on board the boat that was now swarming with men in disposable overalls and gloves, sifting through and recording everything, while divers splashed around in the water nearby.

'So, do you think it was your Mr Drugoi – whatever his real name is – who was their intended target?'

Hope was flicking through the other stations to see if she could get more information – preferably in English.

'It seems like a hell of a coincidence if it isn't him. He's only just arrived in St-Tropez and, surprise surprise, so have they. Max mentioned the men to you. You told me. I told Pete, and now this. Yes, my money's on it being Drugoi.'

'Couldn't happen to a nicer guy.' Hope shot Jess a half-smile.

'God, Hope, he's a slimy toad, but I wouldn't want him dead.' She did her best to smile back, although the thought of a gang of murderers on their doorstep was pretty horrific to contemplate. 'A stray shot in the groin probably wouldn't come amiss, but not murder.'

Then, around half past one, they got another surprise. From Hope's point of view this was even more momentous than the discovery that her boyfriend's boat had been used by potential assassins. One of the French national television channels had managed to contact a man in London and they broadcast an interview with him. He appeared to be in his late fifties, heavily built, with a piebald grey and black beard. He was interviewed in English with subtitles, so Jess and Hope heard and understood every word he said.

What stunned both girls was the caption that appeared beneath his name, describing him as the owner of the *Helios IV*.

'The boat has been available to charter through a reputable agency for several years now and this booking came through them. I'm afraid I have no more knowledge than you as to who they are, or where they come from. I've been informed by the French police that my skipper, Max Taylor, is currently helping them with their enquiries, but they stressed that they don't believe he's involved in any way. He's been working for me for two years now and he's always proved to be trustworthy and reliable. I have no doubt he has nothing to do with whatever these men were plotting.'

Jess glanced across at Hope and saw her face as white as a sheet as she took in the ramifications of this revelation. Trying her best to sound positive, Jess reached over and gave her hand an encouraging squeeze.

'That's good news. Clearly, they aren't going to arrest Max or anything.'

'*Trustworthy and reliable*... that's what the man said, isn't it, Jess?' Jess saw her take a deep breath. 'I'm not sure I'd agree with that.' She looked up and Jess saw the tears in her friend's eyes. 'He lied to me, Jess. He told me he owned the boat, and all the time he's just been the hired hand. I couldn't care less whether he owns the boat or not. The fact is that he lied to me. I'm sorry... I...'

Hope jumped to her feet, rushed out of the lounge, and disappeared into her room. Jess gave her a few minutes and then went in after her, accompanied by the dog. As she perched on the side of the bed where her friend was still sobbing, Brutus wandered over and nudged Hope's hand with his nose, his tail wagging uncertainly. After a few seconds, Jess saw her turn to face the dog and pat his head.

'Thanks, Brutus.' Hope collected herself and sat up, wiping her eyes with a tissue. 'And thanks for the support, Jess. Sorry for the tears, but it's all come as a bit of a shock.'

'A *bit* of a shock?'

In fact, all along, Jess had been harbouring the suspicion that Max might not have been the owner of a three-million-dollar yacht, but had kept her suspicions to herself, seeing how besotted Hope was with him. She wondered if alcohol might help Hope and then decided to go for the more traditional English solution to life's problems.

'I'll go and make some tea. All right?'

Hope nodded distractedly, so Jess went through to the kitchen and boiled the kettle. When she returned with the mugs of tea, Hope was sitting on the floor beside the bed, hugging the Labrador in her arms.

'Here... tea.'

Jess handed the mug across and sat down on the side of the bed again. She sipped the hot tea and waited quietly until Hope felt like talking. It took a while.

'Jess, we've been here now for, what, three weeks?'

'We left London exactly three weeks ago today.'

'And we said we'd stay for four weeks, maybe longer?'

'Mrs Dupont is away for another two months, so we could stay until September if we feel like it.'

'I think I want to go home, Jess.' Hope's voice, like her expression, was numb.

Jess nodded, unsurprised at Hope's reaction, but desperately analysing her own thoughts. There was no doubt that the very last thing in her mind was the idea of going home. Now that she was beginning to settle into St-Tropez life, making friends, and getting to know the area, she knew she wanted to stay. But, above all, she knew she wanted to stay close to David and his father. At the same time, she could see that Hope was hurting. Badly.

'And when you get home, Hope? What then?'

'Oh, I don't know. Start looking for a job, I suppose. Anything, just so long as it's as far away from here and from Max as I possibly can be.'

Jess felt awful for her, imagining how she herself would feel if the roles were reversed.

'Well, we're sort of committed to another week, so let's see how we both feel in a few days' time.'

'But you don't need to let this spoil your holiday as well, Jess. Besides, what about Brutus? And then, of course, there's David. I can get a flight home from Nice or Marseille. There's no need for you to come with me.'

'I know, but let's just see how we feel next week. For now, I'm committed to drawing up some plans for George anyway. In fact, I don't know about you, but, although it's past lunchtime, I'm not feeling very hungry, so I think I'll skip lunch and sit down at the computer.'

Leaving Hope to be comforted by Brutus, Jess went back to the kitchen table and opened her laptop. Slowly and meticulously she transferred the measurements she had taken in the villa onto the screen, using the computer-aided design software with which she was so familiar. Gradually, a three-dimensional CAD plan of the villa took shape until she was happy that it represented the villa in its current state. Saving that, she then started working on the changes she proposed, refining ideas in her head as she did so.

It was well past five o'clock when she decided to stop. She spun the model around on the screen, checking the various alterations she was proposing, and then decided to take a break. Closing the computer, she tiptoed back to Hope's door and saw her lying fast asleep on her bed. Hearing footsteps, Brutus raised his head and jumped to his feet. Jess mouthed the word *Walk* to him and he trotted very willingly out with her.

It was another delightful warm day, although the forecast for the next week was a bit more mixed. Mind you, she thought to herself as she and Brutus wandered through the wildflowers, St-Tropez's claim to have more hours of sunshine than just about anywhere else in France appeared to be justified, at least on the basis of her experience so far. Their walk took them across the hillside and back down to the coastal footpath a bit further along the coast towards St-Tropez, passing fairly close to the tumbledown farmhouse she had spotted before. It looked even better close-up, but very dilapidated and definitely abandoned. She could imagine it renovated and extended and she felt sure it could become a spectacular house – for a billionaire.

With a little sigh, she turned for home, encountering a few tricky bits where the path climbed up and down over the rocks at the shoreline, and was delighted to see Brutus managing it without too much trouble. He was definitely looking slimmer and much fitter than when they had started and his energy levels were much higher. And his flatulence had also finally stopped – a state of affairs that had come as a considerable relief to both girls. Jess reflected that, if she and Hope did decide to head for home at the end of next week, the dog, at least, would be in far better condition than before.

When they got back to their little beach, Brutus wasted no time in leaping into the water and paddling happily out to sea and back again as Jess threw bits of driftwood for him to collect and fetch. As she sat there, she gazed down into the crystal clear water and, from there, past the happy dog and out towards the distant horizon. The sea was that wonderful aquamarine colour she had come to love, and the sun on her shoulders felt really good. It would be very, very tough to leave all this – not to mention the people she would have to leave. And number one among those was, of course, David.

He was certainly sounding more communicative – still not chatty by any means, but making good progress now. In particular, he appeared much less dejected, and he had even started smiling, albeit weakly. She definitely sensed the same gradual improvement to which his father had alluded, and she hoped desperately he would continue to make progress. On a personal note, she was secretly really pleased that the sight of him earlier that day – although on his crutches – had created a sensation in her that she recognised and welcomed. Today, when he had come into the room, the first emotion she had felt had not been pity, but desire. So her fear that the discovery of his handicap might have made him less desirable was proving to be unfounded. As Hope had said, wheelchair or no wheelchair, he was still a hunk.

As she and Brutus walked back to the guest house, she heard her name being called. She turned to find Antoinette standing at the front door of the villa and went across to her.

'*Bonjour*, Antoinette.'

'Hi, Jess. Listen, there's a man who wants to see you.'

'To see me?' Jess was puzzled. Apart from Olivier and maybe one or two others, nobody knew she was here.

'Yes. He sounds foreign, but not English. He's waiting outside the gate. I don't let people in unless I know them. Do you want to go and see who it is? I'll come with you if you like.'

Together they walked back along the gravel drive to the entrance and Jess peeked out through the gap between the gate and the gatepost. At first all she could see was a big white car right in front of her, and then she spotted two things that clarified the identity of the visitor. The first was the unmistakable silver statuette on the bonnet of the car. Even with her very limited knowledge of vehicle emblems, Jess recognised it as a Rolls Royce. Second, in case she might still have any doubt, was the figure resting against the front wing – Dmitri.

Jess turned to Antoinette.

'I know who it is, but there's no way I'm letting him in here. I'll go outside and see what he wants. Would you close the gate behind me and hang around here, so you can let me in again? Hang on to Brutus as well, would you? I'll knock when I want to get back in.'

'Of course. Who is this man?'

'It's somebody I knew in London.'

Taking a deep breath, Jess opened the side gate and slipped through, hearing it close firmly behind her. As soon as he saw her appear, Dmitri ducked back to the rear door of the car and opened it. As Drugoi stepped out, Jess was relieved to see the front passenger door open and the familiar hefty figure of Pete step out on the other side. He gave Jess an encouraging smile as the interpreter spoke.

'Mr Drugoi has come to say thank you.'

Dmitri gave a half-bow and, to her surprise, Drugoi followed suit. Her surprise increased as Drugoi took a few steps towards her and, for the first time, spoke to her directly.

'Miss Jessica Milton, I come say thank you for save my life.'

His English wasn't perfect by any means, but it was understandable. Jess glanced across at Pete, who was still smiling, before turning back to the oligarch.

'I saved your life, Mr Drugoi? I don't understand.'

In fact, after watching the news on television, she felt pretty sure she knew exactly what he meant. Although his name hadn't been mentioned, she had been increasingly convinced that he had to have been involved.

'If you not speak Peter, my bodyguard, I maybe dead.'

'All I did was to pass on what I had heard. I'm pleased if it helped.'

'You save my life, Jessica Milton. Thank you.'

He actually looked and sounded as if he meant it. To reinforce the message, he held out his hand. Although just twenty-four hours earlier, she would happily have throttled him, she took his hand and shook it.

'Mr Drugoi wants you to have this, Miss Milton.'

Jess turned towards Dmitri, who was holding out an envelope. Inside the envelope she found a banker's draft for ten thousand euros. She stood there for a few moments, staring down at it in disbelief, before making up her mind. She replaced it in the envelope and handed it back again, ignoring the incomprehension on Dmitri's face. She returned her attention to Drugoi.

'I don't want your money, Mr Drugoi. I did what I thought was right, that's all. I'm glad it helped.' She raised her eyes towards Pete. 'Like I say, Pete, I'm glad it helped.'

'Mr Drugoi's right, you know, Jess. That information probably did save his life.'

'Goodbye, Mr Drugoi.'

Jess turned back and tapped on the gate. It opened immediately. With a little smile to Pete, Jess went back in and closed the gate behind her. She and Antoinette remained there, without saying a word, until they heard car doors close and the muted hum of the engine, followed by the crunch of gravel as the Rolls Royce did a three-point turn and headed back up the track. Only when the noise of the car had completely disappeared did Jess glance back out again to check that they had all gone. The coast was clear. The area outside the gate, and the track leading up the hill, were both empty, apart from a few wisps of dust still hanging in the air from the passage of the Rolls Royce.

Jess straightened up and did her best to explain to Antoinette as they walked slowly back towards the house, starting with the events in London that had led to her dismissal, and then her conversation with Pete the previous night. Antoinette listened with rapt attention.

'And he offered you ten thousand euros? I would have taken the money.'

'Ten thousand would have come in very useful, I know, but it's a question of principle. Drugoi and the like think everything revolves around money. I did what I did because I felt it was the right thing to do. Somehow, taking his handout would have demeaned my actions. I'm not sure if I'm making sense, but I'm much happier not having anything to do with his money.'

Back at the guest house, she found Hope awake once more and in the kitchen making tea.

'Want a cup?'

Jess nodded, sat down, and recounted the events of the past few minutes. Unlike Antoinette, Hope immediately understood why she hadn't taken the money and approved.

'While I'd be the first to admit that you could probably do with the ten grand – not least as you're currently unemployed – I reckon you did the right thing. Good for you, Jess.'

She passed over a mug of tea and then handed Jess her phone.

'I got a text message ten minutes ago. Check it out.'

The message was from Max.

Not sure if you've heard, but there's been a bit of trouble. I'm okay. Call me. X. Max.

Jess looked up.

'So, did you call him?'

Hope shook her head.

'No, and I'm not going to. But I sent him a one word text – just *Liar*.'

Jess nodded slowly. She could fully understand. She glanced at her watch and saw that it was half past six.

'Brutus has had a walk and a swim in the sea. Why don't we both go for a swim in the pool? It's still very hot outside – and a lot more humid, too. I think they might be right about rain coming in tomorrow.'

Hope shook her head.

'I'm not really in the mood, Jess, but you go. How does grilled chicken breast and salad sound for dinner? I'll go and light the barbecue.'

Jess changed into one of her new bikinis, wrapped a towel round herself, and went down to the pool. As she got there, she was delighted to find David in the water. His wheelchair was standing by the ladder at the deep end, so when she peeled off her towel, she put it down on a sunbed right beside the chair.

'Hi, David.'

'Hi, Jess.'

She stood on the side for a moment, looking down at him, and then decided to try diving in. The impact of the water almost took her breath away, but as she floated to the surface, she stretched luxuriously, loving the relief from the increasingly sticky heat outside. She took a deep breath and then ducked down, swept her hair back out of her eyes and surfaced again, before swimming slowly across to where he was floating.

'Want to hear the latest on the *Helios* business?'

David nodded, so she told him, up to and including Drugoi's offer of money. David looked impressed.

'Good for you.'

Jess waited for him to say more, but clearly he was once again feeling less than communicative. She felt a wave of disappointment after the positive signs she had noticed in him earlier on, but she was sensible enough to realise that the process of recovery for him was going to be slow and steady, rather than a lightning step change. She decided to give him some space.

'Well, I think I'll go for a swim then, David.'

'Yes.'

She swam lazily up and down the pool ten times and then rested on the bottom step in the shallow end, the cool water up to her shoulders, with just her head above water as she leant back and breathed in the scent of the flowers around the pool.

At the other end, David had evidently decided he had done enough swimming. She saw him pull himself out of the water, up the stainless steel ladder beside his wheelchair. His strong arms made getting out of the pool look easy, but her heart went out to him when she saw the difficulty he then had to haul himself up into the chair. She was just wondering whether to offer to help when she saw him lunge for the arm of the chair, miss his target and pull the chair over on top of himself, leaving him floundering.

Jess jumped to her feet and splashed out up the steps and around the pool to where he was lying. She crouched at his side, a compassionate expression on her face.

'Hey, David, are you OK? You didn't hurt yourself, did you? Here, let me give you a hand.'

Then, to her dismay, he looked up at her from the stone slabs where he was still sprawled and snarled at her – an expression of such fury on his face, she physically shrank backwards and jumped to her feet, so as to get out of his way.

'Leave me alone. I don't need your help. All right?'

'But I...' Her voice tailed off helplessly.

'You heard what I said. I can do it. I don't need your help – I don't need anybody's help.'

Beneath the anger Jess could see the full extent of his anguish laid bare, and it broke her heart. She stood, blankly, looking on, as he laboriously righted the wheelchair and even more laboriously hauled himself up into it. No sooner was he seated than he spun the chair round angrily, and set off back along the slabs at the side of the pool and up the path, disappearing behind the rosemary bushes without a backward glance.

Behind him, he left Jess standing rooted to the spot, tears running down her cheeks.

Chapter 16

The atmosphere in the house the next day was grim. After a broken night, Jess woke to find it raining outside. This time it wasn't a torrential downpour, but a steady, miserable drizzle that occasionally increased to spells of harder rain. The ground was already soaked when she took Brutus out for his walk and even he seemed loathe to venture into the sea – doubtless feeling already quite wet enough. Looking back over her shoulder from the beach towards the hills, she found them masked by low cloud, and the grey surroundings further darkened her mood.

Back at the house, Hope was still in bed, so Jess put the television on with the sound turned down while she rubbed Brutus as dry as possible with an old towel. Once she had finished, she threw it into the washing machine to remove the smell of wet dog. This didn't, of course, remove the smell from Brutus himself, so she opened the door onto the courtyard as she boiled the kettle and sat down to drink her tea to the accompaniment of the sound of a steady stream of water overflowing from the blocked gutters above. The statue of the naked woman in the middle of the courtyard looked as if she had caught a bad cold, with regular drips running off the end of her nose.

As she sipped her tea, Jess suddenly saw a familiar scene flicker onto the screen. It was St-Tropez harbour and, judging from the rain, it was live footage. She pushed the kitchen door closed and turned the volume up a bit. Her French comprehension was improving, but she couldn't follow much of the commentary, but what she did see was that the police cordon had been removed and life appeared to have returned to normal on the quayside. Of Max, there was no sign, but she didn't blame him. After all the fuss and bother the previous day, he was no doubt keeping his head down. The reporter had just handed back to the studio when the kitchen door opened.

'Hi, Jess, is that fresh tea?'

'Hi, Hope. Yes it is. Did you manage to get some sleep?'

Hope shook her head. 'Not a terrific amount, to be honest. The mind's a funny thing, isn't it? Why can't my brain just accept that I don't want anything more to do with that lying bastard? Instead, I seem to have done nothing but think about him all night long.'

Jess did her best to suppress the memory of David's outburst that had been troubling her all night and concentrated on her friend's problems.

'The fact is, Hope, your brain belongs to you and it's you thinking all these things. Maybe you're not over him as much as you imagine. Let's face it – you were head over heels in love with him until less than twenty-four hours ago. You can't just switch that stuff off, you know.'

Hope nodded disconsolately as she poured herself some tea.

'Has Brutus had his breakfast?'

Jess shook her head. 'Not yet. We've just come in.'

She watched Hope dig out a handful of biscuits for the dog and refill his water bowl. As she did so, Jess had time to reflect on what she had just said to Hope and how it applied, equally, to her.

David's aggressive outburst had hurt her deeply, although the pragmatic part of her brain knew she shouldn't really blame him for it, or take offence. She tried – as she had been doing for some days now – to picture herself in his shoes, suddenly transformed from active, self-confident, alpha male to a cripple who couldn't even manage to climb into a chair. She could imagine only too well how he felt, but it didn't stop his words from hurting.

Hope sat down on the other side of the table – with the dog happily crunching his biscuits at her feet – and took a mouthful of tea. After a minute or two of complete silence, apart from the low background babble of the TV news which had now moved on to the previous day's football scores, Hope looked across at Jess.

'What about you? Any more thoughts on David?'

'Thoughts? Loads of them, but they haven't got me anywhere apart from a bit weary. I suppose I'm coming round to thinking that maybe the best thing to do might be what you said yesterday. When the month is up – and that's less than a week away – maybe we should think about going back home. I can come back in two months' time to pick up the car and the dog in time for Mrs Dupont's return from her cruise.'

As she spoke, Jess felt the same internal struggle that had kept her awake for hours that night. Yes, she still felt attracted to David, but pretty clearly he wasn't in a fit state to reciprocate, even if he did find her attractive. What was the point in flogging a dead horse? Maybe being apart was the best solution – at least for her.

'Did you get a reply to your text to Max?'

'Loads – one after another. I switched my phone off after a bit.'

'So, what was he saying?'

Hope wiped her bleary eyes. 'Just the same thing over and over again, really. You know – he hadn't wanted to hurt me. He was just being a stupid prat. He loves me, he wants me. You know… the usual crap.'

'He said he loved you?'

'Over and over again.'

'Wow.' Jess was truly surprised. 'Hope… do you maybe think you should at least sit down and talk to him?'

Hope shook her head. 'And give him the satisfaction of seeing me crying my eyes out over him? I've got a damn sight more pride than that.'

Jess decided not to press the point – at least not for the moment. Instead, she went back to her room, showered and changed, and then settled down to finish the plans for George. By eleven she reckoned she had got things pretty much as she wanted them, so she went over to the villa to show him. As she did so, she noticed that David's car was missing and she had a hard time analysing how this made her feel. On the one hand, there was a feeling of relief that she wouldn't have to face a potentially embarrassing confrontation, but along with this was the memory of the bleak expression in his eyes that had reached deep inside her.

She went round to the kitchen door and found Antoinette hard at it, preparing lunch.

'*Bonjour*, Jess. Sleep well?'

'Fine, thanks.' Jess was determined not to show weakness. 'Is George available?'

'Yes, he's in the lounge. Go on through and I'll bring you some coffee.'

Jess went through and found George sitting by the window, reading a book. From in here the view was even more depressing than from down on the beach. It was almost impossible to make out the far side of the bay and there wasn't a living soul to be seen anywhere. Fortunately, when George looked up and saw her, he gave her a cheery smile that was in distinct contrast to the weather outside.

'Whenever I get a day like this I keep telling myself how badly the gardens and the fields need the rain. Have you and Brutus been for a swim this morning?'

Jess mustered an answering smile. 'No, unless you count getting soaked going for a walk.'

'Come and sit down, my dear.'

'David gone out?'

George nodded his head. 'He must have got up very early. His car was already gone when I got up. I'm not sure where he's gone on a day like today.'

This didn't sound very good to Jess, but she did her best to hide her concern.

'I've drawn up some plans for you to see. Have you got time?'

George beamed. 'Absolutely.'

Jess opened her laptop and together they went through the alterations she was proposing. George declared himself very happy with everything and thanked her profusely. Finally she emailed him a copy of the plans for David to print out when he got back.

'That's terrific, Jess. Thank you so much. Now, how much do I owe you for all your work?'

'Nothing at all, George. Of course not. After all the hospitality we've had from you, it's the least I could do.'

'Now, that's not fair. Well, if you won't let me pay you, I'll have to see if I can come up with some other way of saying thank you.'

'Absolutely no need, George. Really.'

'I got the quote from Antoinette's husband for the electrics. It all looks fine and, even better, he reckons he could start as early as the middle of July – in two or three weeks' time, he said. Oh, yes, and he says he can easily work round us, so there's no urgent need to move out.'

'Very good news. And what about the bathrooms, the building work and tiling and so on? Does he know other tradesmen?'

'Yes, indeed. He said he'll speak to his cousin, the plumber, and to a close friend of his who's supposed to be a really good builder.'

'Excellent. If they all know each other it'll make things a lot easier on site.'

'So, Jess, would you be able to keep an eye on things once the work continues? You will still be here, won't you? David and I would really like you to stay on here, you know.'

Jess had been dreading this. She thought desperately for a few moments before taking refuge in Hope's current troubles.

'Erm, I hope so, George. It's just that Hope's having a tough time at the moment after finding out that her boyfriend lied to her about being the owner of the yacht he works on. Hopefully she'll pull herself together, but at the moment she's talking about going home.'

'Poor thing.' George shook his head. 'It's like I said – you've got to watch the sailor boys. Do try and persuade her not to go. But, anyway, if she really does decide to leave, you could stay on, couldn't you? Please.'

'Let's give it a few days and see how she feels later in the week. Maybe she'll change her mind.'

'I do hope so. I'd dearly like you to stay on, Jess – not for the building work, for the pleasure of your company – and I know David feels the same way.'

'You do?'

'Of course. We'd both miss you a lot.'

As Jess walked back across to the guest house, she turned George's words over in her head and wondered just how his son really felt. She was crossing the parking area when she heard the unmistakable sound of gravel crunching beneath car tyres and the long bonnet of David's lovely old Jaguar appeared. For a moment the coward in her toyed with the idea of scuttling off into the walled garden and back to the guest house, but then she stiffened her back and stopped to say hello. Although the drizzle had almost stopped, here under the big pine tree large heavy drops of water were falling all round and she felt a good few of them land on her. Even so, she stood her ground.

She saw the driver's door open and then David's feet emerge. With a practised manoeuvre, he caught hold of the side of the windscreen and hauled himself to his feet. Resting with one hand on the roof, he shuffled round until he was facing the car and then looked across at her. Jess did her best to analyse his expression. After a struggle, she plumped for *sheepish*, and it turned out she was right.

'Hello, Jess. Could you come over here a moment, please?'

His tone was anything but confrontational. Jess walked across and saw him make his way gingerly, steadying himself against the canvas roof, but without the aid of his crutches, until he was at the rear of the car. He opened the boot and reached inside.

'These are for you, Jess. I owe you an apology.'

Carefully, he lifted a massive bouquet of flowers wrapped in clear cellophane from the floor of the boot and held them out towards her.

'I would have been back sooner, but both florists here were closed. Must be because it's a Monday morning. So I had to drive round to Ste-Maxime.'

'David… there's no need.' Jess was genuinely touched – not least because he must have had an hour and a half's drive just to get the flowers.

'There's every need. I behaved atrociously, and I do hope you'll forgive me.'

'There's nothing to forgive, David. Really, you shouldn't have.'

She took the flowers from him and, for an instant, their fingers touched. She looked up and saw his clear blue eyes looking intently at her. A particularly large raindrop landed on her cheek and she felt it run down her face, but she resisted the urge to wipe it away.

'Jess, I'm very, very sorry. It was frustration, sheer blind frustration. I don't know if you can imagine how absolutely infuriating it is for me to find myself in this state. From time to time it gets the better of me and, like I say, I'm just very sorry that you were on the end of that particular outburst.' He hesitated for a moment. 'I felt like an absolute worm afterwards. If it helps, I hardly slept a wink last night as a result.'

'Neither did I, David.' She saw what might have been surprise in his eyes. 'Not because I was angry with you, but because I could feel your unhappiness.' Now it was her turn to stare into his eyes. 'I'd like to help, David, any way I can.'

'Thanks, Jess. You already are – more than you realise – just by being here.'

Another raindrop landed on her cheek and she was secretly pleased. She was as close to tears as she had ever been in her life and she didn't want him to think he was to blame. Of course he was the reason her eyes were welling up, but not because of anything bad he had done. She dropped her eyes to the bouquet so he wouldn't see the emotion on her face.

'That's the very best thing I've heard since I arrived here, David.'

'Thank you.' There was another pause. 'I can't thank you enough.'

Jess was readying herself to reach out towards him with her hands, arms and maybe even her lips, when she saw him turn and make his way back along the side of the car once more. Rubbing a hand surreptitiously across her eyes, she followed him. He reached into the car and removed his crutches. He didn't ask for help and she didn't offer.

'Again, Jess, please forgive me.'

'You are forgiven.'

Chapter 17

As Jess walked back through the walled garden towards home, she felt her heart soar. The fact that David had taken the trouble to go out and buy her the flowers was great, but his obvious contrition and, above all, the fact that he had been able to talk to her, albeit briefly, about his feelings had left her in absolutely no doubt about one thing. There was no way she wanted to go off back to Britain and leave him now.

This left the problem of Hope. If she remained heartbroken and convinced that all she wanted was to get away from Max, then Jess felt pretty sure nothing she could say would stop her friend from making tracks for home sooner rather than later. She wanted Hope to be happy and somehow felt sure she would be happier here than back in London all alone. As Jess reached the little pergola in the middle of the ornamental garden, she glanced down at the flowers in her arms and had an idea. She hesitated, mulled it over, and then decided to take a chance. She set the bouquet down on the wooden bench – almost hidden by the mass of bougainvillea and clematis that was running wild across the structure – and left it there, heading through the little door and back to the guest house.

Jess found Hope sitting at the kitchen table, staring glumly at her phone. As Jess came in, she looked up and attempted a little smile.

'How did it go with the plans?'

'George liked them. And it sounds as if he's got tradesmen lined up to do the work.'

'So are you going to stay on and supervise?'

'I don't know.' Not for the first time in her life, Jess was glad she hadn't been born Pinocchio. Affecting a change of subject, she glanced out of the French windows into the courtyard. 'The rain's stopped. Any of that chicken left from last night? Fancy another barbecue?'

Hope took a bit of persuading but, finally, she agreed, and went out to light the barbecue. As Jess had hoped, she left her phone on the kitchen table. It was the work of a few seconds to pick it up, check through, and copy down Max's phone number. Replacing the phone on the table, Jess called out into the courtyard.

'I'll just take Brutus for a quick walk. Back in ten minutes.'

She and the Labrador hurried out, round the side of the villa, and down to the beach. Brutus wasted no time in splashing into the water while Jess wasted no time in calling Max's number.

'Yes, hello.' His voice sounded unusually subdued and Jess took this as a good sign.

'Max? It's Jess.'

'Jess… thank goodness. I've been trying to get in touch with Hope ever since yesterday and she's not taking my calls.'

'Do you blame her, Max?'

'I know…' He sounded totally deflated. 'I'm a stupid bastard.'

'Her feelings exactly. And mine. She feels absolutely betrayed, Max.' She hesitated, needing to be sure of just how he felt. 'You have no idea of how much you've hurt her.'

'Oh, God, Jess, I know. She's the best thing that's ever happened to me, and I had to go and screw it up.'

'So, you're regretting the whole "I'm a millionaire, I've got a yacht" thing now?'

As she said it, Jess realised that somehow Max's actions were even more despicable than Drugoi's. At least the Russian hadn't been pretending to be something he wasn't.

'Yes, of course. I'm not proud of what I did, Jess, but the thing is, I really, really like her. I was so immediately attracted to her when I saw her, I knew I had to do anything just so as to get her. And that included lying to her. The more serious it's become between me and her – and it really is serious, at least as far as I'm concerned – the worse I knew the consequences would be if she found out, so I put off saying anything.'

'But you had to know, deep down, that sooner or later she would find out.'

'And now she has.' She heard a catch in his voice and took that as an even better sign. 'Is that it, Jess? Is that what you're phoning to say? Is it all over between us?'

Jess paused for thought. At that moment Brutus appeared with a piece of driftwood in his mouth and Jess picked it up and threw it back into the water for him. As she watched the dog paddle strongly out towards the open sea, she reached a decision.

'Listen, Max. Hope has no idea I'm making this call. She's my very best friend and I hate to see her hurting. And I would really hate it – and you – if she got hurt any more.

Tell me, honestly, have you any idea how broken up she's feeling right now?'

'Yes, if it's anything like I feel, it must be awful for her. I've never felt so bad before. I really, really regret what I did.'

'So you're telling me you feel really bad, that you regret what's happened?'

'Totally, Jess. I'd do anything to get her back.'

'And when you say "get her back", you're not just talking about some sort of causal short-term hook-up?'

'Jess, if I told you I think I've fallen in love with her, would that satisfy you?'

'It might, but Hope's the one you've got to tell that to.'

'That's what I've been trying to do, but she won't answer. Jess, could you help? Speak to her? Maybe ask if she might be prepared to see me?'

'I'll speak to her, Max.' She heard his intake of breath. 'I think a meeting between the two of you on neutral turf might be the answer.' She paused, searching for a suitable venue. 'Do you know Senequier?'

'The café on the quayside? Yes, everybody knows that place.'

'Unless you hear from me to the contrary, could you be there today at, say, three?'

'Of course, any time.'

'Then I'll do my best to set it up, but Max…'

'… I know, Jess. Don't screw it up. Tell her everything. And I will, I promise.'

'That's good. That's what's needed. Now, listen. I'm going to give you a hand – but you'd better not disappoint me. You've just sent her a big bouquet of flowers.'

'I have?' He sounded bemused.

'Yes, they've just arrived. Don't ask… all right?'

'Um… all right.'

'And, Max, when you see her, tell her what you've told me. All right? And remember, if she gets hurt again, the next bunch of Chechen gangsters on your boat will be out for *your* blood. Understood?'

'Understood, and, Jess, thank you. Thank you so much. You can't imagine how grateful I am to you for what you're doing. I promise you won't be disappointed in me.'

Jess called Brutus, managed to avoid getting soaked as he shook himself, and together they walked back to the house. Glancing up, Jess saw a patch of blue sky appearing and took this as yet another good sign. Maybe the universe was back on her side. And Hope's.

Retrieving the bouquet, Jess checked to see that David hadn't included a note and then carried the flowers back to the house. Brutus's nose told him Hope was outside by the barbecue and Jess followed him into the courtyard.

'Here, Hope. Take a look at these.'

Jess saw Hope's eyes widen as she saw the bouquet. Unmistakably, the expression on her face was one of yearning.

'Wow, what an amazing bouquet!'

Jess took a good look at her friend, surreptitiously crossed the fingers of one hand, and took a deep breath.

'Yes. They've just arrived. They're for you.'

'For me?' The yearning was more obvious now, and alongside it was delight.

Jess passed the bouquet across to her.

'There's no note, but the guy who brought them gave Antoinette a message. He asked if you could meet him at Senequier at three o'clock.'

'The café on the quayside?'

'That's right.'

'And who was the guy who brought the flowers?'

'Antoinette didn't recognise him, but I think we both know, don't we?'

'Max was here?'

'That's what it sounds like. So, are you going to meet him?'

'I don't know, Jess.' Hope was staring at the flowers, which were gorgeous, and had no doubt cost a fortune. 'What would you do?'

Jess did her best to look inscrutable. 'I don't think you've got anything to lose by meeting him. At worst, it'll give you an opportunity to slap his face.'

'And if I were to decide to stay here for the rest of the summer, after all, what about you? After what David said to you yesterday, weren't you thinking of leaving?'

'Things have moved on a bit. I've just seen David. He said he was sorry, and I believe him.'

'So you wouldn't mind staying on?'

'Not in the slightest.'

–

Jess walked into St-Tropez with Hope. By this time the sun had come out again and the ground was already drying out fast as the temperature rose steadily. As they walked round the coast path, as ever passing the ruined farmhouse, Jess breathed in the fresh perfume of the flowers and wild herbs – their scent revitalised by the rain – and found herself smiling. She looked out to sea and saw that, magically, a flotilla of yachts with white sails had appeared in the blue waters of the gulf. Across on the far side, Ste-Maxime and the wooded hills beyond were clearer than they had ever been. It had turned into a delightful day and Jess hoped things would continue to improve – and not just as far as the weather was concerned.

When they got to the harbour, Jess led Hope along the waterfront to the red awnings of Senequier and left her there. This was the best-known café in St-Tropez, famous as a meeting place for celebrities from all over the world. Max was going to find the drinks expensive there, but Jess reckoned that paying for a few pricey cups of tea was the least he could do after the grief he had inflicted on Hope. Jess herself set out for a stroll around the town, determined to visit the old citadel, although she knew this would involve quite a steep climb, and the temperature felt as if it was rising by the minute.

She walked up through the narrow streets, seeking out the shade wherever possible, until she saw the bulk of the old citadel, its sheer stone walls rising up into the now almost completely cloud-free blue sky. Huge cactus plants and tall palm trees gave the place a North African feel, and she could almost imagine soldiers of the Foreign Legion leaning out of the gun slits or pointing rifles down at her from the battlements. She bought a ticket and walked in through the arched entrance with its massive wooden gates. The path climbed steadily, passing through more gates, until she reached the main fortress itself. This handsome white stone building sat inside what had maybe once been a moat – now grass – and it had clearly been designed to be impregnable. High on the ramparts, the flags of France, Europe and the red and white flag of St-Tropez flew proudly in the breeze.

She took some photos of the castle before turning her attention to the view down over the town and the gulf. The roofs of St-Tropez itself were predominantly weathered terracotta, the faded pink mixed with an orangey-ochre, and the deep blue of the sea beyond really stood out clearly in contrast. Peeking up amidst the roofs, the iconic church with its square pink tower – capped by a yellow cupola – was unmistakable, with the harbour and breakwater directly behind it. Jess thought she could just about distinguish the *Helios* down there and she spared a thought, and a prayer, for Hope's meeting with Max.

Finally, she walked across the bridge into the fortress itself – and there she got a surprise. A group of university students were huddled in the shade on one side of the quadrangle while their teacher told them all about the place. To Jess's delight, the teacher was Olivier. She settled back against the wall, out of his sight so as not to put him off, and did her best to follow his lecture.

In fact, she understood disappointingly little of what he said. Although her French comprehension was improving by the day, she really wasn't up to following academic language, although she did manage to work out that over the four centuries since it had been built, the citadel had protected the town from aggressors – notably the Spanish and the English. She reflected that nowadays the restaurateurs and bar owners were wreaking their revenge for past aggression with their prices, particularly down on the waterfront. Once again this made Jess think of Hope and Max and she crossed her fingers that they would sort themselves out.

After a quarter of an hour or so, Olivier finished his lecture and the students began to get up and head off in little groups, presumably investigating what they had learned. Seeing him on his own, Jess went across and gave him a kiss on the cheek.

'*Bonjour, Monsieur le professeur.*'

His face broke into a smile.

'Hi, Jess. Don't tell me you've been listening to my talk.'

'Listening, yes. Understanding, no. At least, not much. I did get the bit about the nasty English being the enemy, though.'

'Ah yes, perfidious Albion. But that all died out years ago.' He glanced at his watch. 'Well, I've finished for the afternoon. I'm having dinner with my parents tonight before driving back to Aix, but why don't I buy you an ice cream this afternoon?'

'That sounds like a lovely idea, but *I'm* going to buy *you* the ice cream. It's my turn and it's the least I can do.'

Back down the hill again, he led her to an ice cream shop on the quayside. He told her it was the best ice cream shop in the town – maybe the whole country. It was packed out with people buying all manner of ice creams with flavours ranging from strawberry to bubble-gum and liquorice. Jess decided to opt for a decadent mixture of white chocolate and salted caramel, while Olivier chose lemon tart and yoghurt flavour. They took the tubs and two bottles of ice-cold water across to the edge of the quay and sat on the warm slabs, dangling their legs over the edge, listening to the gentle slap of the water against the stone wall. The sun was warm, the air clear, and the atmosphere relaxed. Jess stretched and breathed deeply.

'Going back to London after this is going to be really tough.'

'So, don't go back.' Olivier gave her a grin. 'Stay here forever.'

Jess grinned back. It was a wonderful, if impossible, dream.

'One minor problem, Olivier, what do I live on? At the moment I'm living rent free in a wonderful place, but that won't last forever. And when that finishes, where do I live and what do I do?'

He shook his head sadly.

'You're right, of course. St-Trop is a very expensive place to live in.' He gestured back over his shoulder. 'You can bet your life the vast majority of the people working in the ice cream shop, or any of the shops, can't afford to live here. They probably live across the bay and commute every day by ferry, or live further inland and travel to and fro by bus or scooter.'

'See what I mean? And then, there's the question of work. I'm not sure I'd enjoy serving ice cream for the rest of my life – even if I could get a job in the first place. The thing is – I'm an architect and I enjoy being an architect.'

'They need architects here, you can be quite sure. You've seen how much building and renovating's going on all over the place. If I were you, I'd check that out. You never know, with your experience of high-end clients, it seems to me you'd be perfect here.'

'Apart from the fact that my French isn't anything like good enough.'

'I wouldn't worry about that. I've heard your French – it's pretty good, you know – and the longer you stay here the better it'll get. Besides, having a native English speaker might be a positive bonus for a firm here. So many of the properties belong to people who speak a lot less French than you do.'

Jess carried on slowly eating her way through her gorgeous ice cream, dreaming of somehow managing to make this temporary moment of bliss last a lifetime. Maybe she would check out architectural firms in the area as he had suggested. Then, as she took a big mouthful of mineral water and gazed out across the harbour, a thought occurred to her.

'You know, Olivier, for years now I've been laughing at Hope. She's always been dreaming of St-Tropez – almost for as long as I've known her. But you know something? She was right. This place really is wonderful, and now I've caught the bug. I'm the one who's dreaming – dreaming of staying here.'

The thought of Hope made her look up and search along the harbour for the *Helios*. In fact, the yacht was less than a hundred metres or so from where they were, and she wondered yet again how Hope's meeting with Max had gone.

Chapter 18

Hope's meeting with Max went very well.

As Jess was walking back to the villa later on, she got a text:

> All good with Max. Am staying on the boat tonight. See you tomorrow. X

Jess sent back a smiley face and rejoiced for her.

When she got home, it was almost six o'clock, but the sun was still hot. She found the ever-slimmer and more energetic Brutus delighted to see her and even happier to go for a swim in the sea. This time, she decided the water was warm enough for her to join him, so she pinned her hair up, changed into a bikini, and followed him down to the beach. As the dog splashed excitedly into the water, she waded out until she could duck down and let the cool water cover her shoulders. It felt wonderful. Compared to the pool, the salt water was very buoyant, and it was easy to swim lazily out in the wake of the Labrador. When they were a good distance from the shore, she rolled over and floated on her back, doing her best to keep her hair out of the water, and looked up at the villa on the hillside above.

There was a figure on the terrace, but she couldn't make out if it was David, his father or Antoinette. Now, for the first time since he had given her the flowers, she allowed herself to think about David, and she felt a warm glow of happiness spread throughout her body – in spite of the cool sea water. He had sounded positive, contrite and caring. Of course, he had in no way declared undying love for her, but his attitude had been friendly, maybe more. She thought back on the words he had used and did her best to analyse them.

He had apologised, then he had thanked her, and he had said that thing about her helping him 'more than she realised', just by being here. Surely this implied a depth of feeling towards her that he maybe couldn't bring himself to admit. Or did it?

The trouble was, of course, that they were two very different animals.

David was a millionaire, probably a multi-millionaire. His background, upbringing and lifestyle up to the accident had been very, very different from hers. She had already had the experience of dating a millionaire in London and it hadn't worked out. Terri at the beach bar had been in no doubt that there had been a long line of girls only too willing to hook up with him – and, no doubt, a lot of them had done just that. Jess herself had never had a line of men chasing after her – or, if she had, she wasn't aware of it – and she certainly hadn't leapt in and out of relationships with abandon. Very much the opposite, in fact.

At university there had been a couple of relatively serious boyfriends, but they hadn't lasted and, since qualifying and settling into the job in London, there had only been Rafael. Although she had launched into that relationship with enthusiasm and optimism, the difference between their two lifestyles had gradually eroded the love she had felt for him. In consequence, she now found herself on her own and up to now, she really hadn't minded. She had had her parents, good friends like Hope, and her job. Now, suddenly, she found herself with the free time to consider what she really wanted out of her life, and two things were emerging from the pack.

Put simply, she wanted to live in this little piece of paradise forever and she wanted David – irrespective of his wealthy background. But she was pragmatic enough to realise that neither looked like a realistic proposition. Both were lovely dreams, but dreams – unless in fairy tales – rarely come true.

Her meditations were interrupted by the arrival of a big furry lump. Delighted to find her down at his level, Brutus appeared from behind her and did his best to climb onto her shoulders, pushing her head underwater and soaking her hair in the process. She emerged spitting and coughing and subjected him to a withering look.

'Brutus, you don't do that to a girl who only washed her hair this morning. Shame on you.'

He looked anything but ashamed and paddled back towards her and nuzzled her with his nose. Unable to maintain the stern expression, she patted his head and started swimming back to the shore. One thing about dogs, she thought to herself – you're never alone when you've got one.

She climbed out of the water and rubbed her hair with the towel, feeling it stiff with salt, before stretching out on a flat rock to dry out in the sun. The rock was hot, but tolerable, and she felt cosy and relaxed. Beside her, the dog rolled around on his back in the sand, making happy grunting noises, and Jess reflected she would no doubt have to wash not only her hair, but the dog as well, when they got back to the house.

She had been lying there for ten minutes or so and her bikini was already almost dry when she heard movement from Brutus and then a voice.

'Hi, Jess, had a good swim?'

She looked up and smiled. George was crouching on the beach, saying hello to the dog.

'Hi, George. Yes, I've had a lovely time.'

'All right if I join you?'

'Of course.' She sat up and moved across so he could sit down beside her, both of them looking out to sea.

'I've just had a bit of good news.'

Jess looked across at him.

'What's happened?'

'At lunch today, David was looking and sounding more cheerful. He really does seem to have bucked up since you got here. The good news is that he told me he's spoken to his doctor, and he's going to start an intensive course of physiotherapy.'

'That's good, but I'm surprised he hasn't been doing that already.'

'He's done some, but not as much as he should be doing. They've been at him for weeks to start making a real effort, but he's been so depressed, he's been putting it off. Anyway, starting on Wednesday, he's going to have regular daily sessions.'

'Well, that really is good news. I'm so glad for him.'

'I've said it before and I'll say it again – a lot of the improvement is down to you. Thank you once more.'

'I'm sure it's not me, really, but you – and he – are very welcome if I have had a hand in it. Anyway, I've got some good news as well.' She told him about the text she had received from Hope. 'So it seems pretty definite we're going to stay on for the rest of the summer, if you're sure we won't be in the way. And of course I'll be happy to keep an eye on the works on the villa.'

'Excellent news. I'll ring Mum and tell her. She'll be delighted. And, Jess, I've got some news of my own. Last night, I went out.' He saw her eyebrows raise. 'Yes, out into the big, wide world.' He smiled at her. 'All on my own.'

'George, that's amazing. Fantastic.' Jess beamed back at him. This really was progress.

'When I was out for a walk with the dog yesterday, I bumped into a couple of my oldest friends.' His smile turned to one of regret. 'I've hardly seen anybody since Babette's funeral. We stood and chatted for half an hour or more and they managed to persuade me to come round to their house for dinner. I decided to go and called a taxi. We had a lovely evening together and I really enjoyed seeing them again and getting out and about for the first time.'

'I'm so pleased, George. That really is terrific.'

'Anyway, when I got home again, I did a bit of thinking. I reckon the time is maybe ripe for me to start living my life again. God knows, I've been a hermit here for long enough. I thought I'd do a bit of ringing round and see if I can get a bunch of people to come over for drinks in a few weeks' time. As you know, July 14th is Bastille Day, and that's a big day here in France. Babette and I always used to invite people round the day after, so as to keep the celebrations going. So, would you and Hope be able to come on the fifteenth?'

'I'd love to, thank you, George. The wonderful thing about being on holiday is that my calendar is completely free. I have no idea what Hope's plans are, but if she can, I know she'd love to come.'

'Splendid. And tell her to bring her sailor boy if she wants.'

—

Hope arrived home late that night, but Jess was still up, waiting to get her news. Hope sat down and recounted everything that had transpired between her and Max and it was evident that they had cleared the air between them.

'It's like I told him, Jess. I couldn't care less whether he's a prince or a pauper. I just want him to be honest with me.'

'So you're no longer thinking of going home in a few days' time?'

Hope shook her head emphatically. As Jess had supposed, she was now dead set on staying on for the summer, maybe longer. In fact, circumstances had changed.

'Jess, if I were to move out of here and onto the yacht for July and August, would that be a pain for you?'

'Wow, July starts next Saturday. That's a bit soon for moving in together, isn't it?'

'Well, to be honest, this would be a business arrangement.'

Jess raised an eyebrow. 'You're going to have to explain.'

'He wants me to be his hostie. The girl who was all set to start this weekend has just cried off.'

'Hostie?'

'That's what they call it. You see, the boat's fully booked throughout both months and he needs a deck hand – a deckie – and somebody to look after the guests, the food, the laundry and so on – the hostie. Sort of like a glorified housekeeper, I imagine.'

'Deckie and hostie, eh? I suppose that makes him the skipper-ie. So, he's offered you the job?'

'That's right, and it would mean living on board – apparently we'll probably sail off along the coast to Italy or even across to islands like Corsica or Sardinia.'

'That sounds amazing. And the deckie?'

'The same guy who's been helping him this month. His name's Steve and he's a Brit. I've met him. He's a hoot.'

'Sounds like fun. And of course I don't mind. I've got my faithful hound to look after me.' She glanced down at the freshly-bathed Labrador. 'Besides, the work on the villa will be starting in a few weeks, so I'll probably have my pick of hunky builders to invite back to my lonely bed.'

'Yeh, right. That'll be the day.' Hope knew her too well. 'Anyway, of course, you'll have your hunk with the sexy old sports car to keep you company.'

Jess told her the good news about David's physiotherapy and passed on the invitation to the drinks party. Hope shook her head. 'I expect I'll be off with Max on the boat, but I'll check with him. I'll go and see George anyway and thank him for the invitation. It certainly sounds like he and David are moving in the right direction.'

'I sincerely hope so.'

Chapter 19

The next two weeks flew by. Jess saw very little of Hope as she flitted between the house and the yacht, getting everything ready for the busy summer season. Jess even had to run the Range Rover out on one occasion – just about the first time she had driven the car for weeks – to take Hope to a ship's chandlery to collect all manner of bits and pieces. She was pleased to find that she really rather enjoyed driving it, particularly now she felt confident finding her way around St-Tropez and its narrow streets. As a result, in the days that followed, she started taking the rejuvenated Brutus up into the forest for walks, short at first, but increasing in length as it became clear that his energy levels were once more approaching normal for a five-year-old dog, rather than a geriatric fatty.

Feeling that it was time she started experimenting, she found wonderful fresh fruit in the weekly market and tried her hand at making summer pudding and homemade custard. She invited Antoinette to come and try it with her and was delighted with the reaction. Antoinette looked and sounded impressed.

'This is an English recipe?'

'My mum's own recipe. I phoned her last night to get it.'

'Over here in France we often joke about English food being terrible, but this is delightful.'

At her feet, the expression on the Labrador's face made it quite clear that his nose agreed with her.

'That's good to hear. I know I can't compete with your skills in the kitchen, but I'm glad you approve.' She felt relieved and she gave Antoinette a big smile. 'Maybe I should make another one and invite David and George along to try it.'

'You know what they say about the way to a man's heart being through his stomach.' Antoinette smiled back and Jess wondered if she, like Hope, had realised the way she felt about David.

Unfortunately, however, she saw less of David. Now that he was having his physiotherapy – apparently in Toulon – he was out for most of the day, and she only glimpsed him on a couple of occasions, but didn't have the chance to talk to him. She did, however, spend a lot of time thinking about him. It would have been rather nice to be able to sit down and chat to him, but he had made no move to contact her and she felt it better not to intrude.

Then, one day, towards the middle of July, she was in St-Tropez, walking up the narrow street by the tourist information office, when she spotted a familiar shape coming towards her. Although her knowledge of cars was far inferior to Hope's, she couldn't mistake this one. The long sleek bonnet was unmistakably an old silver Jaguar E-Type and the only person she knew round here with one of these was David. She heard the throaty burble of the engine as he reached the corner and, as he did so, he must have spotted her. To her delight, he slowed and stopped. The overnight rainstorm had passed, and the streets were mostly dry again, so the car roof and windows were down. As she walked over to him, he looked up at her from the driving seat.

'Hi Jess. Can I give you a lift somewhere?' There was quite definitely the hint of a smile on his face.

'That's very kind. Where are you going?'

'Wherever you want to go. I'm just out for a drive.'

'Well, I don't care where we go, and I'd love to have a ride in your wonderful car.'

As she went round and opened the door on the passenger side, Jess distinctly felt the eyes of a number of the passers-by looking on enviously. She had little doubt that a lot of them were jealous of her getting a ride in such an iconic classic car, but many of the women were quite possibly more interested in the driver – just as she was. She shot a glance across at him and checked out his suntan, his strong forearm resting on the top of the door, and the immaculate pink shirt stretched tight across the muscles of his chest. Yes, she thought to herself, if it weren't for the crutches stowed behind the front seats, he would definitely have been fighting them off – and she wouldn't have stood a chance.

Getting in proved to be tricky. She had chosen to wear a light dress today, rather than shorts, and she soon realised that it was virtually impossible to get in gracefully. Unlike the Range Rover, you didn't climb into the Jaguar. You fell into it. Or at least she did. Although he had seen her numerous times in her fairly skimpy bikini, she was as red as a beetroot by the time she had settled in and tugged her skirt down from where it had ended up around her waist. She found herself almost lying horizontal in the car, her legs stretched out in front of her. It certainly took a bit of getting used to.

Politely he made no comment and waited until she was settled before pulling away and glancing across towards her.

'How about going out of town? Maybe up for a drive in the hills?'

'Oh yes, please. It's lovely up there. And I might be able to show you the places where Olivier told me there used to be German bunkers during the war.'

It took a few minutes before she began to realise that he was driving without using the pedals and she remembered he had told her the car had hand controls. Presumably his crushed legs were still too weak to press down hard. She debated for a moment whether to remark on this and then decided to air the topic. As his father had said, the main thing was to get him talking about the accident, his injuries and his experiences.

'So let's see if I've got this right. You pull the level towards you to accelerate and press down to brake. Is that right?'

'That's right. All done with my right hand. Luckily the car's automatic, so there's no clutch to worry about.'

'And did you buy the car like that?'

He shook his head. 'No, I've had this car for five years. I got a specialised firm to modify it for me after the accident.'

At that moment they approached a roundabout and she watched as he expertly manoeuvred the controls – braking and then accelerating away again. She gave it another few moments and then risked a more personal question.

'So how long's it going to be before you can use the pedals again?'

'I'm not sure.' His voice was low.

'Well, you can obviously put pressure on your legs again – I've seen you walking without your crutches and now you're doing all that physiotherapy – so, presumably it won't be long.'

He didn't answer immediately and she feared she might have overstepped the mark. It came as a considerable relief when he responded.

'I hope I'm getting there. The legs can take my weight now, but the nerves and muscles haven't quite recovered enough to make everything work. Hopefully that'll come. The physio says she's pleased with my progress, so fingers crossed.'

Jess decided not to press him any more, but was pleased he had been prepared to talk about his problems. She relaxed and enjoyed the ride. After a couple of kilometres, he turned off the main road and they started to climb. Jess loved the sensation of speed that the low-slung car produced as it swung though the corners, although the long bonnet made it difficult to see what was ahead. David was a good driver – fast, but not reckless – and she felt safe in his hands. As they climbed up from the coast into the thick pine forest, she found she recognised a number of the places Olivier had pointed out. One, in particular, gave her an idea.

'David, up there, a hundred yards ahead, can you slow down and see if you can turn onto that track? But it may be too bumpy for this car. See what you think.'

'Are you looking for the wartime bunkers? They're down there.' David obediently slowed and turned off the road into a lay-by. 'The track doesn't look too bumpy, but it does look very muddy after the rain. I'm afraid this car has no grip at all on mud, so we'd probably better not risk it. I wouldn't want us to get stuck.'

Jess looked across at him. 'Of course. So, do you know where the bunkers are?'

He nodded. 'Some of them. As kids we used to cycle up here and play around in the woods. We found a few old gun positions, but all the hardware was removed years ago. If you come up here with the dog one day, try going along this track for the best part of a kilometre until you see the ruins of an old stone building – probably a shepherd's hut before all the trees were planted. Turn right and you'll find bunkers and gun pits up there. But be careful – a couple of them are quite deep.'

Jess was genuinely astonished to hear him deliver the longest speech she had ever heard from him and she smiled back warmly.

'Let's hope your physiotherapy does the trick and then you can come up here for walks with me and Brutus.'

He looked up and caught her eye for a second.

'Thank you, Jess.'

'For what?'

'Thank you for giving me something to dream about.'

'The trick is to turn the dreams into reality.'

'That's some trick.'

He pulled the funny T-shaped gear stick into Drive once more, and started off up the hill again. Jess felt very happy with him up here in the forest, occasionally catching glimpses of the blue of the sea and the pink roofs of the houses of St-Tropez down below. After the rain, it was still very clear and there was a wonderful scent of resin in the air from all the pine trees. She reached up, joined her hands behind her head, and stretched luxuriously. As she did so, she felt pretty sure she saw his eyes checking out her body and that same, now familiar, frisson of desire ran through her.

They drove through Ramatuelle and on from there to Gassin, perched on another little hilltop. David was able to get right into the middle of the village, and as they climbed out of the Jaguar, he tapped the blue disabled badge on his windscreen and produced a creditable attempt at a smile.

'It's amazing what some people will do to get a parking space up here.'

Jess smiled back. 'So, what's the plan, chauffeur? Do I get to buy you a drink?'

He shook his head. 'The drinks are on me. Dad says you've refused to take payment for drawing up the plans of the villa. You should, you know.'

Jess shook her head. 'Absolutely not.'

'Then the least I can do is to buy you a drink. There's a restaurant and a bar up in the square. I should be all right to get up there on the crutches.'

Jess was impressed, and delighted, to see David walk the hundred yards or so into the square with the help of the crutches, no longer the wheelchair. The square itself was situated right on the top of the hill and dominated the surrounding countryside. As they took a seat at a table in the shade, Jess let her eyes roam out across the tree-clad hills, down to the deep blue of the sea in the far distance. It was a charming view and she felt very happy to be here – particularly with him. She turned back towards David and saw him looking at her.

'Like the view, Jess?'

'It's stunning.'

They were interrupted by a woman's voice.

'David, mais c'est toi! C'est bien toi!'

Jess looked up and saw a very glamorous, dark-haired woman at an adjoining table leap to her feet and rush across to David's side, where she draped herself all over him and proceeded to shower him with kisses – and not just restrained, friendly kisses. This woman looked as if she was going to eat him, and Jess felt a sudden surge of a quite unfamiliar emotion. And the emotion was, without a shadow of a doubt, jealousy.

David fought off the woman's attentions and emerged from beneath her suspiciously pert bosom.

'Hi, Mireille, it's me all right. It's good to see you. Let me introduce you to my friend, Jessica. She's English.'

Jess was pleased to find that she had little or no trouble in understanding David's French. She did her best to lower the hackles that had so unexpectedly raised themselves and smiled sweetly at the other woman, checking her out as she did so. Designer top, perfect tan, freshly-manicured fingernails and a small fortune in gold hanging around her neck and wrists – this, Jess realised, was the type of woman David would have frequented before the accident. And, presumably, as and when he recovered, this would be the sort of woman who would once again have him in her sights. And there was no way Jess would be able to compete.

'Pleased to meet you, Jessica.'

As she spoke, Jess saw Mireille's eyes flick down for a couple of seconds before coming back up again safe in the knowledge that Jess's summer dress hadn't cost more than £29.99. Jess smiled back at her – hoping it didn't look too much like a grimace – and shook her hand.

'And you, Mireille.'

The other woman's attention immediately transferred itself back to David.

'I was so worried when I heard about your accident. You poor thing. Are you on the road to recovery now?'

'I sincerely hope so, Mireille.'

'When you feel better, we should meet up again.'

'We should.'

At that moment a waitress appeared to take their order and Mireille – after appearing to do her best to tear David's ear off with her lips – returned to her friends at the other table.

'So, Jess, what can I get you?' Rather self-consciously, David wiped his ear with his hand. 'A glass of champagne, maybe?'

'To be honest, I'd love a cup of tea.' She addressed the waitress in French. 'Could I have a tea with some cold milk, please?'

The girl nodded. '*À l'anglaise.*'

'*À l'anglaise* indeed. Thank you.'

David decided to have the same and the waitress left. As she did so, he shot a glance across to Mireille's table and then leant forward towards Jess. The sheepish expression was back on his face again.

'Sorry about Mireille – she does tend to be a bit effusive. I've known her since school. She's married to a solicitor in Aups, but she hates the place, and spends most of the time – and most of his money – down here at St-Trop.'

'She seems very fond of you.' Jess kept her tone studiously even.

'She thinks she is. So fond of me she didn't get in touch when she heard of the accident.' He was smiling, but Jess could see it was only a thin veil. 'There's nothing like being reduced to a wheelchair for sorting out who your real friends are.'

Jess was determined not to let his mood – which had been quite buoyant up to now – deteriorate into melancholy once more.

'Well, you're not in a wheelchair now, are you? I was very impressed to see you make it up here without much difficulty.'

'So far so good. I really hate that thing.'

'The wheelchair?'

'Yes, it sort of symbolises everything I've lost.' Before she could say anything comforting, he continued. 'Do you know something? Weeks ago, when Antoinette told me two pretty girls had come to stay, I started hiding the chair when I went down to the pool, so you wouldn't see it.'

'Now you say that, I realise there was no sign of it when I first went to the pool.'

He nodded. 'It was shoved behind a bush. Damn thing, I hate it.'

Just then their teas arrived and Jess was glad of the interruption, just as it looked as if he might be about to slip back into his depression. The idea of him feeling ashamed of his wheelchair was tough to swallow, but she valued this new, tiny insight into his inner feelings. As soon as the waitress left them, she studied him across the table and waited for him to look up and catch her eye. It took almost a minute but, finally, he looked up, and she launched into some encouragement.

'Well, you've pretty much finished with the chair now, haven't you? And soon, hopefully, you'll be able to ditch the crutches. Tell me, David, are you a betting man?'

He shook his head.

'Well, if you feel like taking it, I have a bet for you. I bet you you'll be up here, walking the dog, before the end of the summer. Bet?'

'I haven't heard the stakes. Are we talking big money?'

Jess hesitated, deliberately taking her time over her next mouthful of tea. There were a lot of things she knew she would love to do to him if he won, and lots of things she knew she would love him to do to her if she won, but she decided to leave sex out of it – at least for now. She set her cup down again and made a suggestion.

'How about, if I win, you have to come with me to the beach bar and dance with me?'

'And if I win?'

'You won't.'

'I wish I had your confidence. But just suppose my legs don't make the grade and you don't win, what do I get?'

'Wash your car?'

He snorted.

'Wash your car in my bikini?'

He raised an eyebrow, but didn't comment.

'Hope and I both wash your car in bikinis?'

He smiled – a lovely relaxed smile that lit up his face.

'That's an enchanting thought, but I've got a better idea. If I win, you have to stay on here until Christmas and help me put my shoes on every morning.'

'Sounds fair to me, but you aren't going to win.'

She held out her hand, looking him in the eye.

'So, have we got a deal?'

He caught hold of her hand and held it for a few moments before shaking it. 'It's a bet. And I really hope I lose – although the help with the shoes would have been good.'

'I hope you lose as well, and I'm sure you will. As for the shoes, we'll see about that. Maybe I could be persuaded to help out with those anyway.'

'In your bikini?'

'We'll see about that.'

Chapter 20

Jess decided she had better dress up a bit for George's drinks party and it didn't take long for her to work out that the stuff she had brought from England wouldn't cut it. This was definitely going to be more than a shorts and T-shirt affair. She did a rapid calculation of her finances and was encouraged to realise that she still had a sizeable chunk of the euros given to her by Mrs Dupont and hadn't needed to dip into any of her savings so far. In fact, she had spent very little. Conscious that many, probably most of the other guests would be out of the Mireille mould, she decided to throw caution – and a whole heap of money – to the wind, and go dress shopping in St-Tropez.

As she walked slowly down the narrow streets in the very centre of town, gazing apprehensively at the clothes on display in the boutiques and big-name designer stores, she began to have second thoughts. Most of the nicest clothes had no price on display – and she knew what that meant. Where there *were* prices, they were very, very scary. One boutique, in particular, caught her eye. The window was almost empty, but all three of the dresses on display were absolutely gorgeous – lightweight and stylish – one white, one red and one blue – the colours of the French flag. Needless to say, there were no prices to be seen anywhere, although she was slightly heartened by a discreet red and white notice indicating a sale. It wasn't a big notice, so presumably it wasn't going to be a big sale, but she decided to go in and try – after having a coffee to bolster her courage first.

She went into a little bar and stood at the counter to drink her espresso. A few moments later, she was joined by a familiar figure.

'Hi, Jess, what brings you into town today?'

She looked round and smiled. It was Pete – today wearing a dark suit that, if anything, highlighted his muscular form. She reached up and kissed him on the cheeks. Living in France, she had already worked out, meant doing a lot of kissing. She rather liked the habit.

'I've got to do some shopping. What about you?'

'I'm on duty in half an hour. I've got a new client arriving from the USA.'

'But you can't tell me his name…' Jess was grinning.

'Or hers.' Pete grinned back. 'So, what sort of shopping? Food, clothes, jewellery?'

'Clothes.' She explained about George's party and the rather nice dresses she had seen in the boutique window. 'The thing is, I'm scared stiff of going in there. They'll probably take one look at what I'm wearing and laugh me out of the place.' She pointed down. 'I'll give you a clue – the top came from the Tuesday market here, and the shorts came from the supermarket back home in Britain.'

'You don't want to be intimidated. It's the same in my business. First impressions count. If you walk in looking as though you own the place, normally they roll over and behave.'

For a moment, Jess had an image of a Chechen gangster lying on his back, legs and arms in the air like a little puppy, while Pete scratched his tummy.

'It's difficult to look as though you own the place when your whole outfit – and I'm including my underwear and sandals – cost less than a good meal here.'

Pete glanced at his watch.

'Listen, I've got a bit of time. Let me help you out. Have you decided which shop you want to visit?'

'Yes, it's just a few doors up the road from here.'

'Fine. So how much do you want to spend?'

'As little as possible. What do you think for a summery dress? Something smart.'

Pete reflected for a moment. 'I've done quite a bit of shopping around here with various clients, and you can pay anything up to three or four thousand euros for a dress if you try hard enough.'

'Blimey. I've never paid more than a hundred pounds for a dress in my life. I was thinking of maybe twice that in a place like this.'

Pete shook his head. 'I reckon we should be able to get you something nice, but you might need to spend a bit more than that. What's your absolute max?'

Jess had been thinking about this all morning. She really had been very frugal so far and she still hadn't even started to dip into her severance pay. This was possibly going to be the dressiest event she had ever attended and she wanted to look good. And, of course, she knew she particularly wanted to look good for David. She took a deep breath, hardly believing what she was saying.

'Absolute tops – five hundred euros.'

As she said it, she found herself wondering what her mum would say if she knew her daughter was contemplating spending that much on a frock. Yes, living in a place like St-Tropez could seriously affect your sense of proportion.

Pete nodded approvingly.

'That sounds fine. Now, are you going to pay cash or by card?'

'Either, really.'

'Have you got a flashy gold card or something like that?' Jess shook her head. 'Then you need to pay cash. I tell you what, let me have it. The very rich don't carry money.'

Jess took ten fifty-euro notes out of her purse and passed them across. She was surprised to see Pete remove a thick bankroll from his pocket and add her notes to it. Catching her eye, he explained.

'In my business, it's necessary to have a certain amount of cash on hand for emergencies. Also, like I was telling you, it helps with maintaining the illusion. Now, when you find what you want and it's time to pay, just give me a sign and I'll do it.'

'What sort of sign?' Jess was beginning to enjoy the intrigue.

'Something dismissive. You know – superior to inferior. Try something like this.'

He half-raised one arm and clicked his fingers. 'I'll be standing behind you. That should do it.'

Jess experimented until Pete declared himself satisfied.

'Excellent, but remember not to smile at me. I'm part of the furniture. You're a princess. I'm just a foot soldier. Got it?'

'Got it.'

'Right, finished your coffee? Fine. Now, have you got a pair of shades?'

'Shades?'

'Sunglasses, sweetheart. The mega rich don't go anywhere without them – even at night. One of my clients walked into a lamppost last year because he wouldn't take his shades off while we were walking through Cannes at midnight. He was still wearing them in the emergency room.'

Jess giggled, pulled out her sunglasses and put them on. She saw Pete remove a pair from his top pocket, shake them open and follow suit. They walked out of the bar and up the road. As they approached the boutique, Pete leant towards her and lowered his voice.

'Now, you wait out here. I go in, check it out and then call you. Once inside, I'll lurk in the background. You ignore me and make sure you say as little as possible and try not to be too nice.'

'Nice?'

'You're always so smiley and friendly and nice, Jess. But not in the face of the enemy. We're going into a combat zone here. Stay alert and remember what I said – act as if you own the place or as if you could buy it with your small change.' He caught her eye. 'And for God's sake stop giggling.'

When they reached the door of the boutique, Pete parked her outside and went in. Jess's giggles were replaced by nerves by now and she was feeling quite apprehensive once more by the time Pete appeared at the door and waved her in.

'All clear.'

He could have been waving her into a property recently occupied by insurgents. Jess took a deep breath and stepped inside. Pete followed, closing the door behind them and stationing himself beside it, arms crossed, impassive.

'*Bonjour, Madame.*'

The woman behind the counter was immaculately dressed and looked as though she was most probably the owner. She was every bit as elegant and daunting as Jess had suspected, but she was looking nervous and Jess took heart.

'Good morning.' She made no attempt to speak French.

'Good morning. How can we help you today?' Unsurprisingly, the woman's English was fluent.

Jess didn't reply. Instead, she just stalked around the shop, affecting only minimal interest in the gorgeous clothes on display until she reached the window. Very casually, she glanced at the backs of the dresses on display and was relieved to see price tags on two of them. She glanced casually over her shoulder and saw the woman watching her anxiously. Just beyond her, the monolithic presence of Pete in his suit and shades was having the desired effect.

'If there's anything I can do for you, Madame, please just say so.'

Again, Jess didn't reply, but she leant forward and ran her fingers over the material of one of the dresses. It felt like silk and it was absolutely lovely. As she did so, she managed to get a closer view of the price tag. The first figure she saw was 999 euros and she almost had a heart attack. Then, to her immense relief, she spotted a thin pencil line crossing this out and, below it, somebody had written *499 €*. She felt a wave of relief that she could just about afford it. Turning away, she completed her slow tour of the shop until she returned to the woman at the counter.

'Have you seen anything you like, Madame?'

'The blue dress in the window – do you have that in my size?'

By this time the shopkeeper must have checked her out and she nodded, scuttling off to return almost immediately with the dress. She was leading Jess to a changing room, when they were interrupted.

'One moment, please.'

Pete came past them and opened the door to the changing room, his right hand inside his left breast pocket like in the films, and Jess felt an overwhelming urge to giggle again. Fortunately, she managed to keep a lid on it, for now.

'Clear.' He stood aside.

The shopkeeper ushered Jess inside and withdrew. Jess saw the comforting shadow of Pete against the louvred door as he took up position outside and she hastened to try the dress on. It fitted perfectly, it felt wonderful, and it looked stunning. It was very simple, cornflower blue, with the thinnest imaginable shoulder straps, and she really did feel like a princess in it. After a couple of whirls and turns, she slipped out of it once more and returned to her supermarket clothes.

The shopkeeper looked up hopefully as Jess emerged from the changing room and walked over to the counter, accompanied by her faithful bodyguard.

'I'll take it.'

Remembering her lesson in the bar, she raised one hand and clicked her fingers. Immediately a large shadow fell across the counter and Pete stepped forward. Jess glanced at the shopkeeper's face as she watched him pull the hefty bankroll from his pocket and peel five hundred euros off the roll and place them on the counter. It was not dissimilar to the expression on Brutus's face when his food was being prepared. Jess did her best to keep a straight face as the shopkeeper folded the dress and slipped it into a very fine-looking bag, along with a card.

'If Madame requires anything else, please feel free to call me any time.'

'Thank you.' Jess reckoned she owed the lady at least a word of thanks. The one euro change was left, disdainfully, on the counter.

As she walked towards the door, Pete sprang into action, opening the door and stepping out to check the street in both directions before turning back with his usual, 'Clear.'

Jess made it as far as the bar once more before the dam burst and she slumped down at a table, erupting into a fit of the giggles that had the other customers looking across at her curiously.

'You're a natural, Jess. Brilliantly done.' Pete sat down opposite her and joined in the laughter. 'And I was very impressed to see that you kept the shades on even when you were changing. That's real devotion to the cause.'

'You saw me changing?' She caught his eye.

'It's my job to see everything.' Pete was still grinning. 'By the way, you might like to invest in some new underwear. A dress like that needs something really minimal underneath. There's a gorgeous lingerie shop just a few doors down.'

In fact, Jess had been thinking along the very same lines. She took a second look at the big muscleman. The way he was talking wasn't in the least bit suggestive or offensive. In fact, it sounded like very sensible, impartial advice. She suddenly began to see him in a whole new light. Could it be that underneath the hard man façade he was really made of much softer stuff?

'Pete, you're a star. Thank you so much for helping me out. I'm sure I couldn't have done it without you.'

'You're very welcome, Jess, and the dress looked fabulous on you – a real princess.'

'A phoney princess, but what the hell? By the way, how come she kept calling me *Madame*? Do I look that old?'

He grinned. 'Not at all. The thing is, *Madame* is the usual way of addressing any woman these days, irrespective of age. *Mademoiselle* is being used less and less. No, it's not because you look ancient.'

'Well, that's a relief. Anyway, thanks again, Pete. I owe you.'

He shook his head. 'Wrong. *I* owe *you*. If you hadn't told me about those guys on board the *Helios*, I might have lost a client – and that's really not very good for business.' He gave her a wink, before a much more serious expression appeared on his face. 'Besides, from what the police told me about the heavy artillery they were carrying, a lot of other people might have got hurt as well. And that would probably have included me.'

Jess reached over and caught hold of his powerful forearm.

'I wouldn't want anything to happen to you, Pete. You're a sweetie.'

He gave her a smile. 'By the way, Jess, I've been meaning to say – I was very, very impressed that you didn't take Drugoi's money.'

'The less I have to do with Drugoi and his money, the better.'

'He and his little friend, Dmitri, were still discussing it when they left. It must be the first time somebody's refused his money.'

'They were discussing me in English?'

'No, in Russian.' Pete caught Jess's eye. 'It's a pretty important language in my profession, along with Arabic.'

'So, you speak Russian and Arabic, as well as French of course?'

He nodded and grinned. 'Brains and brawn, eh, Jess? Now I bet you wish I was straight, don't you?'

Chapter 21

Jess went over to the villa just after six o'clock on Sunday. She had followed Pete's instructions and invested not only in new underwear, but in new shoes – not as expensive as the dress, but a major investment nevertheless. She rarely wore heels, but somehow the new dress seemed to be crying out for them. On George's instructions, a freshly washed and brushed Brutus was also invited to the party and he trotted happily alongside her as she cautiously negotiated the gravel path over to the house.

The parking area was already crammed with cars, many of them probably worth as much as David's Jaguar, and she began to feel a bit nervous. She walked round to the kitchen door and let Brutus lead her in. She found herself in the midst of a hive of activity. Antoinette was directing oper-ations, while two pretty, teenage girls were preparing trays. Antoinette looked up as she heard the door and beamed approvingly.

'Jess, you look wonderful! That dress suits you down to the ground. Here, say hello to my daughters – Chantal and Marie-Hélène.'

Jess shook hands with the girls and asked if she could help. Antoinette gave a very definite shake of the head.

'In that dress, Jess, absolutely not. I'd never forgive myself if it got messed up. Thank you for the offer, but we'll manage.' She smiled happily. 'I'm so very pleased this is happening. We used to do a lot of entertaining back before Babette got sick, and the post Bastille Day party was a regular annual event. It didn't happen last year – so soon after her death – so it's wonderful that George feels like doing it again. I'm sure that's your influence, you know. Now, you go on through to the lounge. Jean-Pierre's in there with champagne.'

'You've got your husband working as well? It really is a family affair, isn't it?'

Jess and Brutus walked through to the lounge as instructed and found it almost empty, although she could see a crowd of people out on the terrace. Jean-Pierre was standing at a side table that was covered with glasses and bottles and he held out a glass of champagne towards her.

'*Bonsoir, Jess.*' He raised the fingers of his other hand to his lips and kissed them appreciatively. '*Comme vous êtes belle!*'

Jess blushed as she took the glass from him.

'*Merci bien, Jean-Pierre. Vous êtes très gentil.*'

She let the dog lead her out of the French windows onto the terrace where she found George waiting for her. He was looking very smart in a pair of immaculate light grey trousers, sky blue shirt and a linen jacket. His reaction to her appearance was not dissimilar to the one she had received from Jean-Pierre. He reached out, took hold of her free hand and gave a quiet whistle.

'Jess, my dear, you look breathtaking. Oh, to be thirty years younger!'

Jess kissed him on the cheeks and thanked him for the compliment, secretly very pleased that he, too, seemed to think she looked all right. She let her eyes roam across the twenty or so people standing out on the terrace, pretending to look for faces she recognised, but really checking to see where David was.

George didn't miss much.

'David's down the far end. I'm sure he'd love to see you. Why don't you go and chat to him and then I'll introduce you to a few people a bit later on?'

Jess gave him a big smile and followed his directions, slipping in and out among the other guests with the dog, feeling a number of curious eyes on her and checking out the clothes of the other women. One thing was for sure – she was in no way overdressed. And, she thought to herself, if a few Chechen gangsters happened to come around, they could no doubt make themselves a small fortune by collecting the jewellery on display – although she was wearing none at all. She returned a few smiles, but recognised nobody, until she reached the end of the terrace and heard his voice.

'Hello, Brutus. You've come to the party, have you?'

David was sitting at the far end of the terrace in an ordinary chair, not in his wheelchair, and Jess felt a rush of happiness for him. It felt really good to see him again. She hadn't spoken to him for almost a week. As she reached his side, he was bending forward over the dog, giving him a stroke. She touched him lightly on the shoulder.

'Hello, David.'

'Hi, Jess...'

His voice tailed off as he glanced up and took a good look at her. As his eyes met hers, she suddenly realised why her new dress had appealed to her so much – it was the exact same colour as his eyes.

'Jess, I really don't know what to say. You look absolutely devastating. That dress, those shoes, your hair... you look wonderful.'

Jess leant down and kissed him on the cheeks.

'It's amazing what can be done with smoke and mirrors. Besides, you don't look too shabby yourself.'

He was wearing a soft white cotton shirt and immaculate dark blue trousers. His hair had been freshly cut and with his suntan – broken nose or no broken nose – he looked like a Hollywood idol himself. She reached over and clinked her glass against his as the dog sat down between them.

'Cheers – it's good to see you, David.'

'And it's really good to see you.' He sounded as if he meant it. 'So, what's your news?'

She sat with him, chatting, telling him about the latest messages from Hope on the *Helios* – now somewhere off the Italian Riviera coast – and how the skipper and the hostie were getting on like a house on fire. She also told him about Pete's invaluable help at the dress shop and was delighted to hear him laugh. As he did so, his face changed so radically from the glum expression to which she had become accustomed, and she felt a wave of optimism for the future – his future.

And maybe hers.

After a while, she managed to persuade him to stand up and, with the support of his crutches, accompany her on a tour of the other guests. She could see the effort – mental rather than physical – that it cost him, but she felt sure it was the right thing to encourage him to do. In the course of their slow progress along the terrace, she was introduced to a load of people whose names she felt sure she would never remember, and she got a close-up view of some of the finest jewellery she had ever seen. Most of the people were of George's era, with a few younger exceptions here and there. Roughly half of them were French, and she found herself speaking French to a couple of the older ones. The others a mixture of nationalities, from Canadian to Indian, with a handful of Brits thrown in. By now she counted upwards of thirty people out here and her progress along the terrace seemed interminable.

Just as they were finally reaching the end, George appeared with a man who was probably around the same age as him at his side. This charming, smiley gentleman was introduced to Jess as Philippe Mailly, one of his near neighbours. George and David then went off together, leaving Jess to have a long chat with M. Mailly – partly in French and partly in English – in the course of which she told him about the changes they were going to make to the inside of the villa. He appeared very interested – particularly when she told him she was an architect and had worked in London for some years. When he finally moved on to talk to other people, she wondered whether she might find him knocking on her door sometime soon for some architectural advice about his own property.

Brutus had a wonderful time, being thoroughly spoilt by everybody. Jess was pleased to find that he stayed close to her, so she was able to divert most, although not all, the treats that people were intent upon giving to him. Antoinette's two girls were doing a grand job of circulating with trays of delicious nibbles and Brutus's nose was permanently cocked upwards, his eyes ever-hopeful. He really was looking noticeably slimmer and fitter, so Jess decided a few extra calories wouldn't hurt him – just this once.

After a while, she spotted David heading indoors, so she and the dog followed him into the lounge. For a moment, she thought he might be about to take the lift – which, she noticed, now boasted a fine piece of carpet on its floor – and disappear upstairs, but he didn't. Instead, he settled down on the very upright armchair he normally used and stretched his legs out in front of him. She went across to him.

'Do you mind if I join you?'

'Please do. I just needed a sit down.'

Jess took a seat on a stool beside him and Brutus flopped down at her feet.

'So, how's it been, David?'

'Physically – surprisingly easy. Mentally – a bit wearing.'

At that moment, Jean-Pierre appeared with a bottle of ice-cold champagne. Without being asked, he topped up their glasses and he was just moving off when Jess caught his attention and asked when he would be starting the electrical work. His answer was just what she wanted to hear.

'*Demain matin, Jess.*'

She gave him a big smile and, after he had left, she looked across at David.

'So, tomorrow morning the rewiring starts. I hope that isn't going to interrupt your work with your computers too much.'

David shook his head. 'No, it's all sorted out. First thing he's going to do is to set up a separate temporary circuit for Dad and me to use while he rips the old wiring out. I should be fine. I'll still be contactable.'

'Do lots of people contact you?'

He nodded. 'You wouldn't believe how many.'

'Business or pleasure?'

'Almost entirely business, I'm afraid.'

'What is it you do, exactly, if you don't mind me asking?'

'I sometimes ask myself the same question. Things have got so complicated over the past few years.'

'Computery stuff, isn't it?'

He smiled – a lovely light, happy smile – and she found herself smiling with him.

'That's right – computery stuff.'

He then went on to attempt to explain what he did and Jess was flabbergasted. Not only had she heard of his company, she actually used the internet messaging service he and his company had designed. As he talked, she remembered reading about the secretive boss of the company, who rarely appeared in public. Clearly, she was sitting next to a twenty-first century icon.

Suddenly she began to realise that, however rich his father might be, David was in another league entirely and, by the sound of it, he had done it all himself. She was sitting alongside a man who was most probably on first name terms with presidents, prime ministers and household names like Bill Gates. She was so totally gobsmacked that the Labrador must have sensed her stupefaction, as he pulled himself to his feet and laid his head on her knee.

'You all right, Jess?'

David sounded concerned. She did her best to shake herself out of her amazement as she scratched the dog's head.

'I'm fine, thanks. It's just taking me a bit of time to get my head round the fact that I'm sitting alongside a legend. Wow, David, I had no idea.'

He smiled gently. 'A legend with broken legs, don't forget.'

She waved a finger dismissively. 'A legend's a legend, period. Besides, hopefully the legs are getting better.'

'I hope so, but I'm not holding my breath. I've got another scan and a meeting with the specialist in Nice next week. We'll see what she says.'

'I'm sure it'll be good news.' Jess was pleased to hear him talking about his legs, but she sensed a change of topic was called for. 'So, before the accident, where were you living? In the US?'

He nodded. 'I've got a place in California – that's where my head office is – but I prefer it over here, to be honest.'

'I've never been to California, but I can well see how you'd like this area. I love it. So what's the plan? Once your legs are fixed, are you going back to the States or are you going to buy yourself somewhere in St-Tropez?'

'St-Trop if I can find somewhere. There aren't many places available, but I've got lots of feelers out.'

'Wonderful. Remember, if you find somewhere, and you want me to pull my architect's hat on again and take a look, just say, won't you?'

He leant back and subjected her to a long, lingering look that sent a thrill of raw desire through her whole body. She swallowed hard and waited for him to speak. Finally, he gave his verdict.

'I reckon you'd look good in a hat. Mind you, you look good in anything. Tonight, in this amazing dress and the killer heels, you look like a Hollywood movie star.' For a moment she glimpsed the confident, athletic, desirable man who had surely had a pack of women baying at his heels before the accident. 'I've dated a few movie stars in my time, so I know what I'm talking about.'

Jess could feel her cheeks burning with embarrassment and she searched for the right words to brush off the compliment, while her brain was reminding her, not for the first time, that if the accident had never happened, he and she would almost certainly not be sitting here like this. He was so far out of her league, he wouldn't even have recognised her existence. But before she could say anything, he carried on.

'Sorry if I'm embarrassing you, Jess. The thing is – you're more than any movie star I've ever met. Yes, you look amazing, but the big difference is inside, out of sight. First of all, you've got a brain, but along with being bright, you're kind and selfless, and you've never even heard the word *ego*.'

'Please stop, David, before my head explodes. I don't think I've ever been so embarrassed.'

'You shouldn't be embarrassed. It's true.' He caught her eye. 'Please don't change, Jess.'

'I'm too old to change.'

'How old's that?'

'I'm twenty-nine – but not for much longer. And you know what comes after twenty-nine. How old are you, then?'

'Thirty-three – but I feel about twice that age these days.'

'So how old were you when you set up your company and it all took off?'

Jess was glad to turn the conversation round to him and she felt her cheeks begin to cool. Inside, her head, and her heart, were in turmoil. There was no disguising the pleasure his comments – embarrassing or not – had given her. Could it really be that he might even be harbouring feelings towards her after all?

'I had the idea while I was still at Oxford, and I set up the company the day after I graduated. So, that was eleven years ago now. Since then, it's just gone crazy.'

'And so you're busy all the time with work stuff?'

'Yes and no. Yes, we have regular weekly video confer-
ences, and I do get other calls every now and then – for
urgent stuff – but I've got a good team running things now,
and so I've been able to take a step back.' He glanced across
at her. 'Sorry, that's a poor choice of words. Walking
backwards is one of the things the physio's been trying to
get me to do – and it isn't easy. At the moment, what's
occupying so much of my time is the Foundation.'

'The Foundation?'

'Yes, I'm trying to set up an organisation that can give
support to people suffering from life-changing injuries,
caused as a result of sport. There's a lot going on for
wounded military personnel nowadays, but I thought it
would be good to try to help people like me.'

'That's a great idea.'

And it was. Jess was very impressed. She was also
delighted to hear David talking so fluently and openly. Like
his father had said – talking was good.

'Nobody can work miracles, but I want my people
to concentrate as much on the psychological side as the
physical. For people like me, it's not just the physical
consequences of the accident, but the total change of life,
outlook and objectives that something like this brings with
it.' He managed a little smile and her heart went out to him.
'And you never know, if I'm lucky, the Foundation might
even be able to help *me*.'

'I'm sure it will. And, David, in my small way, you know
you can count on me for any help I can give you.'

'I think I've said it before, but you already have helped
– helped a lot. As recently as a month ago, if somebody
had told me I'd be sitting here tonight with a beautiful girl,
talking about this stuff with a smile on my face, I wouldn't

have believed it possible. Jess, if the Foundation could clone you, we'd be world-beaters.'

'David, there's only a certain amount of embarrassment a girl can handle. Could we talk about something else, apart from me?'

'Of course. You know something? I really do enjoy talking to you, Jess. We must do this again another time.'

'I'd like that, David. I'd like that a lot.'

'Do you think I could have your phone number? That way I can give you a call some time, rather than struggle across on crutches, and maybe you might like to let me take you out for dinner?'

'That sounds terrific.'

And it did.

Chapter 22

The work on the villa started on Monday morning with the arrival of Jean-Pierre. The following day his cousin, the plumber, arrived to take a look. He brought what turned out to be his brother-in-law, the builder, with him and Jess discussed her requirements with them, delighted to find them both knowledgeable and friendly. Certainly, it looked like the job was going to be a real family affair. Everybody appeared to know everybody here in St-Tropez and Jess felt pretty sure that the word would soon spread that there was an English architect – and a woman to boot – staying here.

The weather got steadily hotter and Jess even played around with the air-conditioning in the guest house, but soon discovered that by keeping the windows and doors onto the enclosed courtyard open, the temperature inside stayed at an acceptable level. Brutus deserted his bed and slept, stretched out, on the cool terracotta tiles on the floor beside her. Now that Hope had gone, Jess found she really liked having his company – particularly as his flatulence was now a thing of the past. Of course, nice as the dog was, there was somebody else whose company in her bedroom she would have preferred.

To her delight, she got a phone call from him on Wednesday morning.

'Hi, David, how's it going?'

'Fine, thanks, Jess. I'm just about to go off to Toulon for today's session with the physio and I was wondering if you were maybe free tonight?'

'Pretty much. I said I'd send the builder a copy of the plans, and I wanted to mark up all the alterations for him, but I should be able to knock that off this afternoon. So, what did you have in mind?'

'Do you like Italian food?'

'Absolutely. I love it.'

'Have you ever been to Italy?'

'No, never, but that's miles away.'

'Yes, but don't worry about that. There's a really good restaurant – one of my all-time favourites – on the coast just over the border that I'd like you to try, if you feel like it.'

'Wow. Well, if you're sure.'

'Yes, I am, absolutely. I hope you like it and, as for me, it'll be terrific to go out for dinner for the first time in ages.'

'Well, yes, then. Thank you.' Jess had a sudden thought. 'Is it a posh place? Should I dress up?'

She heard him laugh and she found herself smiling for him. 'Yes, I suppose it is a bit posh, but you wear what you like. It's like I told you – you look good in anything.'

'David! That's unfair. You can't tell me it's a posh place and then say I can turn up in shorts and T-shirt. They'd probably throw me out.'

'They wouldn't dare. But if you're worried, why don't you wear that gorgeous blue dress you were wearing the other night?' A thought must have struck him. 'But best if you don't wear heels. Heels and boats don't mix.'

'Boats?' Jess was getting seriously confused. 'Are we going there by boat?'

'Sort of. Anyway, look, I've got to go. Are you okay if we leave at six o'clock?'

'Yes, of course. That's fine.'

'Right. I'll book the taxi for six, and don't forget your passport, just in case, although I don't think anybody'll ask for it. See you later, Jess, and... Jess, I'm really looking forward to it.'

'Me too, David.'

She put the phone down, feeling excited, but a bit bewildered. She opened her laptop and checked what she had suspected. The Italian border was about a hundred miles east of here, just beyond Monte Carlo. The computer suggested that it was likely to take over two hours to drive there. That would mean at least four hours in the car there and back – not exactly a relaxing evening, but it was certainly something different. And she would be with David. Of course, as far as getting there was concerned, he had talked about a boat and a taxi, so maybe he had some alternative up his sleeve.

It turned out that he had.

The taxi collected them from the villa at six o'clock and took them to St-Tropez harbour. Here, a launch was waiting for them. David hadn't brought his wheelchair and Jess was delighted to see him moving fairly confidently with his crutches, and managing to scramble into the boat without too much trouble. They set off out of the harbour, then, to her considerable surprise, as the launch rounded the end of the long breakwater, she discovered exactly how they were going to get to Italy. There, bobbing gently on the light wavelets, was a seaplane.

Jess had never seen one in the flesh before and she certainly hadn't flown in one. The aircraft had a propeller at the front and rested upon two long white floats. It was surprisingly small compared to the commercial aircraft she had flown on in the past. They came up alongside one of the floats, from which a ladder led up to an open door above, and David helped her out of the launch and onto the ladder, hauling himself up afterwards inelegantly, but without too much apparent difficulty.

Inside, there were six seats, but, clearly, they were the only passengers. Two uniformed crew were waiting for them. The pilot shook hands with them and then returned to his seat in the cockpit. Moments later Jess heard the engine cough into life while they sat down and the co-pilot went through the safety information with them. He made it all sound very safe, although his revelation that seaplanes tended to end up upside down in the water in the event of a crash sounded a bit scary. However, he reappeared a moment later with a bottle of champagne and Jess decided to go with the flow. She was with three men who clearly weren't worried, so why should she be? Even so, as the engine note rose to a roar and she felt the aircraft start to slice through the water, she gripped David's arm and hung on for dear life.

After a remarkably short run-up, bumping far less than she had expected across the water, the spray outside the windows suddenly stopped and they were airborne. Compared to jets she had flown on in the past, this little aircraft appeared to be travelling at little more than walking speed, but it nevertheless gained height pretty quickly and they soon had an amazing view inland across the tree-covered hills, as far as the peaks of the Maritime Alps in the distance.

'So, what do you think of it so far? I hope that wasn't too scary.'

David's voice was gentle. Jess turned back from the window towards him, and realised with a start that she was still hanging onto his arm with her right hand. She slowly unclenched her grip, noticing the imprint of her fingers on the tanned skin of his arm.

'I'm so sorry. I hope I didn't squeeze too tightly. I'm fine now, but I was a little bit scared as we took off. Are you sure I didn't hurt you?'

'Not at all. I'm glad to be of service. It's a bit different in a seaplane, isn't it?' He smiled at her. 'If it helps, I took an old friend up in one of these once, and she was sick in my lap. Cheers.'

He clinked his glass against hers and they both sipped their champagne. As they flew along the coast, she could see the captain and co-pilot at the controls, separated from them by just a curtain. The two men were drinking coffee out of a flask and the little plane appeared to be flying itself. Jess took another, bigger, mouthful of wine and decided to place her trust in their ability, and concentrate on the handsome man alongside her.

He was wearing an impeccable light blue linen shirt, grey trousers and deck shoes. He looked happy and she was very pleased to see him like this. Had it not been for the crutches lying across the seats behind them, he looked every inch a fortunate member of the privileged classes – and, of course, that was exactly what he had been until the accident. When Jess had arrived in St-Tropez, she wouldn't have been seen dead in the company of somebody who used a private aircraft and yet, here she was. As Hope had been telling her all along, it wasn't the fact of being rich that made people objectionable. She made a mental note to try to give people

– even Rafael or the Drugois of this world – the benefit of the doubt before judging them in future.

'So where exactly are we going, David?'

He turned towards her and smiled.

'If you don't mind, I'm using you as a guinea pig.' Seeing her raised eyebrows, he explained. 'I'm taking you to a restaurant on the coast just over the other side of the Italian border, a kilometre or two beyond Monaco. It's a place I used to come to a lot and I'd welcome your opinion of it.'

'Why? Do you think it might have changed over the past few months?'

'It might have, or I might have. That's what I'm keen to find out – with your help. Anyway, I can guarantee you a wonderful meal. Their food is second to none.'

Jess didn't quite follow.

'Well if you're so sure of the quality of the food, what am I supposed to have an opinion about?'

He smiled again. 'Just anything. See what you think.'

She still didn't follow, but she decided to wait and see. Presumably all would be revealed in due course. After a minute or two, she changed the subject.

'So, have you used this sort of aircraft a lot, David?'

'There's been a lot of trouble with helicopters around St-Tropez over the years – you know, noise and so on – and the local authorities have been clamping down on the number of flights, so this is the next best thing. We're flying back later on by helicopter but, to be honest, helicopters are terribly noisy inside as well as out. I quite like this sort of aircraft – besides, I can't fly a helicopter, but I can fly an aircraft, so if the pilot and the co-pilot decide to jump out, I know I can get us down.' He was smiling.

'You can fly?'

'I used to do a lot of flying – and gliding, hang-gliding and parachuting.' His smile faded. 'I fear that's something else I won't be able to do any more.'

Just then the co-pilot reappeared to top up their glasses and to inform them that they would be landing in ten minutes' time. Jess was astounded.

'So less than half an hour. That's amazing. The computer reckoned it would take two hours to drive to the border! Mind you, I imagine you could do it quicker than that in the Jaguar.'

David shook his head. 'And get locked up. There are so many speed restrictions, speed cameras and police patrols on the motorway, it really doesn't matter whether you're driving a Ferrari or a Cinquecento. Besides, don't forget, my Jag's an old lady. A souped-up Cinquecento probably goes a whole lot faster than her. But, yes, it's at least two hours by car, probably more, depending on the traffic.'

Jess sipped her wine and listened as David pointed out iconic places like Cannes and Nice as they flew past. The coastline along here had been heavily developed and there were houses and huge apartment blocks as far as the eye could see, unlike the virgin forests above St-Tropez. From up here in the plane, the clear blue sea below was almost transparent and the boats they spotted looked as if they were hanging in mid-air. It was an enchanting view.

A few minutes later, the co-pilot came out to tell them they were about to make their final descent. Jess swallowed the last of her wine, refused a top-up, and caught David's eye.

'Would you mind if I hung onto you again?'

'I'd be disappointed if you didn't.'

This time she grabbed hold of him with both hands for good measure. Looking down, she clearly saw Monte Carlo, with its crowded harbour and mass of high-rise buildings. The feel of David beside her more than compensated for the slightly bumpy descent – although the actual contact with the water was very smooth – and the beautiful backdrop of the Italian coast also helped to calm her fears.

Where they landed, the mountains came right down to the coast and plunged vertically into the sea. There were far fewer buildings visible here and the area looked really quite unspoilt – no doubt because the terrain was so inhospitable. The engine revved as they headed towards the shore and then, as the captain cut the power and silence descended upon them, Jess saw another launch appear out of a little rocky bay and head out to meet them.

'We'll be at the restaurant in five minutes.' David smiled again as he glanced down at her hands on his arm. Shyly, she removed them.

'Thanks for the support. So the restaurant's near here, is it?'

'Up there. Look.'

Jess followed David's pointing finger and spotted a low building, perched on a rocky outcrop, thirty or forty metres above a beautiful little cove.

The launch delivered them to a stone jetty and as they climbed out, the only sounds were the lapping of the water and the squawks of a handful of seagulls. It seemed unbelievable – so close to the bustle of the Côte d'Azur – to find somewhere so tranquil. She looked up and wondered how they – and David in particular – were going to get up the sheer rock face to the restaurant. She needn't have worried. Tucked into a deep fault in the rock was a glass lift that whisked them up in a matter of seconds. Waiting for them, as the lift doors opened, was a very smartly-dressed, dark-haired lady who gave David a beaming smile.

'*Signore Dupont, buona sera*. Welcome back.'

'Good evening, Stefania. It's good to be back.'

Jess heard a note of insecurity in his voice and shot him a covert glance. For a moment his eyes met hers and she read uncertainty in them. He was looking a bit nervous – presumably as this was his first outing since the accident. She reached over and caught his forearm briefly, giving him an encouraging squeeze.

Stefania led them to a table on a terrace with a panoramic view out over the sea. But it wasn't so much the view that astounded Jess as the other guests. The very first table she passed contained a group that included no fewer than two Formula One world champions, another a very famous – and noticeably very drunk – Hollywood film star on his own, while a discreet table for two in a distant shady corner held what might have been the third in line to the British crown with his fiancée. Jess gulped a few times and tried to remember how to recognise the symptoms of a panic attack.

As David made his way along the terrace on his crutches, a number of people recognised him and stood up to shake his hand or kiss his cheeks and wish him well. He responded to all of them, although the look of discomfort hadn't left his face. As for Jess, her knees were trembling so much, it was all she could do not to keel over. When they reached their table and she could sit down, she felt as if she had just done ten rounds in a boxing ring.

She looked across the table at David in awe.

'A *bit* posh? This place is incredible. I feel like I'm in a dream.'

'Don't worry about the people. It's the food that counts. And, believe me, this place really is incredible when it comes to food. I've been coming here for years and it's always been excellent.'

Jess found herself wondering how many girls he had brought here over the years and whether their reaction had been the same as hers. The thought of herself as just another in a long line of his girls was disconcerting and she had to struggle to keep the distaste off her face. For a moment, the dead eyes of Drugoi's 'companions' crossed her mind and she found herself reflecting that, as far as the other diners here tonight were concerned, she doubtless fell into that same category – something pretty on a rich man's arm. It wasn't a pleasant thought and she did her best to ignore it. But it wasn't easy.

Instead, she directed her attention to the view out across the little bay. The water was clear and transparent at the shore, and a rich deep blue further out. The only sign of human life was the vapour trail of a jet far above them, and a gaggle of expensive-looking speedboats and launches moored at the mouth of the bay – presumably those used by their fellow diners. It was stunningly beautiful but, the more she looked around, the more she felt like a fish out of water – albeit in a seafood restaurant.

'So, first impressions?'

'It's just it's all so… so amazing.'

He must have picked something up from her tone. She saw him nod.

'But you don't like it.'

'No, David, no. Of course not. How could anybody not like a place like this? It's just that it's a bit…' Her voice tailed off uncertainly as she did her best to think of an appropriate adjective. *Ostentatious* sprang to mind, but she didn't mean to sound rude. The fact was that he was right – she didn't like it. Or rather, she thought to herself, it wasn't really the place, it was the fact of finding herself in the midst of such opulence. She had been out to a fair number of posh restaurants in London with Rafael and his friends, but nothing like this. She didn't belong here, and she knew she was so far outside her comfort zone she could have been on another planet. She saw him nod his head again.

'That's sort of what I expected. If it helps, I feel the same way now. I've been wondering about it for ages and it struck me forcefully the moment we walked in here. It's a lovely place and, like I said, the food is to die for, but I no longer feel comfortable here – and it's not because of my legs. Once upon a time I felt at home in environments like this, but that's all changed. And I'm glad you feel the same way.'

To her surprise – and delight – he reached across the table and caught hold of her hand in his.

'I owe you so much. I wanted to give you a treat. That's why I thought I'd bring you here, but it was also to prove something to myself. You may think you feel out of place here, but so do I now. I realise that. Those months in the hospital really affected me. They changed me.'

At that moment, a waiter appeared with menus and a wine list, and this meant that she had to relinquish David's hand – with a feeling of regret. There were no prices marked on the menu – at least not on the one given to her – but in a place like this, that didn't come as a big surprise. She scanned through the different dishes on offer – all written in three languages: Italian, French and English – and wondered what to choose. There were so many things there she had never

ever tried, and several that meant nothing to her at all. What on earth was *Amberjack tartare on watermelon ice crush with coffee powder*? After a few minutes, she looked across at David.

'What do you suggest?'

'The menu here changes regularly so there are some dishes on the menu tonight that I've never had. It depends how you feel. Personally, I think I'm going to go for stuff I've had here before and loved. I'll start with their mixed seafood antipasti, followed by deep-fried zucchini flowers with caviar. If I'm still hungry after that, I might have something simple like a plate of pasta or sea bass.'

'Zucchini… courgette flowers?'

'That's right. They have a big bright yellow flower. Here they deep fry the flowers and serve them with caviar and warm toast. It's exquisite – at least I think so. And the seafood starter is really not to be missed. It's sort of their signature dish.'

Jess shut her menu and dropped it on the table.

'Then I put myself in your hands. I'll have what you're having.'

'And what about wine? White suit you? They've got a stunning Menetou-Salon – at least they used to have. Would that do?'

'I have no idea what a Menetou-Salon is, but, like I said, I'm in your hands.'

Menetou-Salon turned out to be a white wine from the Loire Valley, near Sancerre, and this one was quite simply the best wine Jess had ever tasted. It was crisp, it was dry, and yet it left a rich, lingering taste of honey in the mouth after every mouthful.

The seafood antipasti were a voyage of discovery. First, Jess and David were each brought a small plate with three large prawns in a spicy, rusty red sauce. These were delightful and Jess ate them with relish, wondering what the courgette flowers for the next course were going to taste like. However, she had a long wait before they reached the courgette flowers. No sooner had they finished the prawns than their plates were removed and replaced with new plates, this time with a cold salad of tiny octopus in olive oil. These were followed by sashimi with homemade green wasabi sauce. After this came three exquisite grilled sardines, arranged in the shape of a triangle with a lone scallop in the middle, and so it went on. And on. And on.

After almost an hour, Jess watched the final little plate of starters disappear back into the kitchen and gave a deep sigh.

'Now I understand why you brought me here. That food was unbelievable.'

'So you liked it?' David's expression was inscrutable.

'I loved it, David. All of it. Even those spiny black things with the slimy yellow innards.'

He laughed. 'The sea urchins. Here in Italy they call them *ricci di mare* – "sea hedgehogs". They're a real delicacy, but I'll grant you they wouldn't win any beauty contests.' His eyes met hers for a moment. 'So are you happy we came here?'

Jess nodded emphatically. She glanced around and saw that the tables were now almost all full, but she didn't dare check out the faces of the new arrivals in case she found herself even more embarrassed. She looked back at David.

'It's without doubt far and away the best food I've ever had in my life, and the view is terrific. And my dinner companion's pretty great as well.' She reached over and caught hold of his hand. 'You'll have to excuse me if I was a bit overwhelmed at first. This sort of thing is all so new, so different.'

To her delight he raised her hand to his lips and kissed her softly on the knuckles.

'Nothing to excuse. In fact, I'm delighted we both feel the same way – not that I always did.' Seeing the expression on her face, he went on to explain. 'Before the accident – back in my previous existence – I used to do a lot of this sort of thing. I once flew to Marrakesh for dinner and back again, just for the hell of it. You do stupid things when you've got stupid amounts of money.'

He was still holding her hand in his and his eyes were trained downwards onto it as he continued.

'The accident didn't just affect me physically. It made me do a lot of thinking about my life.' Just for a moment he raised his eyes towards her. 'I spent all my life before then thinking I was immortal. I did all sorts of crazy things, took appalling risks, without the idea of dying, or being injured, even crossing my mind. Now, over these past months – most of them lying on my back – I've had a lot of time to think.'

He kept hold of her hand as a waiter appeared, removed the bottle from the ice bucket, replenished both glasses, and then disappeared again like a ghost.

'Coming here is something I've been dreaming of for months. You know you said Hope used to spend ages dreaming of St-Tropez? Well, when I was at my lowest ebb – and believe me, that was low – the one thing I kept dreaming of was this place, and the antipasti we've just had.'

'I can believe that. It's been amazing. Yes, I can imagine you lying there in your hospital bed, dreaming of this fabulous food. And, like I say, I'm having a wonderful time – it just took me a little while to acclimatise. But above all, I'm

266

honoured – and very grateful – that you chose me to come with you on your first outing.'

'I'm the one who's honoured. And I hope it won't be the last.' He released her hand as a waiter approached. 'Well, anyway, next time, you choose where we go.' He caught her eye for a few seconds. 'That's if you want there to be a next time?'

'Do you need to ask?'

The bright yellow courgette flowers were lightly fried and so delicate in texture and flavour, they almost melted on the tongue. The taste of the caviar was amazing. She took her time over the dish, savouring every mouthful and glancing over, from time to time, at the man across the table from her. After a while, seeing him looking as relaxed as she had ever seen him, she decided to ask something a bit more personal.

'So, when you were lying in hospital, what else did you dream of – apart from this place? What about people?'

He had just cleared his plate and he sat back, taking a big mouthful of mineral water before replying.

'I thought about my mum. You know she died last year. And I thought about my dad. He's had a tough time.' He caught her eye. 'I now realise I could have done so much more for both of them.'

'In what way?'

'I used to fly back over here for a few days when I could, but I spent most of my time in California working – or enjoying myself. Even when I knew she was sick, I could have made so much more time to spend with her, but I didn't. And after her death, I could have been – should have been – so much more supportive of my dad, but I wasn't.'

Jess could hear the guilt in his voice and she did her best to reassure him.

'They both knew about your job. You've done so amazingly well – that needs an awful lot of time and effort. I'm sure they understood that.'

'I wish I could believe that.'

Jess did her best to move the conversation on.

'And what about all your friends?'

Jess would dearly have liked to add the words *girlfriend* or *wife*, but she didn't dare. As it was, he answered her unspoken question without needing to be asked.

'I used to have a lot of friends – male and female. There was one girl I was very fond of, but, looking back on it, I treated her terribly.'

Jess looked up in surprise.

'Why, what did you do?'

'I neglected her. Of course I bought her stuff, I took her places, I helped her career – she's an actress – but I see now that she was never the most important thing in my life. She wanted kids. I thought they would slow me down too much, so I said no. She wanted me to spend more time with her, but I was far more interested in building up the business and in all the crazy things I was doing. I worked around the clock and I used to dump her in a heartbeat if somebody called up and suggested climbing El Capitan, or if there was a powerboat race coming up.'

'And what happened?'

'The inevitable – she left me. That was a few years ago. At the time I was devastated, but, thinking back on it, she did the right thing. It turned out all right for her. I've seen her from time to time since then. She got married a year or two ago and she's got a gorgeous little baby girl.'

'So do you think you're different now? Does the idea of a family appeal now?'

'If you'd asked me a year ago, I'd probably still have said no, but, after everything that's happened, the new David Dupont – let's call him Dupont 2.0 – would say yes.' He took a sip of wine and looked across the table at her. 'You see, the results of the accident aren't just the physical ones you can see. I've changed, Jess. A lot. I've grown up. I'm a lot different now from the selfish, immature person I was before. I'm pretty sure that if you'd known me before the accident, you wouldn't have liked me.'

'I can't believe that.'

'It's true. All I was interested in was myself, my work, and all the things my money allowed me to do. You find yourself living in a crazy world, among crazy people, doing senseless things, and you start to believe that it's what you want. Months in a hospital bed and legs that don't work are a pretty brutal form of cold turkey, but the result is what you see before you. Whether we're talking about work, relationships or children, I really have changed.'

He took another sip of wine and looked across the table at her.

'What about you, Jess?'

'What? Work, babies or boyfriends?'

'Any of them.'

'I haven't really thought much about men for a while.' She caught his eye. 'I had a boyfriend for a couple of years, but that fell apart back before Christmas, and this year I've been concentrating on my career more than anything – until that bit of unpleasantness with the Russian. As far as babies are concerned, a normal prerequisite is a man, and I haven't got one of those any more. If I manage to find the right one of those then, yes, I think babies might be a rather good idea – as long as I can juggle family and career. I enjoy being an architect, you know.'

The waiter appeared to clear their plates and he enquired if they would like anything else. David glanced across at Jess.

'Some fish? A steak? Some pasta, maybe?'

Jess shook her head. 'Nothing, thanks. All that fish for starters has filled me up. But I'd be happy to watch you, if you're still hungry. And I suppose there's a chance I might be able to squeeze a little bit of dessert down a bit later on.'

'How about I get a plate of pasta and two forks? You can have a forkful or two if you like the look of it.'

'You go ahead, but the way I'm feeling at the moment, I doubt if I'll feel like even tasting it.'

In fact, when the plate of pasta appeared, Jess couldn't resist trying it. David pushed it into the middle of the table and handed her one of the two forks the waiter had brought. Apart from the thin strips of homemade pasta, the plate was laden with clams, mussels, langoustines and chunks of what was unmistakably lobster. It was utterly delicious and, in spite of her conviction that she was full, she managed to eat several big mouthfuls before admitting defeat. As David finished the rest, she sat back and let her mind roam.

She was delighted that he had opened up to her tonight, even telling her about his inner feelings and the sea change he claimed to have undergone as a result of the accident – not to mention his treatment of his former girlfriend. He looked as handsome as ever, although she knew full well just how vulnerable he still was. Holding his hand had felt very good, and the touch of his lips had sent shivers throughout her body. She glanced around the terrace, observing the rich and famous people who surrounded her, and wondered if he really meant it when he said he had finished with such ostentatious company. Certainly, he had sounded sincere and she tended to believe him.

It was fully dark by the time they left. After the restaurant's version of Death by Chocolate as a dessert, Jess felt sure she wouldn't be able to eat again for a week. The launch ran them round the headland into the bay of Monaco and from there they took the helicopter home. As David had said, it was very noisy, but they were provided with headphones. She hung onto his arm all the way home and she would have leant her head against him, but for the headphones.

They landed quite a way outside St-Tropez and a sleek Mercedes taxi was waiting to drive them back to the villa. When they arrived home, Jess was amazed to see that it was still only eleven o'clock. They had travelled two hundred miles by car, boat and aircraft, and had a long lazy dinner, all in a matter of a very few hours.

As the taxi drove off and silence returned, Jess looked across at him. He was standing in the middle of the gravel parking area, resting on his crutches, the floodlights in the umbrella pine shedding an orange glow across his head and face. She went up to him and gently laid a hand on his arm.

'Would you like to come back to the guest house for coffee?'

His expression was difficult to read. For a few moments he didn't reply, before, evidently, arriving at a decision.

'Thanks, Jess, but I'd better get back to the computer and see what's happening in California. Some other time, maybe.'

Doing her best to contain the wave of disappointment that surged through her, Jess reached up to kiss him goodnight. At the last minute he turned his head and her kiss landed on his cheek. She kissed him primly on the other cheek and then stepped back. For whatever reason, he was keeping things friendly, nothing more.

'Goodnight, Jess, and thank you.'

His voice was warm, but low.

'I'm the one who should be thanking you, David. That was a totally memorable evening. I'll never forget it for as long as I live.'

'Next time, you choose.'

Jess shook her head. 'Next time *you* choose. You know me well enough by now.' She glanced across at him in the lamplight and smiled. 'And I know you a lot better now, too. Goodnight, David, and thanks again.'

Chapter 23

Jess didn't sleep well that night. This might have been partly because of the exotic foods she had eaten, but she knew full well that it was her brain that was causing her insomnia. She eventually got up and took Brutus for an unusually long walk in the starlight, but even this didn't help. She then found herself lying wide awake in bed into the small hours, running through the events of that night over and over again.

She had felt sure she had read attraction in his eyes, and the touch of his hand against hers, as well as the kiss of her fingers, had been sensual rather than just sociable. Apart from her initial wobbly moment when she had found herself catapulted into the midst of the great and the good – or not so good – it had been a warm, cosy evening and she had come away feeling a whole lot closer to him. Where the evening would have led if he had accepted her invitation for coffee remained to be seen but, deep down, she knew she would have been happy if it had led to her bed. And yet, he had turned her down. Why?

Was there somebody else? He and his girlfriend had split up 'a few years ago', so there would have been ample time for him to form other significant relationships since then. But as Hope had pointed out, if there was another woman, where was she?

And if it wasn't another woman, was it something physical? For a moment she wondered just how damaged he had been. Maybe his injuries extended to other parts of his body as well as his legs and he was afraid, ashamed, uncertain if he was capable of forging a physical relationship? The ramifications of this kept her awake for a considerable time, but without leading her to any firm conclusion.

And, then, of course, there was the other explanation. Maybe, seeing her there in the restaurant, like a fish out of water, he had realised just how deep the gulf between them really was. He had invented all that stuff about being a changed man to hide the fact that he had worked out that she just wouldn't fit into his lifestyle.

She finally must have drifted off to sleep some time around dawn, but she was rudely awakened at eight o'clock by her phone. She picked it up and was pleased when she saw who was on the other end.

'Hello Mrs Dupont. How lovely to hear from you. Where are you now?'

'Jess, my dear, how good to hear your voice. We're in the middle of the Pacific Ocean. We left the Galapagos Islands yesterday and we're heading west. So, how are you getting on?'

She and Jess chatted for a few minutes under the watchful eyes of Brutus, who was waiting for his morning walk. Jess gave her a progress report on her beloved dog, and then she moved on to the humans. She described the works that had started in the villa and how George and David were looking and sounding so much more positive. When she told her about the drinks party there had been on the fifteenth, Mrs Dupont sounded delighted. Jess had already told her the tale of Hope's relationship with Max and its crushing termination, followed by its resurrection from the ashes, and now she told her how happy the two of them appeared to be together on the yacht. Mrs Dupont sounded pleased for Hope, but, clearly, was more interested in Jess.

'So what about you, Jess? Have you found yourself a handsome man as well?'

'I'm fine, Mrs Dupont. To be honest, I'm spending a good bit of time with David.' Remembering the way things had finished the night before, she was quick to add clarification. 'But, don't worry, there's nothing romantic going on there. I just enjoy spending time with him and he's really starting to come out of his shell.' She went on to give a brief account of the previous evening's outing, but without any mention of touching, kissing or emotions. To her surprise, Mrs Dupont made an unexpected confession.

'I'm so glad you're spending time with David. I'll be totally honest and let you into a little secret. When I asked you to go over to St-Tropez, it wasn't just for Brutus's sake. I'm sure you'll think I'm just a meddling old busybody, but I just knew you'd be good for David. You're pretty, you're bright, and you know your own mind. And from what you've said, your influence is working wonders. And, just between the two of us, if romance were to blossom between you and David, nobody would be happier than me.'

'Well, somehow, I don't think anything's going to happen on that front. His life and mine are so very different.'

'My point exactly.' There was a triumphant note in the old lady's voice. 'He needs to make a good few changes to his lifestyle.'

'I'm afraid his accident has already done that for him.'

'Of course, but I'm not just talking about all those crazy sports he was doing. He needs to realise that he's not a young man any more. He needs to settle down.'

'We had a good long talk last night. I think he realises that himself.'

'You see? That's your influence, Jess.'

By the time the conversation ended, Jess was thoroughly confused. She climbed out of bed, greeted the effusive Labrador, and pulled on an old T-shirt and shorts. As she and Brutus walked down to the beach, her brain was still churning – now adding this latest revelation to the mix.

So Mrs Dupont had had her earmarked for David from the start. That in itself was unexpected enough, but even more unexpected was the revelation that the old lady wanted Jess to help David change his lifestyle. How she was supposed to do that, and what David's reaction might be, remained to be seen.

Back at the guest house after Brutus's walk, Jess was in for another surprise. When she opened her laptop to check her mail, she was amazed to find one from Graham, her former employer, sent the previous evening. As was his way, it was long and convoluted, but the upshot was that things had changed at work. They now wanted her back, in a more responsible position, with a hefty increase in pay – to begin as soon as she was free.

Absently, she gave Brutus his breakfast, made herself some coffee and toast, and sat down at the outside table. She could hear birds singing in the trees beyond the house and a wonderful scent of roses floated in all the way from the walled garden. The morning sunlight still hadn't reached the ground and it was shady and cool out here, although the cloudless sky promised to produce another scorching hot day. At her feet, the happy dog was rolling around on his back, rubbing himself dry on the flagstones. It was an idyllic scene and this was an idyllic place, but now, with the arrival of this email, reality had returned – with a bang.

How on earth could Graham possibly expect her to docilely return to the fold after being booted out so unceremoniously? And, more interesting still, what had brought about this change of heart? At the same time, the chance to leap up a grade and find herself earning a good bit more than before wasn't to be sniffed at. What on earth did all this mean? She needed help, so she picked up her phone and called her best friend.

'Hi, Hope, it's me.'

'Hi, Jess, how's it going?'

'Fine, thanks. Where are you?'

'Monte Carlo.'

'Wow! I was there just last night.'

'With you-know-who?'

'With David, yes.'

'And is he still with you now, or has he done the walk of shame back to his room?'

'No, Hope, nothing happened. He slept in his bed and I slept in mine.' Although, Jess reflected to herself, she had done precious little sleeping – but not for the reason to which Hope was alluding.

'But you're still friends?' Hope sounded concerned. 'You didn't do a Drugoi on him and thump him, did you?'

'Why does everybody think I thumped Drugoi? And, no, I didn't thump anybody – especially not David. And he and I are definitely still friends, very good friends.' Just how good remained to be established. 'But let me tell you about this email I've just opened.'

She related the contents of Graham's email to Hope and waited for her response. It didn't take long.

'I reckon it's him – your Russian friend – Drugoi.'

'Drugoi?'

'Yes. You saved his life – well actually I had a hand in that as well, but what the hell. You wouldn't take his money, so he found another way of thanking you. I reckon he must have contacted Graham and told him to give you back your job – or else. After all, he's the one who got you fired in the first place.'

Jess turned the idea over in her mind and, the more she thought about it, the more she had to agree that Drugoi might indeed have had a hand in it.

'You might well be right, Hope.'

'So, what are you going to do, Jess? Do you tell Graham to stuff it, or do you go back there? It's more money, after all.'

'After the way Graham treated me, I really don't know.'

'Business is business, Jess. We're halfway through the summer already. Before long it'll be time to head back to the UK and return to reality. You need a job. He's offering you what sounds like a pretty good one.'

Hope was right. In less than a month and a half, it would be time to up sticks and head for home again. At that very moment, a beautiful zebra-striped butterfly flew past and settled on the head of the statue in the middle of the courtyard, flexing its wings gently up and down in the first rays of sun to reach down to it. Jess took a long, nostalgic breath. It was going to be very, very tough to leave this little piece of paradise.

'I really don't know, Hope. I'll sleep on it before replying, anyway. So, what about you? What happens to you in six weeks' time? Are you coming home with me and Brutus?'

'Good old Brutus. I miss him, you know. How is my big hairy friend?'

'Your big hairy friend is a very happy dog. And, just this morning, when he came out of the water, I could count all his ribs. Don't get me wrong – he isn't as thin as he should be yet, but he's getting there. He's currently lying on his back at my feet, grunting to himself – can you hear him? Anyway, what about you, then? What happens at the end of August?'

'Some interesting developments on that front, Jess.'

'Such as?'

'I'll tell you on Saturday if you're around.'

'I'll be here. Does this mean you'll be back at St-Trop this weekend?'

Jess was delighted at the prospect of catching up. Hope had been away now for almost three weeks.

'Yes, we're heading back to St-Trop today, as there's bad weather forecast for Friday. We'll be fairly busy tomorrow and Friday but, as the next charter party doesn't get here until Sunday afternoon, Max and I wondered if you and David might like to come and join us on *Helios* for lunch on Saturday. I was going to ring you this morning to ask, but you beat me to it. We thought we might invite a few other friends along and make a little party of it.'

'That sounds brilliant, Hope. Yes, I'd love to, and I'm sure David will come along if he's free.'

'And do bring my big hairy friend as well.'

–

After a day spent washing clothes and mowing the increasingly dry, yellow lawn, Jess was pottering about in the kitchen when her phone rang. Her heart lifted as she saw who it was.

'David, hi. Good to hear from you.'

'Hi, Jess. Look, I know it's a bit last minute, but I wondered if you felt like coming out for dinner tonight?'

'Dinner again? Are you trying to fatten me up or something?' His voice had sounded a bit tense, so she was doing her best to lighten things up.

'No, it's just that I reckon I know the right restaurant for you – for both of us. And it would be good to see you.'

'It would be great to see you too, David. Well, if you're sure, I'd love that. What time do you want to go?'

'Leave here at sevenish, say. And, Jess, you don't need to dress up for this one, I promise.'

He was doing his best to sound cheerful, but Jess could hear something else in his voice and she wondered what was bothering him.

'Seven it is. Do you want me to drive tonight? I'm quite a good driver. I promise I won't frighten you too much.'

'That's very kind, but you know I love driving my old girl. We'll go in the Jag – if that's all right with you. And it's not because I'm scared of your driving.'

'Well all right, if you insist. Now I'd better go and get changed.'

'Shorts and a T-shirt will do just fine.'

Jess decided on shorts and one of her new tops. This one revealed a bit more skin than she was used to, but she knew there wouldn't be many occasions when she would be able to wear something as skimpy as this when she went back to London. Besides, she told herself, it might even stir some interest in David. As she stood in the shower, she wondered what she had heard in his voice. She knew him well enough by now to realise that there was something bothering him.

She was still pondering this as she walked through the walled garden to meet up with him. The box hedges and flower beds here were looking much more presentable now. George's hard work was clearly paying off and Jess was delighted – more for him than for the garden. Knowing that he was getting out into the fresh air and enjoying his former hobby was definitely a very good omen for the future.

David was already sitting in the car when she got there. The roof was down and he looked as handsome as ever. She lowered herself into the car and was delighted to see his eyes run across her body as she did so. She leant across towards him and kissed him on the cheeks. Then she drew back, but only a few inches, and gently lifted his sunglasses up onto his forehead so she was looking right into those magnetic blue eyes of his.

'Hello, David. You look good.'

'Not as good as you. You look amazing.'

For a moment a hint of a smile appeared on his face, but disappeared as soon as it had come. Jess could definitely see that something was worrying him and she wondered what it might be. She sat back in her seat as he started the engine.

'So, where are you taking me? And, please, after last night, could I be allowed to pay this time?'

David shook his head. 'Sorry, that's not negotiable. But I really hope you'll like the place we're going to. It's about half an hour away, in the hills.'

It was a delightful evening with hardly a breath of wind and not a cloud in the sky. It was hard to believe the weather forecast she had just heard. As always, weather was a safe topic of conversation, so she took refuge in it.

'Have you seen that we're supposed to be having a hurricane tomorrow?'

He glanced across at her as they waited for the electric gates to open fully.

'Not quite that bad, but there's a vicious-looking front coming across. It shouldn't be around for too long, but it'll certainly get very windy and unseasonably wet. They're talking about a month's rainfall in a few hours.'

'Well, at least tonight should be fine. So, tell me more. Where are we going?'

'It's a cellar.'

'A cellar? What, complete with rats, I suppose?' She grinned at him. 'Are you sure it's the right place to take a young lady?'

'It's the right place to take this young lady, I'm sure. It's a restaurant in the cellars of an old chateau. And it's all right – it's not a glitzy sort of chateau. I'm not taking you to Versailles. This place is pretty ramshackle, but the people are lovely and the food's great – not as fancy as last night, but I'm sure you'll like it.'

'If I'm with you, I know I'll enjoy myself.'

He made no response.

The restaurant was not so much a cellar as a series of rooms on the ground floor of an old fortress that perched high in the wooded hills. The ceilings were low, the walls rough stone, and the floors centuries-old terracotta tiles scarred by the passage of thousands upon thousands of feet. It was lovely and cool in there, as well as being very picturesque, and Jess immediately fell in love with it. They were shown to a little table for two in one of the inner rooms and Jess, after sitting down, looked across the table admiringly.

'So you really do know me well! This place is perfect, David. Thank you so much.'

He managed a smile and looked relieved. The owner was hovering in the background and, once they were seated, she stepped forward with a verbal menu. Jess listened hard and managed to understand at least half of it. By the sound of it, the speciality of the house appeared to be meat cooked on a charcoal grill. That suited Jess fine. Once again she and David decided to both have the same and they chose a wild mushroom salad, followed by a mixed grill. Jess put in a plea for small portions, but her pleas fell on deaf ears.

The raw mushroom salad, served with shavings of mature goat's cheese and local olive oil, was delightful, and Jess had no trouble clearing her plate. Then the meat arrived on a wooden platter – not a lot smaller than a dustbin lid – and it tasted as good as it looked. In consequence, conversation was fairly limited during the meal and when Jess finally set down her knife and fork and admitted defeat, she looked forward to hearing what was bothering David.

She decided not to burden him with her job offer, and her uncertainty about how to respond to Graham. That could wait until she got to the bottom of what was bothering him. All the way through the meal he had been caring and attentive, but she could tell he had something on his mind. She waited until he, too, gave up on the mountain of food and then she did a bit of digging.

'You're very quiet tonight, David.'

'It's difficult to speak and eat – and there's certainly been enough to eat. Did you enjoy it, Jess?'

'I loved the food and I love the place. You've got it dead right – this is my sort of place.'

'I'm sorry last night was so different. Like I said, I wanted to give you a treat, but neither of us fit into a place like that anymore.'

'Last night was amazing, memorable, unforgettable, but I'd be lying if I said I felt comfortable there among the glitterati. Somewhere like this suits me down to the ground. Like I say – you really do know me well now. Besides, from what you were saying, this sort of place suits you down to the ground as well.'

For some reason this caused him to drop his eyes and start talking vaguely about tomorrow's storm. Jess gave him until their *crèmes brûlées* arrived before taking another stab at it.

'Is something bothering you, David? You seem a bit down.'

'I'm fine.'

As answers went, this was pretty non-committal and it only increased her suspicions, but it took until they got back to the villa before he finally opened up – a bit.

When they got back and he parked underneath the umbrella pine, he switched off the engine, but made no attempt to get out. Jess could feel the tension in him and she sat quietly, waiting for him to say what was on his mind. It took all of four or five minutes of silence before he turned towards her. His eyes sparkled green in the orange light shining down from the tree above them.

'Jess, I like you a lot, an awful lot.'

To her delight, his hands reached over and landed softly on her shoulders.

'I like you an awful lot, too, David.'

Jess could hear the emotion in her voice and he couldn't have missed it. He leant towards her and gently pulled her so that their lips met. Her eyes closed as he kissed her more tenderly than she had ever been kissed before. This time the tremor that went through her wasn't so much physical desire – although that was strongly there as well – but something much more elusive. Never in her life had she felt anything like this before and she could feel her eyes welling up under the force of the emotion she was experiencing.

Finally, he drew back a few inches and she opened her eyes again. The light sparkled in his and she saw the raw emotion on display. She caught his hands in hers and gave them a gentle squeeze.

'That was really lovely, David.'

'It was.' She felt his lips brush hers again and then, finally, he started speaking.

'Jess, there's something I've got to say to you, and it isn't going to be easy. I wish things could be different, but they aren't, I'm afraid.'

Jess felt a cold stab in her stomach as she listened to his words. What on earth could he mean…?

'I'm leaving on Saturday. I'm flying back to the States and I don't know when I'll be back.'

'You're leaving?'

'I'm afraid so.'

'What's the matter? Is it a business thing? Is there a problem?'

He hesitated. 'Something like that.'

She picked up on his hesitation.

'Is it me, David? Is it something I've said or done? Tell me if it is. I certainly didn't…'

His lips pressed gently against hers once more.

'It's not you, Jess. You're perfect.'

'But if I'm perfect, why do you have to go off and leave me?'

'I just do, Jess. I'm sorry, very sorry, but I have no choice.'

Jess didn't know what to say. She had never felt so abandoned. Even the shock of being told she had lost her job didn't even begin to approach the feelings now coursing through her body. She heard him clear his throat.

'I've loved getting to know you, and being with you and, like I say, I wish things could be different, but I have no choice. I have to go.' He was keeping his voice studiously expressionless. 'Thank you for everything you've done. Thank you for being Jess. I'll always remember what you did for me.' Releasing her hands, he caught her cheeks between his fingers and his mouth pressed hard against hers as he kissed her with real passion. In spite of her bewilderment, she felt a wave of arousal that only further confused her. Then he drew back, released his hold on her and opened the driver's door. Remarkably nimbly, he swung himself out and onto his feet and by the time Jess had undone her safety belt and got out in her turn, he was already resting on his crutches. His eyes met hers for a second or two and she read what could have been despair in them.

'Goodbye, Jess, it's been wonderful knowing you.'

He turned and made his way across to the front door of the villa and disappeared inside, leaving Jess feeling totally numb.

Chapter 24

Jess did manage to sleep for a few hours that night, but that was only because she hadn't slept much the previous night. When she woke, however, she didn't feel rested, she felt drained – physically and emotionally. All night long she had been wrestling with what he had said, analysing his words, doing her best to read between the lines, and make some sense of what might be behind his decision. She had felt tenderness and passion and definite attraction. Why, then, did he tell her he had to leave? Why had he said, 'I have no choice. I have to go'?

She heard the clicking of Brutus's nails on the floor tiles as he came in to tell her it was time for his early morning walk, so she pulled on some clothes and followed him out. The sky was no longer clear today. A few patches of blue remained, but a strong wind was blowing and an ominous bank of dark grey clouds was building over the hills. It looked as though the weather forecasters had got it right – something nasty was coming. The grey conditions further served to dampen her already gloomy mood.

She had cried a lot overnight – more than she had cried over any man, even back in her years of teenage angst. Even before he had kissed her in the car, her feelings towards him had been strengthening. But that kiss had pushed her over the edge, spinning her irresistibly towards a depth of emotion that was completely new to her. And then, just like that, he had pulled the rug out from underneath her and left her with nothing – not even a clear explanation.

She sat in the shelter of a big rock, her back to the wind, and watched the dog swimming happily, without a care in the world – apart from where his next meal was coming from – and she envied him. After a while, she glanced back towards the villa in the hope that George might be about. Maybe he would be able to shed more light on just what was driving David's sudden decision to return to America. But, for once, the terrace was empty and there was no sign of father or son.

As Jess and the dog tramped back up the slope, Antoinette appeared at the kitchen door.

'Hello, Jess. You've got a letter.'

Jess's eyes widened. 'A letter for me?' She hadn't received any mail since arriving here. 'Who's it from?' For a moment she wondered if it might be from David – maybe with an explanation he hadn't been able to articulate face to face.

Antoinette shook her head. 'I don't know, but it was hand delivered. Look, it's just got your name on it.'

Jess took the long white envelope from Antoinette and saw that it was simply addressed to:

Jessica Milton
Villa les Romarins

She realised she had never seen David's handwriting, but, somehow, this looked a good bit more flowery than she would have expected. Nevertheless, although she could see Antoinette was fascinated to know who had sent the letter,

288

she decided to read it when she was alone, just in case it was from him, and it brought about a further emotional reaction.

'Thanks, Antoinette, I'll read it back home. Brutus is dying for his breakfast.'

True to her word, Jess waited until she was home and had given the dog his breakfast. She even delayed opening it a bit longer while she made herself a cup of coffee. Finally she sat down at the kitchen table and opened the letter.

It wasn't from David.

It was a typewritten letter on headed paper belonging to a firm called *PM Design*. The name meant nothing to her, so her eyes flicked down to the signature at the bottom and a ray of light began to dawn. It was signed Philippe Mailly. This, she suddenly remembered, was the name of the smiley older gentleman she had met at George's party. It appeared that he was the senior partner of a firm of architects here in St-Tropez and, as she read down the page in amazement, it became clear that he was offering her a job. As an architect. Here in St-Tropez.

She read and re-read the letter several times, checking a couple of the words in her French dictionary, to be sure she had got it right. But there was no doubt about it – he was offering her a job and inviting her to telephone to arrange to meet him and his colleagues to discuss this offer in more detail. She remembered how George had introduced her to M. Mailly and she also remembered how a few weeks earlier – when she had refused payment for drawing up plans for the alterations to the villa – George had told her he would have to see if he could come up with 'some other way of saying thank you'. Somehow she felt pretty sure the introduction to Monsieur Mailly, leading to this job offer, was indeed George's doing and she smiled at the thought of his kindness.

However, if her head had been spinning before, this further confused her. If this letter had arrived a day or two earlier, it would have been the very best news she could have imagined. Now, after David's bombshell last night, she didn't know what to think. She loved St-Tropez and the idea of living here forever had been uppermost in her mind for weeks now – that and a certain Mr David Dupont. Now, just as she had been refused one, the other appeared. What on earth was going on and what was she to do?

She pulled out her phone and called Hope.

'Hi Hope, it's me – I've got a problem.'

'What's up, Jess?' Hope must have picked up on Jess's tone, and she sounded concerned for her.

'Have you got a few minutes? This could take a bit of time to explain.'

'As long as it takes. I've already done the breakfasts, so I'm sitting on the deck with a coffee, enjoying the last few rays of sunshine before the big storm hits.'

Jess glanced at her own coffee – still untouched.

'Well, Hope, it's like this…'

Hope listened in silence as Jess told her everything David had said to her the previous night in the car, and then about M. Mailly's job offer. Finally, she ground to a halt with a simple, but fundamental, question.

'What do I do now?'

She picked up her cold coffee and took a big mouthful.

'Do you want the job?'

'I don't know.' Jess could hear the pathetic note in her own voice and tried again. 'The thing is that I'd love to live in St-Tropez, but then David…'

'Jess, let's just say for a moment that David carries out his threat of going to the USA and he never comes back.'

'But his dad's here…'

'Forget short visits. Just imagine he's gone back to the US and you never see him again. Try to erase him from your mind completely for a moment. Which would you prefer, St-Tropez or London? Don't forget, you've got job offers in both places now.'

Jess glanced out of the French windows into the courtyard where the dog was wriggling about on his back on the flag-stones like a freshly-landed fish, grunting happily to himself. The perfume of roses was, if anything, even stronger today – strong enough to blot out the wet dog smell – and the birds were still singing. She knew she loved this place, the beaches, the sea, the wildflowers on the hillside and so many people she had met. It really was a wonderful place to live in, but, of course, if she took the job here, she would almost certainly find herself living in a tiny flat across the bay in Ste-Maxime, or even further away. She wouldn't be in a wonderful house with a private pool, only a few steps from the beach. It could never be like this again.

'I really don't know, Hope. On the one hand, I suppose the sensible thing would be for me to go back to London and accept Graham's offer. At least I know what I'd be letting myself in for there. What if I don't like working for Monsieur Mailly? By refusing Graham's offer, I'd be burning my boats.'

'All right, then, let's turn the question round. Supposing David were to come knocking on your door in ten minutes' time, pledging eternal love and asking you to marry him.' She ignored Jess's snort of derision. 'Would you take the St-Tropez job or the London job?'

'Well, ignoring the fact that that isn't going to happen, there's no doubt about it. I'd take the St-Tropez job without a moment's hesitation.'

'Well, if you want my advice, I'd say you have to speak to David before he goes off to America. Get him to tell you just what's behind this sudden disappearing act and tell him you've been offered the job here. See what he says. If he tells you he's got a wife or a boyfriend in San Francisco, at least you'll know where you stand. Maybe it really is just a business thing and it can be sorted out soon. And, if he knows you're going to be here for a while, he'll be able to come back, say, in the autumn and you can pick up where you left off, sitting in his lovely old Jaguar, with his tongue down your throat.'

They talked for another few minutes, but without Jess managing to come to any firm conclusion. Deep down she felt sure Hope was right with her suggestion that she and David should talk some more, but his last words to her had been a final farewell. If he had wanted to spend more time with her before taking the plane to America, he could easily have done so. The fact that he hadn't spoke volumes. Pretty plainly, he didn't want to see her again.

Jess went out into the garden and took a good look at the sky. It was getting darker and darker, but it was still dry. The temperature was already high and it felt increasingly clammy. It was almost ten o'clock and the forecast had been for heavy rain, starting mid-morning. She decided that some fresh air before they got cooped up by the weather would be good for the Labrador and good for her, but the sooner they set off, the better, or they risked getting soaked. She made a snap decision, grabbed the car keys, and hurried across to the Range Rover with Brutus. David's Jaguar was still parked there, but there was no sign of him, and she wasn't sure if she was pleased or sorry. She wouldn't have known what to say if she had seen him. She still badly needed to make up her mind about that. She opened the boot door and, this time, Brutus had no trouble in jumping up into the car. This, more than anything else, was the living proof that his new lifestyle was working out.

The thought of changing lifestyles made her think of her telephone conversation with Mrs Dupont the previous day. The old lady had asked her to see that David changed his lifestyle and settled down – with or without Jess – but that was now looking less and less likely. Maybe his lifestyle was what was calling him away. Maybe he had seen that Jess didn't fit into his billionaire's lifestyle and so was heading back to other people – other women – who matched his tastes. She sighed to herself as she slammed the boot shut and got into the driver's seat.

She decided to head for the wooded hills, in the hope of finding shelter from the increasingly blustery wind. She took the road towards Ramatuelle and turned off when she came to the track that David had told her would lead to the wartime bunker. The Range Rover easily coped with the rutted surface as they ran down into the forest and she stopped when she reached the old stone house David had described to her. She parked alongside a tall stack of logs at the side of the track and opened the boot. Brutus came charging out full of vigour, no doubt delighted to find himself with a whole lot of new smells, and the two of them started making their way up a narrower track into the trees. From time to time there were piles of logs, evidently freshly cut, and the scent of resin was heavy in the air. It was steep, but it had clearly been used by a tractor fairly recently and it was easy to follow.

As they walked through the trees, the noise of the wind in the branches above them gradually increased and, as they emerged into a wide clearing where forestry work had recently been completed, Jess was physically blown back by the strength of it. She glanced up at the sky – now a scary battleship grey – the clouds low and so full of water they were almost black. Jess looked back down again at the dog who was standing, waiting to be told which direction to take.

'I think that's it as far as today's walk is concerned, Brutus. Back to the car.'

As they turned and headed back into the trees, she felt the first rain on her bare legs, blown in almost horizontally by the wind. Seconds later there was a loud rumble of thunder and, almost simultaneously, a flash of lightning that almost blinded her and had the dog cowering against her legs. The rain steadily increased in intensity until Jess and the dog were both drenched. The thunder and lightning were right over their heads and Jess began to feel a bit scared. The temperature was dropping like a stone and the ever-stronger wind was evaporating the water from her skin, making her feel really cold. She increased her pace, almost running down the hillside, the track now streaming with water, the dusty soil transformed into thick, unpleasant mud.

Then, just as she was sliding down a particularly steep part of the track, she sensed a movement out of the corner of her eye. As she turned her head, she glimpsed a whole chunk of the steep bank behind her collapse in a mudslide, coming crashing down against one of the piles of freshly-cut logs. To her horror, the whole pile lurched and seconds later she found herself running for her life as tons of timber came rolling down the hill behind her. Just as it appeared she was going to be crushed, she toppled forwards into a hole, landing heavily on her knees and elbows. Above her, the rumble of falling timber continued for some seconds until all movement had ceased.

Jess raised her head and looked around. She had fallen into a rectangular concrete trench, not a lot wider than her shoulders, the length of a bed, and deep enough for her to kneel, but not stand up. Above her, the light was almost completely obscured by a mass of wet timber that had landed across the opening and which, if the pit hadn't been there, would no doubt have crushed her to death. She gave a sincere sigh of relief when she realised what had happened.

Her relief didn't last long.

Raising herself onto her knees, she tried to shift the logs out of the way, but couldn't get them to move an inch. Presumably there were more logs piled on top and the weight was pressing down, imprisoning her in this concrete box. She wriggled about until she found a thin gap between two logs where she could see a little bit of foliage outside but, try as she might, she was unable to budge them. She could just about get one hand through the gap, but that was it. Then, just as the penny was dropping that she was trapped, the light was almost obscured by a familiar face.

'Brutus, you're all right.'

The dog's tongue reached down and licked her fingers as she took stock of her predicament. At least Brutus was all right, but she definitely wasn't. For the first time she inspected her knees and elbows and her hands came away covered in blood. She was able to move easily enough, so hopefully nothing was broken, but she had clearly scraped away a lot of skin and cut herself as she fell. She scooped up some water from the floor of the pit and washed the cuts as best she could. It was as she was doing this that she suddenly realised the significance of the water.

Outside, it was still pouring with rain – in monsoon proportions – and water was streaming in, down the sides of the concrete, and she could see that the trench was gradually starting to fill up. A wave of panic swept over her as she realised that when the water reached the top of the walls, she would drown. For the first time in her life, Jess found herself in a life-threatening situation. It was absolutely terrifying. She crouched there, shivering with fear and cold for some moments, before common sense kicked in. She needed help. Badly.

She wriggled about until she could remove her phone from her pocket and muttered a silent prayer of thanks when she saw it turn on. She knew that the emergency phone number here in France was 112, but as her fingers reached down to start dialling, she realised that she didn't really know how to describe to them where she was. The road to Ramatuelle, a forest track, then another forest track, and then an old wartime bunker almost completely hidden by bushes and, now, a pile of logs. By the time they worked that out, she would be dead.

Her brain was working overtime. Just as she was desperately trying to rehearse her story in French before phoning for help, she came up with a better idea. It had been Olivier, and then David, who had told her about this place. Without hesitation, she called David, praying that he would answer.

His phone rang and rang, and she had almost given up when, to her eternal relief, she heard his voice.

'Hello, Jess?' He sounded hesitant – no doubt after the way things had ended between them the other night.

'David, thank God. Listen, I'm in a hell of a mess. I'm trapped.'

She went on to tell him where she was and what had happened. As she was speaking, she felt the water reach her thighs. It was still pouring in.

'And the thing is that I'm trapped in a sort of concrete box and it's filling with water. Unless you can get somebody to get me out of here, I'm going to drown.'

'Listen to me, Jess.' His voice cut through her rising panic. He sounded calm and in control. 'Nobody's going to drown. I'll ring the emergency services now and we'll be with you in a matter of minutes. I know exactly where you are and I'll guide them to you. I'll call you from the car in a few minutes when I'm on my way, so just stay cool until we get there.' He paused for a moment. 'I'm not going to let anything happen to you, Jess. Trust me.'

The line went dead and Jess stared down at the phone, praying that he was right. As for staying cool, she was freezing. She became aware that she was shaking like a leaf, but there was nothing she could do to warm herself up. As much for Brutus's sake as for hers, she put her mouth to the gap between the logs and called the dog. He appeared straight away and she felt glad he hadn't run off. She crouched there for a few minutes, talking to him and, from time to time, putting her fingers up through the gap to be licked. It was very comforting to have another being alongside her, even if he was powerless to help.

Suddenly her phone rang and she almost dropped it in the water that had now reached her bottom.

'Hello, yes, David?'

'Hi Jess. It's all in hand. I've spoken to the fire brigade and they'll be with you in ten to fifteen minutes. I'm already

297

on the hill and I should be with you in five. Just hang on in there. All right?'

Jess felt a massive sense of relief. 'Yes, I'll be fine now. Just a bit cold. Thanks, David. Thank you so much.'

'So what about the dog? Is he in there with you?'

Jess sensed that he was trying to keep her talking and she did her best, even though her teeth were chattering by now.

'Brutus is right outside. When you see him, you'll know that I'm close by, under a pile of logs.'

'I told you when it rains here, it really rains. It's like driving through a waterfall.'

'All I can hear is falling water.'

'Dad did say the gardens need some rain.'

She knew he was trying to take her mind off her present predicament and she loved him for it.

'Maybe not quite this much – all in one go.'

'I'm turning off the road now.' There was a momentary pause. 'Listen, the track's very slippery, so I need two hands on the wheel. Sit tight. I'll be there soon.'

Jess tucked the phone into her breast pocket along with the car keys in an attempt to keep them out of the water. This was still rising steadily and she could now feel it almost up to her waist. Hopefully, he would be with her soon and she would be all right. Of course, she thought wildly, David wouldn't be able to do anything to help. Even if he managed to get his car along the forestry track as far as where she had left the Range Rover, there was no way the Jaguar would get up the slope to where she was, and he wouldn't be able to manage it on crutches. She just had to hope that the fire engine got there soon. At least David would be able to show them where she was.

She knelt there for what felt like an hour, but which was probably only a few minutes, doing her best to stop herself from shivering all over. She tried thinking of sunny beaches, hot cups of tea and that wonderful passionate kiss with David the other night. She didn't stop shivering, but it occupied her mind and stopped her from thinking about what was going to happen to her if the fire brigade didn't get to her in time.

Then she heard something other than running water. It was Brutus and he was barking, something he had hardly done since leaving London. She put her ear to the gap in the logs and strained to hear something other than the rain. Suddenly, she heard a splashing sound and she started shouting, waving her fingers through the hole. Seconds later, a strong, warm hand caught hold of hers and gave it an encouraging squeeze.

'Jess, it's me. Listen, have you get the keys to the Range Rover?'

'Yes, hang on a second.'

As she was scrabbling for the keys, she saw his face above her and his eyes looked down into the pit. The water was just below her shoulder blades by now and she really hoped the fire brigade would get here soon. Grabbing the keys with both hands, terrified that her trembling might make her drop them, she squeezed them out through the gap between the logs and felt him take them.

'Good. Now, listen, Jess. I'm going to get the Range Rover and bring it up here. It's about the only vehicle that can manage something like this. It's what they were designed for. When I get to you, I'll use the car to push the logs out of the way. You're almost free, Jess, all right? Got that?'

'Yes, yes, thank you so much.'

She hear a splashing sound and then he was gone. She crouched in her concrete coffin, wondering just how he intended to drive the car when his legs didn't work. Maybe he had some firemen, or possibly George, with him. She certainly hoped so, as the water had just reached the tops of her shoulders and she felt it cold against her throat.

She listened hard, hearing nothing but running water until, miraculously, she heard the sound of a powerful engine. It came closer and closer, revving hard and then there was a hefty impact above her and, suddenly, light flooded down into the pit.

'Jess, can you get out?'

She could just about hear his voice, calling to her from the car. She tried to pull herself to her feet, but her frozen legs refused to work. She was still struggling to get her circulation going again when she heard splashing and then felt two strong arms reach down and catch her under the arms. There was a massive heave and Jess found herself out of the trench, spread-eagled on the ground, with, just a few inches from her, two smiling faces. One was a very happy dog, and one was David.

He was covered from head to foot in sticky mud and he looked as exhausted as she felt. His eyes met hers and he smiled – a warm, open, uncomplicated smile that reached deep inside her, in spite of the circumstances.

'Come on. Let's get you into the car.'

She saw him haul himself, crab-fashion, up the steep slope and then felt his hands catch hold of hers and lift. She struggled to her knees and together, grabbing hold of branches to support themselves, they crawled across to the car and sat down on the edge of the boot. For a moment she wondered why he wasn't opening the side doors, but then she noticed that the car was firmly jammed into the woodpile. He must have rammed it at considerable speed, as the front of the car – as far as the rear doors – was almost invisible under the pile of timber. Presumably, he had scrambled out of the car over the back seats. Even in her present befuddled state, she found herself wondering just how he had managed it. Indeed, how had he managed to get up here in the first place to get the car keys from her.

'Here, you're frozen. Get inside and let me hold you.'

Jess felt his hands on her body, tugging her into the car, where the back seats were folded forwards. As they did so, the car shook as Brutus jumped in to join them. David crawled back to her side and his arms encircled her body and hugged her tightly to him. At the same time, a very wet, but still remarkably warm, dog snuggled up against the other side of her. She wrapped her arms around David's neck and then, without any warning, she burst into tears.

He held her tightly, cradling her like a little baby, as she sobbed her heart out. Beside her, she heard the dog whining and it was this, as much as anything else, that gradually brought her back to her senses. Only as her brain started working again did she realise that David was running his hands all over her head and her face, making comforting noises, and then down across her body, pulling her tightly against him so that she gradually began to feel his warmth. She snuggled her head against his powerful chest and felt the rapid beat of his heart after his exertions. She sobbed and sobbed, until finally, she managed to stem the flow and rubbed her face against his shoulder before raising her head and opening her eyes. She found herself looking up into his amazing blue eyes at very close range.

'I'm sorry about that. I really don't know what to say, David. You've saved my life.'

'Thank God I did. I don't know what I would have done if anything had happened to you.'

'How did you manage to get up here from your car?'

His face broke into a weak smile. 'I crawled. If there's a crawling race at the next Olympics, I'm your boy.'

'Oh, you're my boy all right.' To emphasise her point, she stretched up until she could kiss him softly on the lips. 'I owe you my life. I owe you everything.'

'I'm just glad I got here when I did. Listen, can you hear them?'

Jess raised her head a little so that she could listen with both ears. Almost obscured by the drumming of the torrential rain still pouring onto the roof of the car, she could definitely hear something in the far distance. It was the unmistakable trumpet sound of the French emergency services – still some way away, but approaching.

'Should we try to go down and meet them?'

David shook his head wearily. 'I don't know about you, but I'm exhausted. I think we should both just wait for them. They can follow the Range Rover's tracks.' Jess felt his lips in her hair. 'Remind me to phone my grandmother tonight and apologise for making a bit of a mess of her car. And I'll compliment her on having had the very good sense to buy just about the only vehicle that could have managed to make it up that slope into a torrent of mud and water. So if anybody saved your life, it was Land Rover. And Grandma.'

'How did you do it, David? How did you manage to drive it up the slope?'

The smile returned to his face. 'I'm not sure the road safety people would recommend it, but I used one of my

302

crutches to press down on the accelerator. I didn't need the brake – the woodpile looked after that.'

She felt him hug her more tightly and this time his lips pressed against her forehead and she felt him kiss her softly. She lay back in his arms, no longer shivering, slowly beginning to warm up, glad to be alive and loving being with him. By now, the sirens were still some way off, but were definitely getting nearer.

'David, can I ask you something?'

'Anything.'

'Why do you have to go off and leave me?'

There was a moment's silence before he answered.

'I have to go, Jess. I just have to.'

'Please tell me. I need to know – to know if there's any way I can convince you to stay.'

She released the back of his neck, and let her hands slide forward to his cheeks. Looking deep into his eyes, she repeated her plea.

'Please tell me. You see, David, it's bad enough that you're leaving, but without knowing the reason…'

She saw his eyes close for a moment, but then he appeared to come to a decision and he caught and held her gaze.

'Jess, we've only known each other for a matter of weeks, but I knew it from the very first time I saw you down at the swimming pool. You're something very, very special, and I've never felt this way about anybody before. I feel a connection with you, an understanding, as if we've known each other for years, not weeks.'

He hesitated for a few moments, during which she was still trying to digest what he had just said. If he felt this way about her, how could he possibly want to leave her? She was still pondering this when he resumed his explanation.

'Jess… the reason I have to go is quite simple, really. I think I've fallen in love with you. In fact, I know I have, but I also know that's not fair on you.'

Jess's smile, which had been growing throughout the course of his revelation, now stalled.

'What's not fair?'

'My wanting to be with you. You're bright, you're beautiful, you're caring, you're perfect – I said it before and I meant it then, just as I mean it now. It isn't fair for me to expect a gorgeous girl like you to saddle herself with a helpless cripple like me.'

'You're not…'

'Jess, yesterday I saw the specialist.' His voice was serious. 'She had the results of the latest scans, and it doesn't look good. The improvement the physiotherapy has been making is minimal.'

For a second, he paused to catch his breath. In the background, the ever-louder sirens suddenly stopped. Presumably the fire engine had reached the bottom of the slope, but this was insignificant to Jess now. There would be time later for her to reflect on the length of time it had taken them to get here, and the speed with which her concrete coffin had filled with water. But, for now, she was only concentrating on his words, and these were far more important than the likelihood of her having drowned in a concrete tomb.

'I almost told you last night, but I stopped myself. The thing is – it's now quite clear that I'm going to be on crutches, or sticks, for the rest of my life. Asking you to get involved with somebody as useless as me isn't fair on you. You've got your life to live – go and live it. I've had thirty-three terrific years, but that's all over now.'

She saw his eyes bright with emotion and her heart went out to him. But he still hadn't finished. He swallowed hard and carried on.

'Jess, I'll always love you. I want you to believe me when I tell you that. And it's because I love you that I know the only fair thing to do is for me to go off and let you get on with the rest of your life.'

Jess's fingers had been slowly stroking his cheeks as she listened to everything he had to say. When he finally finished talking, she tightened her grip, pulled his lips towards her, and kissed him more urgently and more passionately than she had ever kissed anybody before in her life. When she finally drew back a few inches, she saw him slowly open his eyes.

'David Dupont, you are a moron.'

She saw his eyes open wider.

'For a brainy man, you can be very, very stupid when you want.' She kissed him again and felt his whole body respond. 'That's not the way love works. Love is being with the person you love, helping them, cherishing them, caring for them. And, just for the record, I never want to hear any more of that "somebody as useless as me" crap. Do you realise that you have just dragged yourself up a hundred-yard slope, slid back down again, driven a car which you shouldn't have been able to drive, and saved me – the girl who loves you so very, very dearly – from a watery grave? So, please, get a grip and face facts, will you? David, you are anything but useless, and it's you, and only you, that I want.'

This time it was David who crushed his lips onto hers and pressed his whole body against hers. After a wonderful, tender, passionate kiss, he struggled to sit up and, as he did so, the dog also jumped to his feet, tail wagging, and looked out of the back of the car towards the sound of rapidly approaching footsteps, splashing up the slope towards them. David glanced back down at her.

'I really did hear you right, didn't I? I didn't just imagine you saying that thing about you being the girl who loves me?'

'You heard right, and I meant it.' She reached up and kissed him again just so there could be no possible doubt. 'So does this mean you might not be going off and leaving me any time soon? I don't want you to go. Read my lips: I do not want you to go.'

'Are you sure?'

'Of course I'm sure, you idiot. Now, just tell me you're staying.'

'I'm staying.'

Chapter 25

Jess was woken on Saturday morning by birdsong from the courtyard and a cold, wet Labrador nose against her bare shoulder. She smiled down at the dog and then shook her head.

'Good morning, Brutus. You might have to wait a little bit for your walk. Go back to your bed. Go to your bed, Brutus.'

As the dog trotted obediently back to the kitchen, Jess rolled over and reached for her man, burrowing her head into his muscular chest and kissing him softly. Her other hand ran lightly down his side and across his taut stomach.

'Good morning, Jess.' He was smiling all over as he reached for her in turn. 'I can't think of a better way of waking up.'

Neither could she.

It was a good bit later when the long-suffering dog finally managed to persuade her to get up and take him out for a walk. The sky was cloud-free and that wonderful clear blue colour that reminded her of David's eyes. The ground beneath her feet had almost dried out and there was little trace left of the big storm, apart from a few leaves and branches still scattered about. It was warm, the views were stunning, the air was full of the scent of the flowers, and the only sound was the gentle lapping of the waves. Altogether, it felt really, really good to be alive and she knew there was a smile on her face.

By the time she got back, she found David in the kitchen, clad in just a towel, busy at the coffee machine. Jess's smile broadened as she went over and gave him a hug and a long, lingering kiss.

'I knew there was something missing in this kitchen.' She gave him a grin. 'I must make sure I specify one of these in all of the kitchens I design from now on. And I'm not talking about the coffee machine.'

'So, have you made your mind up about your next job?' It was a rhetorical question. They had discussed this the night before and both of them already knew the answer.

'I'll contact Monsieur Mailly this morning and set up the meeting. And I'll send an email to London, thanking Graham for his kind offer, and politely refusing.'

'You see? That's what I mean. You're such a kind, well-mannered person. After the way he treated you, I'd have told him where to stick his job.'

'He'll get the message. Thanks.' Jess took her cup of coffee and set it on the table. After giving Brutus his breakfast, she sat down and took a sip. 'Excellent coffee. I'm pleased to inform you, Mr Dupont, that you're hired.'

'Talking of jobs, might you have a bit of spare time to check out a house?'

'You've found one?'

He nodded. 'Ironic, isn't it? Just as I was thinking about leaving, I get a call telling me there's a house coming up for sale.'

'Ooh, how exciting. Near here?'

'It's in a wonderful position. You pass it every time you walk into St-Trop on the coastal path. You've probably never noticed it. It's terribly dilapidated. It's quite small, tucked away on a…'

'… on a headland. A tumbledown stone farmhouse with an absolutely enormous umbrella pine behind it? I know the house. I've lusted after it ever since I got here.' She reached over and squeezed his hand. 'So that makes two things I've been lusting after.'

'It isn't very big, though.'

'You have to be talking about the house.'

'But of course.' He gave her a wink.

'As long as it's got a bedroom, I don't care.'

He raised her fingers to his lips and kissed them one by one.

'So, I'll phone and make an appointment to view it next week?'

'Absolutely.' Jess felt the dog's nose against her thigh and reached down with her free hand to scratch his ears under the table. 'Of course, it'll need a new kitchen – with the essential element I've just been talking about.'

'You decide what you want, and I assure you it'll be there.' He glanced across at the clock on the cooker. 'Did you say we're invited for lunch?'

'That's right. Twelve o'clock down at the harbour.'

'Then I'd better go back to the villa and check my emails. Shall I book a taxi for twelve?'

'Perfect.'

–

Hope was waiting for them on the quay. When she spotted Brutus, she ran forward and dropped to her knees to hug him. Then she straightened up again and came over to greet Jess and David.

'Hi, you two. It's great to see my hairy friend again. And I gather things got a bit hairy up there in the woods on Thursday.' Jess had already phoned her with the news. 'Let's see your wounds, then.'

The sun was high in the sky now and Jess had opted for just a light summer dress. The white dressings on her knees and elbows looked a bit incongruous against her suntan, but she didn't mind.

'It's all healing up well. Compared to what might have happened, I got off very lightly. Apparently I have Range Rover and David's grandma to thank for that. And somebody else, of course.'

Hope led them across the gangplank and onto the boat. Jess was pleased to see that David managed it without too much difficulty. Somehow, he was looking more confident after his exploits on Thursday. Up in the lounge – Jess remembered she should refer to it as the saloon – they found Max dispensing drinks. There were a dozen or so people there and Jess found she knew most of them. There was Olivier standing alongside Pete – now a very happy couple. Terri and Louis from the beach bar were there, as was Steve the deckie, and a handful of other familiar faces. Jess went round, shaking hands and dispensing kisses, and she was delighted to see David greet the others with hugs and kisses as well. He looked genuinely happy to see them all again, as was she.

They stood around and chatted for a while. Everybody sounded very pleased to hear Jess's news that she was going to be staying on in St-Tropez, and then Hope gave her own news.

'Max has spoken to Christian – the owner of *Helios* – and they've made a deal. This winter, for the first time,

Helios isn't going to stay in the Med. When the autumn comes, we're sailing across to the Caribbean for the winter and staying over there until the spring.'

Jess caught Hope's eye. 'So, does this mean you're a full-time hostie now?'

Max stretched his arm around Hope and answered for her.

'She's not only accepted the offer of a full-time job, but another offer I made.'

Hope was smiling now. 'They say that husband and wife teams make the best crews.'

Jess grabbed first Hope, and then Max, and hugged them warmly.

'That's fabulous news. Congratulations, you two!'

Max returned Jess's hug and gave her a wink.

'And I owe it all to you.'

After a while, David decided to sit down. Everybody else followed suit and Jess found herself perched on the arm of the armchair alongside him. She reached across and clinked her glass against his.

'Feeling good?'

'Feeling great.'

He was smiling. It looked as though he was about to say more, but they were interrupted by Hope, who had come to collect.

'Right, then, Jess, let's have my hundred euros.'

Jess looked up in surprise and then the penny dropped.

'Of course, our bet. Look, Hope, I haven't brought any cash with me, but I'll pay you next time I see you.'

Hope grinned. 'No sweat. Your credit's good with me.'

David looked up suspiciously. 'So what was the bet about?'

Jess felt herself blushing. 'Nothing special…'

But Hope wasn't going to let her get away with that.

'This was my prediction, David, way back in June, just after we'd arrived in St-Tropez – that Jess and you would end up together.'

'Is that so?' David grinned at Jess's discomfort. 'So was I worth losing a hundred euros for?'

She reached down and caught hold of his free hand. 'Worth every cent.'

He was grinning more broadly now.

'You and I had our own bet, didn't we, Jess? Something about us dog-walking together by the end of the summer?'

'Ah, but I didn't specify which summer.'

'No cheating. Maybe by next summer we'll be able to walk together. Who knows? But in the meantime you've lost your bet, so there's something you've got to do for me.'

Jess sighed theatrically and dropped to her knees in front of him. Behind her, she heard Hope giggle.

'Jess, please! Not in front of Brutus.'

Jess ignored her friend and reached for David's foot.

'So which shoe would you like me to help you with first?'

Acknowledgments

With many thanks to Michael Bhaskar and the whole team at Canelo for their support and encouragement.

Thanks also to my old friend Phil Mason who has the great good fortune to live on the Côte d'Azur and who is a mine of useful information.